THE WIFE'S REPUTATION

RACHEL BRIMBLE

Boldwood

First published in 2022 as *A Very Modern Marriage*. This edition published in Great Britain in 2025 by Boldwood Books Ltd.

Cover Design by Colin Thomas

Cover Images: Colin Thomas

A CIP catalogue record for this book is available from the British Library.

Paperback ISBN 978-1-83703-098-9

Large Print ISBN 978-1-83703-097-2

Hardback ISBN 978-1-83703-096-5

Trade Paperback ISBN 978-1-80656-122-3

Ebook ISBN 978-1-83703-099-6

Kindle ISBN 978-1-83703-100-9

Audio CD ISBN 978-1-83703-091-0

MP3 CD ISBN 978-1-83703-092-7

Digital audio download ISBN 978-1-83703-095-8

This book is printed on certified sustainable paper. Boldwood Books is dedicated to putting sustainability at the heart of our business. For more information please visit https://www.boldwoodbooks.com/about-us/sustainability/

Boldwood Books Ltd, 23 Bowerdean Street, London, SW6 3TN

www.boldwoodbooks.com

For my youngest daughter, Hannah, who is always so kind and happy, positive and supportive of her family and friends as she works so very hard at her career as a performer.
I couldn't be prouder of you, sweetheart – I know all your dreams will come true.
Love you forever,
Mum xx

1

Octavia Marshall blinked back tears as her newly married best friend stood alongside her husband outside the green arched door of Bath's town hall. As Nancy and Francis were showered in rose petals, Octavia's lips trembled under the strain of her forced smile, anxiety for her uncertain future tightening her chest.

She despised her selfishness. Nothing but her friends' happiness should be at the forefront of her mind today, but she could not stop fretting about what this wedding meant for the brothel on Carson Street – for her – now that Nancy, who had worked alongside her for so long, was respectably married.

The house meant everything to Octavia. Since her harsh separation from her father several years before, she had gone from being a privileged young girl living in a beautiful home, to homeless and hawking herself on the streets. Then Louisa Hill, the owner of the Carson Street house, had found her – saved her – and their home and workplace became Octavia's haven, her sanctuary – the people living with her there, her saving grace.

Now she feared if the brothel collapsed, she would too.

Why had she allowed herself to believe it would be her, Nancy and Louisa side by side against the world for as long as they could work? Louisa had fallen in love with Jacob, their doorman and all-round protector, over a year before. And now Nancy was wed. Yet the loss of Louisa's heart to Jacob had not affected Octavia as much as Nancy's falling in love with Francis. After all, as madam and owner of the house, it was inevitable Louisa would come to distance herself from the practicalities of the brothel in time.

But with Nancy's wedding came her permanent departure from the house and a ticking clock in Octavia's mind. It was only a matter of time before Louisa wanted to start a family and then the Carson Street house would close for good.

Taking a deep breath, Octavia tried her best to shake off her melancholy and walked closer to her friends. She pressed a firm kiss to Nancy's cheek. 'You look beautiful, darling. Absolutely beautiful.'

'Thank you.' Nancy's cheeks flushed with happiness and her auburn hair, speckled with white flower buds, gleamed beneath her ivory veil. 'I can't quite believe a good-time girl like me is actually married.'

'Married and expecting,' Octavia said, as she nodded towards Nancy's slightly curved stomach. 'All too soon there will be a tiny Nancy or Francis running around and then where will you be?'

Nancy laughed. 'As happy as a pig in sh—'

'Um, darling...' Francis raised his eyebrows. 'Shall we head to the White Hart before your happiness bursts forth in a barrage of unfettered expletives?'

'It's too late to start looking down your nose at me now, Francis Carlyle,' Nancy sniffed, her gaze soft with love even as she feigned a scowl at her new husband. 'Like it or lump it, I'm yours for the rest of our lives. Unfettered expletives and all.'

'And I wouldn't have it any other way.'

As they kissed, Octavia moved away, her smile slipping as Louisa approached. Astute as any human being could be when it came to Octavia's and Nancy's inner feelings, Louisa was stalwart, hardworking and ambitious. Traits that Octavia liked to believe she had now embodied herself, yet her insecurity and current self-loathing proved all too clearly how far she had to go before she was anywhere near as confident and self-assured as Louisa.

She stopped at Octavia's side and gazed towards Nancy and Francis as they walked down the steps and onto the pavement, where a small crowd of well-wishers had gathered. 'What's wrong, Octavia?' Louisa asked. 'Your smile is fooling no one.'

Octavia stared resolutely ahead. 'Nothing's wrong, I'm just thinking.'

'About what?'

'The future.'

'What about the future?'

Octavia turned, saw the concern in her friend's violet gaze but tilted her chin anyway. 'I think it goes without saying that the Carson Street house is not the same place it was when I arrived eighteen months ago. And no doubt it will be different again in half that time.'

'And that's a bad thing?'

'It is when I have nothing else in this city but you and the house. It's time for me to start thinking of what I will do going forward.'

'You have absolutely no need to worry.' Louisa slipped her hand into the crook of Octavia's elbow. 'The house will stay open for many a year yet. Now that I've taken on Adelaide and Eliza, who are that much younger than us. I hope our income will increase and you can continue to work without additional pressure.'

'You know as well as I do that the house will not continue as it has been.'

'Why?'

'What about Jacob?'

Determination clouded Louisa's eyes as she stared towards Jacob where he stood within a small circle of gentlemen. 'I suppose you overheard Jacob contemplating our future. Well, whatever he might say, the house is under my authority and whatever happens with it is entirely up to me.'

Octavia followed her gaze. 'Jacob is a good man, but there is not a man on earth who does not have a need to control a woman once he claims to love her.'

'Don't be absurd. Do you know how bitter you sound?'

With good reason... 'All I'm saying is that a woman should be wary of any man. Do all she can to retain her independence. Work as well as she can. Control her destiny in any way possible. Love leads to weakness. You will eventually be persuaded to Jacob's preferences, mark my words.'

'I will not.'

Despite the annoyance in Louisa's gaze, Octavia could not stem her simmering panic, the unrelenting belief that time was running out and she had to do something to shape her future. 'All right then, what of Nancy and Francis?'

'What about them? Surely you're not concerned Francis will do wrong by Nancy?' Louisa stared at the man in question, her jaw slightly tightening. 'Neither of us will stand by and let Nancy be hurt.'

'Of course not, I think he and Nancy will do well. They have their mission at the workhouse, a nice home and a baby on the way. There is much to keep Nancy busy and absent from Carson Street, which is only right.'

'Then what is it bothering you?' Louisa raised her eyebrows, her gaze stern. 'You sound almost resentful that one of your closest friends is happy and has married the man she loves. This is not like you at all. I was half expecting you to be tormenting Nancy by now and thoroughly enjoying yourself.'

Shame brought heat to Octavia's cheeks, but she would not waver. 'I am happy, just troubled. I feel as though all of us have risen with the success of the brothel, but if it closes, what then? Nancy is now married, and the same will be true of you and Jacob come Christmas. Children will follow, too.'

'Children?' Louisa huffed a laugh and glanced towards Jacob once more. 'I will never be a mother, Octavia. The brothel will forever remain my priority.'

'Does Jacob know that?'

Louisa's expression hardened. 'Yes.'

Tension suddenly hung around her friend like a dark shadow and Octavia quickly turned away, guilt twisting inside of her. The last thing she wanted to do was upset Louisa. She meant as much to Octavia's heart as Nancy and always would.

She squeezed Louisa's hand, forcing a smile. 'I'm sorry. Let's not speak of this anymore. I am feeling horribly morose, which is as selfish as it is misplaced. Come, let's join the others.'

But Louisa neither smiled nor took a step forward. Instead, her wily gaze bored into Octavia's. 'The house is doing well. Our clientele is happy and return with fevered regularity. Your place with Jacob and I will never change. It is yours for as long as you want it.'

'I know that.'

'Then what can I—'

'Nancy is married now, Louisa. Everything is changed, whether you accept that or not. She has not worked for weeks and it is clear she never will again.' Octavia clutched her friend's hand and looked deep into her eyes, praying Louisa did not mistake her musing for malady. 'And I wouldn't want it any other way, but Nancy's marriage has set me to thinking about where these changes leave me.'

'They leave you with the same security and promise I made when you came to the house,' Louisa said firmly, her face set. 'Carson Street will be your home for as long as you want it to be. You can continue to work or not – it's entirely up to you. But know this, Octavia, you are the best girl I have, and I love you. Adelaide and Eliza look up to you, respect you as I do. You have nothing to fear about the future. You are safe. Always.'

Tears burned the backs of Octavia's eyes, reigniting her shame for worrying Louisa. 'I know. Ignore me.' She gently tugged Louisa towards the steps. 'It must be the sight of a red-headed whore dressed in ivory making me doubt whether all is right in the world,' she said, forcing a laugh. 'Come on, let's get Nancy a drink before she starts yelling for one, shall we?'

Louisa's gaze lingered on Octavia's before she gave a firm nod and the two of them walked down the steps to join the jubilant wedding party. Chatter, congratulations and laughter serenaded the group as they strolled along the street and Octavia released her held breath. She had escaped a deeper interrogation from Louisa but was in no way blinded by her friend's brief questioning. Louisa would not be happy until she was entirely convinced of Octavia's contentment.

Louisa wasn't just a madam, she was a mother figure to anyone who worked at Carson Street, and now Octavia had evoked her friend's concern by her ill-timed admission of uncertainty. A selfish, self-absorbed act that only further proved true what her father had said to her the last time she saw him... the last time he had struck her. She was selfish and insular. A person who only really cared about her own wishes. Octavia exhaled a shaky breath. Clearly, nothing had changed in her despite her years away from home, her years on the streets or her months at Carson Street.

Octavia fought the fear that clutched at her heart. She could not falter in her charade of happiness, in her desperation to be so much more than her father had branded her. Yet the truth was she was failing in her pretence and failing badly.

But today was Nancy and Francis's day and she would not be held in any way responsible for dimming their happiness. She had battled to survive the streets and she would survive these new changes, too.

She joined in with the banter of her dearest friends as they walked ever closer to the White Hart tavern. As much as the stinky old pub often distressed her, Octavia's high-class beginnings were a faded and distant memory. The pub stood as the ladies' anchor amid a city that offered little in the way of comfort or security and, as always, Octavia would indulge in a glass or two of wine and then abstain for the rest of the evening.

As for the future... for now, it would have to wait.

2

Seated in the lounge of Tanner's gentlemen's club, William Rose gripped his brandy glass so tightly his pulse thumped beneath his fingers. 'You are missing the point, sir. My mills are on the rise, both in profit and reputation. Rose Textiles is growing from strength to strength. If you wish to invest, now is the time.'

Councillor Lane twirled one end of his grey moustache, his beady eyes narrowed. 'Hmm, I'm not so sure. You are not the sort of man I want to be seen doing business with as I proceed in my own ambitions.'

William opened his mouth to protest but Lane raised his hand. 'Not that I don't like you, sir, and indeed, the standard of your produce is second to none—'

'Then I do not understand your hesitation,' William objected. 'Why did you travel to Manchester in the summer? Why spend time with me at my mills, talk to my workers and display a clear understanding of my vision if you had no intention of investing? It doesn't make sense. Nor do I appreciate my time being wasted.'

'That is by the by.'

'By the by?' Anger simmered inside William as he glared at Lane. 'You have seen how my mills have flourished over the last three years. You have witnessed my progress and hard work. I am a working man, sir. A man from humble beginnings and even humbler parents. A man and woman who have worked their fingers to the bone every single day, raised myself and my sisters to the best of their abil—' William snapped his mouth closed, his emotions rising far too close to the surface. This meeting was too important for his thoughts to drift to the environment in which he had been raised compared to where he was now. 'I have always wanted more, sir, and I still do. By investing in my company, you too shall profit.'

Lane smiled, his dark eyes smouldering with self-importance. 'A lot has changed in the three months since I went to Manchester, Rose. I am no longer just a wealthy businessman looking for a sound investment but a man making his mark in the world of politics. I have goals. Big goals. Governmental goals.'

'And that affects your decision to invest in Rose Textiles?' William took a gulp of his drink as he tried to hold on to his frustration. The meeting between him, Lane and the two other men around the table had gone well... until now. 'What you are saying makes no sense.'

'You are not married, sir.'

'What?' William almost choked on his brandy. 'What in heaven's name does that have to do with my business acumen? My ability to guarantee a profit on your money?'

Lane drained his glass and set it down on the table with a decisive thump. 'I'm sorry, Rose, but my new situation means I must show the world I am a family man. A man who deals in the welfare of family, home and children. Therefore, the people I do business with, whom I am seen with, must reflect those same values. I was willing to come here this evening to hear what you had to say, consider it and, if necessary, dismiss it face to face.' He exhaled a heavy breath and stood. 'I'm afraid I will only be investing with family men from now on. Marriage, family and proper upstanding principles are what matter to my future advancement.' He nodded at the men around the table. 'I bid you good evening, gentlemen.'

William's pulse thudded in his ears, and he gripped the arms of his chair as he watched Lane retreat from the candlelit semi-darkness of the club's lounge into the lobby. Because he wasn't married? That was what had just lost him a huge boost to his company? Good God in heaven. Had the world gone mad?

His anger bubbling dangerously, William faced his friends around the table. 'Can you believe that? He's walking away because I'm not married? It beggars belief.'

The ensuing glances around the room and stares into glasses alerted William to the realisation that Lane might not be a singular problem, but one of possible mass proportions.

He glared. 'What?'

Nicholas Fairham, his good friend and business associate, inched forward and laid his forearms on the table. 'It doesn't look good when a man reaches your age and is neither married nor with children—'

'God man, I'm thirty-two, not ninety-two.'

'People start to wonder what's wrong with you.'

'What's wrong...' William laughed and shoved his friend's arm. 'You're jesting with me.'

'No, William, I'm not.'

William looked to his left and Oscar Daniels, another associate, nodded his agreement with Nicholas. Was this a bad joke? Would a clown jump out at any moment, teeth gleaming as he screamed with taunting hilarity?

'Why in God's name should I even think about marriage if I have no wish for it? My father's commitment to his family and wife meant he could not give the time to both work and personal success simultaneously. He either had to work long, exhaustive hours, forgoing seeing his loved ones, or else choose his family and forgo prosperity. I have made a pledge to provide for my parents and sisters and that is what I will do.'

'And that means what exactly?'

'I will not marry and start a family of my own until my current family's continued comfort is guaranteed.'

'Then you need to accept that certain aspects will be closed to you if you are determined to remain a single man.' Nicholas shrugged. 'That's perfectly fine, but some people may suspect you to be a little averse to commitment.'

'Are you telling me because you're married, you have an advantage over me as far as business is concerned?' William faced Oscar. 'That you both do?'

He was met with dual shrugs.

'What in God's name is happening here?' William drained his glass and stood. 'This could be deemed as some sort of prejudice. Discrimination. Lord above, injustice!'

'Sit down, Will.'

'How can I when men whom I considered intelligent and wise agree with Lane? A man who clearly has his eye on government and far from real life. Business is business. What matters is how I conduct that business, how I run my mills, treat my workers and the profit I garner. Profit, gentlemen. Money. *That's* what makes the world go around, not bloody marriage.'

The others remained silent, each looking at William with varying expressions of amusement. Well, to hell with them.

Snatching his cigar case from the table, William stuffed it into his inside pocket and tugged on the hem of his jacket. 'Fine.

Then I see no further need for this meeting to continue. I declare our business done for the evening. Goodnight.'

'William.'

He halted at Nicholas's firm tone, his heart hammering and the beginnings of a headache threatening. Despite his frustration, William trusted his friend and if Nicholas was irritated, then William could hardly storm out of the club without at least listening to him.

He tipped his head back and stared at the ornate ceiling, silently counting the cherubs sitting among the clouds above him as he concentrated on levelling his breathing.

Dropping his chin, he turned.

Nicholas arched an eyebrow. 'Are you finished?'

William clenched his jaw.

His friend stood and came towards him, firmly grasping William's shoulder, his gaze sympathetic. 'Unfortunately, personal reputation is as important as the professional in the circles you are trying to break open in this city. Marriage and social status matter in Bath, whether you like it or not. If you wish to expand your contacts and connections outside of Manchester, you have to expect to come up against different cultures, obstacles and views.'

'You think I don't know that? Good God, Nicholas, you don't achieve all that I have without facing down adversity, adapting and changing.'

'Maybe not, but sooner or later it will be to your advantage to consider courting a girl and marrying her. Until then...' He smiled and slid a sly wink at Oscar. 'I suggest you come with us to a little place where the women have no interest in marriage but are of the most satisfying company.'

There was no mistaking Nicholas's intention but even as Oscar rose from the table, eagerly finishing his drink, William's headache only escalated. 'I have no interest in being with a woman tonight. *Any* woman.'

'Well, that's too bad,' Nicholas said, urging William towards the lounge doors, his hand still firmly on his shoulder. 'Because you are coming with us to Carson Street. Martin couldn't make it tonight so you can take his place. I'm confident the doorman won't have a problem with that. Come on, man. Forget Lane and shake off your foul mood. There are ladies waiting.'

'And visiting a brothel is your way of showing me marriage is the way forward?' William shook his head. 'Shame on you. On both of you.'

Nicholas laughed. 'Marriage does not mean the end of a man's life, you know. There are women to marry and those to lie with.'

'You're an animal.'

'An animal who can afford to lie with some of the best whores in the city, and trust me, only the very best are found at Carson Street.'

Scowling, William walked with his associates from the club, his mind still reeling with Lane's words and their insinuation. How in God's name could it ever be right that a man's single status was an obstacle to financial success and prosperity? That his married friends not only gained lucrative business deals, but openly betrayed their spouses?

Life was upside down and damn well backwards.

3

'You are both coming along well enough.' Octavia fought to hide her smile as she addressed the two young women sitting in front of her on the sofa at Carson Street. 'But, Adelaide, I advise you to add a little more fun to your ministrations. Believe me, I know what it is like to be naturally serious in nature but that is not what our clients come here looking for.' She forced a frown despite her amusement. 'As for you, Eliza, you need to tease your offerings rather than openly delivering them on a silver platter.'

After three months working at the house, the girls knew Octavia's jesting well enough and laughed.

'Now then,' Octavia continued, slowly walking back and forth in front of them. 'Louisa is impressed with both your work and your willingness to adapt and change to clients' wants and whims so...' She inhaled a long breath, not entirely behind Louisa's latest consideration when Adelaide and Eliza still spent so much time whispering and gossiping with one another. 'She is considering giving one of you Nancy's old room and the other the spare bedroom, although she is yet to make a final decision. Be patient. Things are changing and will continue to change, and I have no doubt Louisa will want you to be a part of what-ever is next for this house.'

Eliza lifted her hand to a stray blonde curl at her temple and tucked it neatly behind her ear, her gaze hopeful. 'Well, that is welcome news! Louisa seems so loyal to her girls. If Adelaide and I show as much promise as you and Nancy, might we one day hope that Louisa will hold us in as much esteem as she does you?'

'I'm surprised you have the need to ask. Hasn't Louisa treated you well and with care for the entire time you've worked here?'

'Well, yes, but...' Eliza glanced at Adelaide, her cheeks colouring. 'When Louisa found us, we were hardly open to her generosity. In fact, it took quite a fight on Louisa's part to convince me that Adelaide and I would be safer here than on the streets where we were independent.'

'Yet she persuaded you. I was the same and had never worked with, or for, anyone else before I came here. The Carson Street house is different, ladies. Louisa runs this establishment on terms that are best for us, not the culls.'

Eliza looked at her folded hands in her lap. 'But I am still so afraid to completely trust Louisa. To believe that she will not one day take our positions away.'

Sympathy rose in Octavia as she looked from one young girl to the other. If anyone understood the difficulty in learning to trust again, she did.

Octavia walked forward and took Eliza's hand, giving her fingers an encouraging squeeze. 'Louisa will not forsake you as long as both she and this house remain your priority. You must demonstrate your loyalty to her as much as she demonstrates hers to you. Reputation is everything to Louisa and as long as you never intentionally do anything to upset our accepted standing within the neighbourhood, you will have Louisa's backing... and mine.'

Adelaide and Eliza exchanged a look so loaded with scepticism Octavia planted her hands on hips, annoyed that they seemed unconvinced by her endorsement of her friend. 'What is it?'

'Well...' Adelaide grimaced. 'When we were shopping this morning, we overheard some people talking in the market.'

'And?'

'And...' She glanced at Eliza who nodded her encouragement, her blue eyes wide. 'There are rumours that the brothels and boarding houses are being watched.'

Trepidation whispered through Octavia as she looked between the women. 'What do you mean *watched*?'

'By certain people. Do-gooders.' Panic showed in Eliza's eyes, her voice rising. 'People likely to get Carson Street shut down.'

'Do-gooders?' Octavia smiled and lowered her shoulders. 'Oh, don't take the slightest bit of notice. Rumours about changes and revolt and goodness knows what else have been directed our way for as long as I have been here. Nothing will come of it. Now—'

The eruption of men shouting in the hallway carried up the stairs, the yelling gathering in urgency and volume. Lifting her skirts, Octavia rushed from the room. She hurried downstairs and made for the front door where Jacob stood, feet planted, his hands fisted on his waist as the trio of men in front of him pleaded their cases for admission.

'We have made appointments!'

'There is no reason Mr Rose here can't take Mr Flanders' appointment if he is absent. Be reasonable, Mr Jackson. We are reg—'

'The answer is no,' Jacob growled, the deep timbre of his

voice commanding in the small space even though it was barely raised. 'Now, you and Mr Fairham are more than welcome to keep your appointments with Adelaide and Eliza, but as Mr Flanders is not here, no one else will be seeing Octavia tonight.'

Although grateful for Jacob's protection, he could sometimes be overly attentive to her and the other girls' wellbeing, meaning that innocents were often caught in the crossfire of his well-intended care and tendency to suspicion.

Octavia calmly walked forwards. 'What seems to be the problem, gentlemen?'

She stared at the men, her attention pulled a little harder towards the stranger standing a little to the left. He was tall, dark-haired with a neatly trimmed beard and moustache, his coat of good quality. An air of quiet yet indisputable maleness surrounded him but, judging by his somewhat uninterested expression as he stared at the walls and then the ceiling, it was clear that, one: this was the Mr Rose whose case of entry was being pleaded, and two: he had found himself at Carson Street under persuasion rather than desire.

Mr Fairham stepped forward, his face set. 'All I am asking is that—'

'Jacob?' The firm clip-clop of Louisa's heels sounded along the hallway tiles until she came to a stop beside Octavia. 'What is going on? I could hear the ruckus from my study. Gentleman, please. Do not cause such a scene on the doorstep. Come in and shut the door.'

Once they were inside, Octavia addressed the men again, her gaze lingering on the stranger's turned cheek as she uncon-sciously willed him to face her. His apathy was becoming vaguely annoying. 'Well, gentlemen,' she said, placing her hand on Jacob's arm. The last thing these visitors would want was for Jacob's fragile veneer to crack. Thankfully, the boxer-turned-brothel-doorman stepped back and disdainfully shook his head. 'Would one of you kindly tell me what is happening?'

'Octavia, Mrs Hill.' Nicholas Fairham cleared his throat with a polite dip of his head to Louisa. 'Myself and my friend have appointments with Eliza and Adelaide; however, as Mr Flanders was unable to keep his appointment with Octavia, I was hoping' – he tossed a glare in Jacob's direction – 'that Mr Jackson would see reason and agree that, as Mr Rose is here in Mr Flanders' stead, it would be all right for *him* to take the appointment.'

'Jacob?' Louisa raised her eyebrows as she looked at her lover. 'Is there anything particularly bothering you about this request I should be made aware of?'

'You mean apart from the fact that Mr Fairham assumes he is so important to us that he can invite all and sundry here without prior warning?'

'Jacob, please. I'm sure this can be sorted out with the minimum of...'

Louisa and Jacob's conversation dimmed as Mr Rose slowly turned his gaze to Octavia. She barely resisted the urge to flinch. His eyes were a lighter shade than his hair, their gaze so intense it was as though he looked to read her thoughts, desires and dreams. The notion was bizarrely unnerving, intoxicating, and a frisson of trepidation – or maybe shameful anticipation – shivered through her. Suddenly it didn't seem such a bad idea to allow Mr Rose's unexpected visit to play out. Yet impromptu admittance was not the Carson Street way...

As Louisa and Jacob seemed too embedded in debate to address Mr Rose and his companions, Octavia cleared her throat. 'I'm sorry, Mr Rose, but it's house policy that no girl spends time alone with a man we do not know. Therefore, I kindly ask that you leave. However, if you wish—'

'Now, now, Octavia,' Louisa said firmly as she brushed past

her. 'I don't think it's necessary to toss Mr Rose so unceremoniously out of our establishment on such a cold and dreary night, do you?'

'Louisa...' Octavia looked pointedly at her friend, her eyebrows raised. 'Jacob is right. Mr Fairham should not have taken it upon himself to offer his friend's unkept appointment to Mr Rose. Therefore, Mr Rose should leave.'

'Mr Rose.' Louisa smiled at the gentleman in question and offered her hand. 'Louisa Hill, owner and overseer of the house. Welcome. If you are a friend of Mr Fairham's, I imagine you too must be of a decent and kindly manner. Am I safe in that assumption?'

Octavia faced Mr Rose and, once again, fought the urge to flinch when she found herself the object of his intense study a second time. She pulled back her shoulders. He had better think again if he thought for one minute she might be intimidated by him. 'Mr Rose? I do believe you were asked a question.'

His eyes lingered on hers before he slowly shifted his gaze to Louisa. 'Mrs Hill. I am happy to leave. I came here under pressure this evening and have complete respect for your rules. I will go.'

'I will not hear of it.' Louisa laughed. 'Jacob and Octavia are correct about how this house is run but I am not beyond bending the rules from time to time. Now then, if Octavia would like to—'

'Louisa...' Octavia stared at her friend in disbelief. Since when had Louisa bent any rules? What in heaven's name was happening to this house, to Octavia's once ordered life? 'Considering the nature of our business, I think bending rules is a mistake, don't you?'

Jacob stepped forward and yanked open the front door. 'I couldn't agree more. Goodnight, gentlemen.'

Louisa squared up to Jacob. Admittedly, Jacob towered over her in both height and width, but Louisa was a force to be reckoned with at the best of times and this was *not* a good time.

Smiling sweetly, Louisa pushed the door firmly closed, her eyes still locked with Jacob's. 'You have one of two options, Mr Rose,' she said, over her shoulder. 'To remain in the parlour with Octavia and enjoy a glass of our finest claret, maybe a cigar or two, while your friends keep their appointments. Or leave.' She faced Mr Rose. 'If you choose to stay, you will not visit Octavia's bedchamber. Nor will you receive any service this evening other than conversation. Now, do you wish to stay or go?'

Protestation battled on Octavia's tongue, yet something in Mr Rose's demeanour intrigued her to know his answer. He seemed agitated yet composed, impatient yet unruffled. The combination was profoundly confusing – and fiendishly delightful. She sensed she might have a little fun with the oh-so-serious Mr Rose...

The silence stretched until Mr Rose gave a curt nod. 'A drink would be welcome.'

Octavia's heart picked up speed.

'Good.' Louisa smiled. 'Octavia? If you'd like to escort Mr Rose to the parlour?'

Before Octavia could respond, Mr Rose faced Jacob. 'Mr Jackson? Is my sharing a drink with Miss Octavia agreeable to you?'

Satisfaction lit Jacob's eyes and Octavia bit her lips together to curb her smile. It was so rare that Jacob showed any mirth in front of a cull, but it seemed Mr Rose's show of respect for their doorman's authority – especially in front of Louisa – was a stroke of genius.

'Indeed it is, sir.' Jacob nodded. 'Octavia will show you the way.'

'Good, that's settled then,' Louisa said firmly, despite her barely concealed annoyance with Jacob. 'Mr Fairham? Mr Daniels? Won't you come this way? Eliza and Adelaide are waiting upstairs in the drawing room.'

Taking a deep breath, Octavia smiled as she met Mr Rose's unrelenting gaze and waved towards the parlour. 'Shall we?'

For the first time since she'd laid eyes on this stranger, Mr Rose smiled. Beautifully. 'Of course. After you.'

Octavia slowly turned, fighting the unnerving difficulty she had in looking away from him before she started along the corridor.

William followed the woman named Octavia into the parlour, leaving the door open behind him. The fact he followed her at all amazed him. Brothels were very rarely on his list of places to visit. In fact, his being in a brothel was so rare, he couldn't remember the last time he'd stepped inside such a house. Yet, here he was, deciding to stay for a drink or two at Carson Street despite a clear opportunity to leave.

The reason he chose to remain was simple.

The challenge in this woman's bright blue eyes had snagged his attention, had unwittingly drawn him from his business frustrations. A feat some might consider wholly unusual. Yet the way he had felt her gaze on him even as he feigned interest in the paintings on the hallway walls, the cornices beneath the ceiling, had been discombobulating enough that William had felt he had little option but to explore its reasons further. Besides, if he had decided to go, Nicholas would have felt duty-bound to leave with him and the last thing William wanted was to incur an extended evening with his sexually frustrated friend. Fornication to Nicholas was like William's work to him. He was insatiable.

'Wine, Mr Rose?'

He snapped his attention to Octavia where she stood by a bureau holding a decanter of claret and a crystal-cut glass.

'Yes. Thank you.'

As she poured their drinks, William wandered to the window and looked out into the darkened street, the glow from the street lamps illuminating the cobbled pavement and muddy road. 'Has this house been open long?' he asked, watching a courting couple stop to share a kiss beneath the gaslight. 'Only my friends have not mentioned Carson Street to me before tonight.'

'We have been open long enough to have established some house rules,' she said, her footsteps soft on the rug. 'Here. I wouldn't get too comfortable if I were you. Louisa's decision to allow you to stay while your friends are occupied is as unusual as it is curious. I wouldn't be surprised if she walks in at any moment telling you she's changed her mind.'

He accepted the offered glass of claret. 'Thank you.' He sipped as he met her eyes above the rim, once again enticed by the challenge in her gaze. 'I sense that if Mrs Hill doesn't do that, you'll be voicing your dissatisfaction at having to speak with me as soon as the front door closes behind me and my associates.'

'Not at all.' She laughed and waved towards the sofa. 'Please, take a seat.'

William stared into her wide blue eyes, noticing the unusual flecks of silver about her irises. There was no doubting the woman's beauty and he found himself full of questions as they sat on opposite ends of the sofa. Octavia, while indisputably alluring, did not strike William as a typical whore. Whatever a typical whore might be. This was a woman comfortable in her own skin, confident in both speech and manner. Sophisticated, interesting and more than capable of keeping abreast of conversation – in fact it could be argued that right now she led the conversation.

'So...' He settled back against the cushions. 'Mr Fairham informs me that this house is one of high calibre. From your and Mrs Hill's attractiveness, I can certainly confirm my friend's assessment.'

'Thank you.' She sipped her drink, then slowly lowered it as she studied him, her brow slightly furrowed. 'And what is it you do, Mr Rose?'

'I'm a mill owner.' Pride swelled inside him, the notion he wanted to impress her neither lost on him nor particularly welcome. 'I run a textile company in the north. Manchester.'

'Well, I can see your business is prosperous.'

William arched an eyebrow, amusement unfurling inside of him that she was so openly presumptuous. 'Oh?'

Much to his surprise and delight, a slight blush darkened her cheeks. Maybe she was not as impervious to his charms as he had been beginning to think. She ran her gaze over him, from his necktie to his shoes, her eyes revealing that she was silently cataloguing everything about him.

She nodded. 'Your clothes are of good quality. You came here this evening filled with neither relish nor horror, which leads me to think you can afford any service that an establishment such as this has to offer. Indeed, you have a quiet confidence about you that I have learned comes with self-sufficiency. With wealth.'

William could hardly argue with her observations. 'I will take your assessment as a compliment, Miss...'

She smiled, her eyes sparkling with a hint of flirtation. 'Octavia, please.'

'Octavia.' He smiled. 'Then you must call me William.'

'Tell me, are you in Bath for very long? Business, or pleasure?'

He sipped his wine and held her gaze. The woman was astoundingly attractive, her thick brown hair already tempting his fingers to touch it, to imagine what it would look like unpinned and tumbling over her bare breasts. Not to mention the magnetism of her eyes. Such a shade of ocean blue, a man could fall into them as he would topple into the sea.

Yet it wasn't just these physical attributes that had caught his interest in Octavia – or strengthened his decision to stay at Carson Street while his friends indulged in what he would not. It was *her*. The woman. Her poise and confidence. The articulate, middle-class way she spoke. The way she openly stared at him without hesitation or deference. Not that she should be deferent to him, but he had somehow expected as much from a whore.

He cleared his throat. 'I am here for two weeks. Business is what takes my time and interest. I rarely have time for pleasure.'

'Surely you allow yourself some pleasures? We met in the hallway of this house, after all.'

'It depends what a man considers pleasure. Work is what defines and sustains me. I feel little need for anything more.'

'Surely all work and no play means little enjoyment of your achievements. Do you not have family? Friends? Business associates you like to socialise with?'

William studied her. Were her questions specifically chosen for him? Or was this just a list of polite enquiries she rolled out routinely? Why did it matter? He would never see her again after this evening. Yet it irked that her conversation with him held every possibility of being nothing more than business. Her business.

'I have friends,' he said before draining his glass. 'I have family and business associates too. But, as I said, work is my pleasure.'

'Are you married?'

He laughed and shook his head. 'For the love of all things holy, please, can we not discuss marriage? Anything at all but that.'

Her brow furrowed, her shoulders ever so slightly rising in an almost defensive gesture. 'Was the question a silly one? You can hardly be surprised that a good number of men who come here are married.'

'Oh, no, it doesn't surprise me at all. Mr Fairham has a wife and a child, in fact.' William shook his head, huffed a laugh. 'No, I avoid your question because the subject of marriage became one of extreme irritation earlier this evening. Let us talk about you instead.'

Her brilliant blue eyes bored into his, ever so slightly narrowing. 'What would you like to ask me?'

William leaned further back in his seat, flung his arm across its back and made a show of appraising her from face to neck to ample bosom. 'Where were you educated?'

Her colour paled, her expression now devoid of the humour he was beginning to enjoy. 'Pardon?'

Removing his arm from the back of the sofa, he looked at her directly, curiosity whispering through him. Such a strange, stilted reaction...

'You speak well, Octavia. Seemingly too well for one in your position. Yet, I can see you are comfortable here. Proud of your work and this house. It's a quandary to me. Why prostitution? A woman like you could—'

'A woman like me?' Her gaze burned with irritation. 'And who is a woman like me, Mr Rose?'

His body heated with a flash of unexpected desire. He could

not remember meeting so forthright a woman, a passionate, quick-witted, intelligent woman who clearly felt able to challenge him on every level. The combination was seductive.

He shrugged, feigning nonchalance. 'A woman who I imagine could easily be a man's mistress if that is what—'

'A man's mistress?' She laughed and stood, before walking to the drinks table and replenishing her glass. She turned, those eyes of hers flashing with unmistakable pride. 'I will never be a man's mistress.'

'Surely you don't believe that you might one day be a man's wife?' William inwardly grimaced at the way the question sounded. Patronising, judgemental, derogatory. 'I mean, this life could hardly lead—'

'To what?' She walked closer until she stood directly in front of him, staring down at him at his lowly place on the sofa, his face level with her stomach. 'To me surviving without a man? You've only just met me. I advise against any kind of assumption as far as my capability is concerned.'

Even though her tone was firm, it was laced with teasing. So much so, he couldn't be sure she wasn't laughing at him. Her manner was commanding, unnerving and, he had to admit, downright arousing. He was unused to such fire in a woman yet found this turn of conversation far more stimulating than the usual banal chit-chat between ladies and gentlemen.

He shifted on his seat and she stepped back, allowing him the space he needed to stand. Slowly, he rose to his feet, his gaze dropping to her lips before he forced his eyes to hers, only to see her pondering his mouth in the same way he had hers. His heart thundered as she lifted her eyes and firmly held his gaze.

William stared at her, not quite believing the strength of his yearning to kiss her, but he would not. Her challenge – her skill – was obvious and there was no way in hell he would be defeated. Turning, he strode to the drinks table. It was patently obvious she had no intention of pouring him a second glass, so he'd help himself.

When he faced her, she had taken his place on the sofa, her eyes shining. He stared, momentarily unable to move. What was it that ran between them like an invisible thread? She appeared entirely unruffled by him. Not that he particularly expected her to be, but he had been told he was better than average to look at and women – most of the time – responded to him.

Then again, Octavia was a whore. A seductress. Yet her predator-like quality only provoked his intrigue of her. It was as though, in that moment, she could reach out, grip his necktie and fling him to the floor before he could as much as utter a curse.

Funnily enough, the scenario wasn't as undesirable as it should have been...

She smiled. 'Do you want to know what I think?'

Blinking from his stupor, William took a fortifying mouthful of wine and walked closer. 'I do.'

'I think as much as you find it impossible to believe that I might make a suitable wife one day, I find it absolutely deplorable that any woman would want *you* for a husband.'

Their eyes locked.

William's heart beat a little faster, a knot of suppressed laughter forming in his stomach until he could hold it no longer. He tipped his head back and laughed, tears filling his eyes as Octavia stood and joined in his laughter.

Wiping his eyes, he smiled down at her. 'Touché, my dear. Touché.'

She touched her glass to his, her smile wide and her eyes shining with fondness and maybe even a little desire...

5

Octavia stood at the front door, her smile strained as Mr Rose's associates shook Jacob's hand before they made their way outside. Rare nerves jumped and leapt in her stomach. She was all too aware that Mr Rose was yet to follow suit. Instead, he continued to stand far too closely beside her. What was the man waiting for? Her unexpected attraction towards him was disconcerting. She had not been drawn to a cull the entire time she had been working as a prostitute, which meant William Rose was quite possibly the most dangerous man she had ever met.

It was imperative she maintained the upper hand, that he did not suspect her extraordinary interest for a single moment.

She abruptly offered him her hand. 'Well, Mr Rose, it was nice meeting you.'

'You, too.' He gently grasped her fingers and raised her hand to his lips, pressing a kiss to her knuckles. It took every ounce of her resilience not to shiver. He met her gaze, his eyes shining with unabashed confidence. 'I appreciate you sharing your time with me. Farewell, Octavia.'

She swallowed and slowly withdrew her hand. 'Goodbye, Mr Rose.'

With a nod, he turned to Jacob, shook his hand and followed his friends into the street.

Jacob firmly shut the door and flung the bolt into place. 'And good riddance. That man was far too familiar considering he hasn't paid a penny for the privilege of spending time with you.'

Octavia continued to stare at the closed front door, her heart not quite beating as it should. 'He is rather self-assured.'

'Self-assured? The man is—'

'So, how was it?' Louisa asked as she came along the hallway to join them, her violet eyes flitting between Octavia and Jacob. 'Let's have a nightcap in the parlour and you can tell me all about it. It's nearing midnight and we have no more clients due tonight.' She looked at Jacob. 'Eliza and Adelaide will come and find you to walk them home when they are ready. Let's talk while we have a few minutes.'

Octavia's mind ran over the evening's events as she entered the parlour. Mr Rose had gone on to explain his dismissal of any marriage discussion by telling her that he had lost a business deal due to his single status. She could not help agreeing with him that the reasoning was entirely ludicrous. Yet his anger about it had seemed exorbitant. As though he found the mere thought of being married more insulting than any loss of money.

The unspoken expectation of matrimony in today's society – in his obvious echelons of society – made his reaction spark Octavia's curiosity deeply. Why would a man of such status – a wealthy, handsome, intelligent and articulate businessman – not wish to marry? Especially if, in doing so, the marriage helped his business aspirations.

'Octavia? Come and have a seat by me,' Louisa said, patting

the sofa. 'I owe you and Jacob an explanation as to why I was so insistent Mr Rose remained here while his friends were busy.'

Walking to the sofa, Octavia glanced at Jacob where he stood in front of the fireplace, his huge hand curled around the mantel edge, his shoulders high as he stared into the grate. Tension knotted her stomach. He was far from happy. She may have lived and survived the streets, slept with more men than most women ever would in a lifetime, but those experiences had done nothing to lessen Octavia's anxiety whenever a man's temper was roused.

She silently cursed her trepidation. Jacob was tall and as broad as a mountain, but he was also their protector. A man who took his job to look after her, Louisa and Nancy seriously. Adelaide and Eliza too. He had barely ever raised his voice to any of them, let alone his hand.

How long would she compare every man's temperament to her father's and judge them accordingly?

She forced a smile. 'What has caught your interest so ardently, Jacob? Haven't you seen a lit fire before?'

Slowly, he raised his head, not looking at her but at Louisa. Still gripping the mantel, he spoke quietly. 'I didn't like the way you overrode me tonight. The door is under my control. You know it's imperative that is always the case if I am to keep you all safe. You had no right to make me look like a damn fool in front of those culls.'

'I did no such thing,' snapped Louisa, her cheeks reddening. 'You should know by now that there is always a reason for everything I do for this house and for you. For all of us.'

Octavia inhaled a shaky breath, then slowly released it. 'Now, now, you two. I have no wish to bear witness to a lovers' tiff at this time of night. Louisa, why don't you tell us your reasons for inviting Mr Rose to stay?'

Louisa collapsed back onto the sofa, a look of exhaustion dimming the fire in her eyes. 'The simple fact is, with Nancy gone, our takings are down.' She sighed. 'At first, I thought having Eliza and Adelaide here would make up the shortfall, but Nancy was popular. Very popular. It's going to take time to replace her income. We simply cannot afford to turn clients away.'

Jacob pushed away from the fireplace and dropped into an armchair, leaning forward to place his elbows on his knees. He carefully watched Louisa. 'And by inviting Rose in you were extending hospitality but still clearly stating that we were not ready for him to be with Octavia.'

'Yes, in the hope he found her enticing enough that he will come back to make an appointment.'

Anticipation twisted inside Octavia at the thought of seeing William again, but she fought against it. The house was all she should be concerned about, not a man who clearly had not wanted to be here and would soon return north regardless.

She cleared her throat. 'I'm sorry for my reaction too, Louisa. I should have trusted you.'

'Not at all. I had to think of something without exposing you to any risk. We know nothing about Mr Rose, and an unknown client lying with you or any of my girls is not a rule I'll break. Whatever our current circumstances. Our days of having to welcome possible difficulties into this house are well and truly over.'

'Still, Jacob and I should've trusted your judgement.' Octavia squeezed Louisa's hand before raising her eyebrows at Jacob. 'Shouldn't we?'

He stood and walked to Louisa before staring deep into her eyes, leaning down and kissing her forehead. He seemed to hesitate before he pressed a firm kiss to her mouth that lasted for far too long.

Octavia rolled her eyes. 'All right, apology delivered.'

Louisa laughed and gently pushed Jacob away. 'Sit down before I forget what I was talking about.'

He grinned and resumed his seat, his eyes still firmly on his lover's face.

Octavia frowned. 'So, if business is not quite as booming as it once was, we will have to see what we can do to rectify that. Especially considering there are rumours flying around that the brothels are being watched.'

Jacob snapped his gaze to her. 'What are you talking about?'

Octavia leaned back against the settee and inhaled. 'It was something Adelaide and Eliza said to me earlier. I have no idea if there is any substance to it, but these murmurings usually start from somewhere.'

Jacob stood, concern furrowing his brow. 'Where did they hear this talk?'

'In the market.'

He looked at Louisa. 'I'll ask around the pubs and clubs. Half the men who drink in those places use a house from time to time. If the constabulary or someone of that ilk is making enquiries, the drinkers and womanisers will be the first to heed any warning of trouble.'

Louisa nodded, disquiet darkening her eyes. 'I'm sure it's nothing, but it will do no harm to be forewarned, forearmed. Not that I can imagine we are included in the number being watched. We have not even had as much as a complaint from our neighbours. Live and let live is the motto of Carson Street, which is why I like it here.'

'So you feel no need for alarm?' Octavia asked, uncertainty

whispering through her. 'I did my best to allay Adelaide and Eliza's fears but I'm not sure we should ignore—'

'I'm not ignoring anything,' Louisa interrupted, waving her hand dismissively. 'I'm just a firm believer in not worrying about something before it's even happened. Now, let's resume our conversation about Mr Rose. It's my hope he will soon join our ledger of returning visitors. He seemed moneyed. Did you manage to find out a little more about him?'

Burying her unease about the supposed rumours, Octavia nodded. 'I did, although I'm not sure that he will be coming back.'

'Oh?'

'He is only in Bath for two weeks before he returns to Manchester. His business is in textiles. He owns a mill or maybe even two. I couldn't be certain.' She smiled, unable to completely hide her immediate and unexpected like of Mr Rose. 'I liked him well enough. He was quite diverting, if I'm honest. He certainly handled my teasing well enough. In fact, I found him quite worthy of my best work. Tormenting him was enjoyable, but I did not get the impression brothels or whores are on his agenda during his time here.'

Jacob sniffed. 'I can't see how any toff who held himself as arrogantly as Rose did can be considered *diverting*.'

'He was here under duress, which accounts for him standing back at the door. The man's reluctance to be in a whorehouse hardly makes him arrogant. Once we were in the parlour, he was forthcoming enough. In fact, his conversation was interesting to say the least. I thought him good company. But, as I said, I do not think he'll be back.'

Louisa's brow furrowed. 'What did he say for you to be so certain?'

'His attention is entirely grounded in his business. Which I think is admirable. He acknowledged that the house is better than most. In fact, he said we are of a high calibre, but he has no interest in anything carnal, as far as I could tell.'

'Then I'm surprised you didn't find him infuriating.' Louisa smiled. 'You pride yourself on your professional abilities as much as Nancy did. The man was clearly impervious.'

Octavia returned her friend's smile. 'I wouldn't go that far. There was definite interest in his eyes whenever he looked at me.'

'Good.'

'And my interest was stirred by him, too. I like a man with ambition. Who wishes to make money. Who is strong and forth-right in his manner. In fact, during the time I spent with Mr Rose, I was reminded that I, too, hold ambition. He is the sort of individual I would like to learn from.'

Louisa glanced at Jacob before facing Octavia again. 'Well, there definitely seems to have been a connection between you.'

Ignoring the curiosity in her friends' eyes, Octavia frowned. 'He doesn't quite fit the expectation of his class. That, too, made him interesting. He isn't one for pleasure-seeking. He's a worker. I would hazard an extremely hard worker. I found him more than a little inspiring despite the short amount of time we spent together.'

Jacob huffed a laugh. 'Men of his class wouldn't know a real day's graft if it was laid out in front of them.'

Stifling the urge to snap at him in William's defence, Octavia kept her attention on Louisa. 'He is rich, I have no doubt of that, but I think he has worked for what he has, holds his mills in high regard and with the utmost care. He was angry about a business deal he'd lost supposedly due to him being unmarried. He didn't take kindly to the implication.'

'What does his marriage status have to do with running a mill?'

'Exactly. I think he was right to be affronted, but I also think his passionate rebuke of the situation was somewhat excessive. After all, marriage doesn't always equate to love and if an arrangement was made to his benefit, then why not take it?'

'He told you he is looking for love?' Louisa raised her eyebrows. 'You two most certainly talked, didn't you?'

Octavia's cheeks uncharacteristically heated. 'He didn't say he was looking for love,' she said, looking towards the window in order to avoid Louisa's stare. 'But his conviction and words led me to believe that he has not yet accepted the basis of what, for many, marriage actually is.' She faced her friends. 'Present company, Nancy and Francis excluded, of course.'

Louisa frowned. 'What do you mean?'

'Convenience.' Octavia shrugged. 'Your first marriage was one of convenience, wasn't it? As are so many others. There is nothing unusual or shameful about such an arrangement. I can't help thinking that maybe Mr Rose should consider marrying if his business is so important to him. A marriage that serves both the husband and the wife has to be worthwhile, does it not?'

'That's a very cold way of looking at the world, Octavia,' Louisa said as she pushed to her feet. 'I didn't believe real love was possible after what Anthony did to me, but...' She walked to Jacob, slipped her hand into his. 'Then I found Jacob.'

When Jacob slid his arm around Louisa's waist, Octavia steadfastly ignored the sudden jolt of loneliness that passed through her. 'And I'm glad for you. Both of you. But the fact of the matter is, marriages of convenience are universally common and, if it helps Mr Rose to achieve his goals in life, then he shouldn't let his pride get in the way of marrying.'

Louisa shook her head. 'Well, with that romantic thought, we'll say goodnight.'

Octavia lifted her hand in a semblance of a wave as Jacob and Louisa walked towards the door. Once alone, she dropped her head back against the settee and closed her eyes.

Love was love. Marriage was marriage. She had liked William Rose, had a quick respect for him even after such a brief meeting. Part of her wished him all the best. He seemed genuine, hardworking and had a good sense of humour. The other part, of course, was more than a little wary of him – especially considering how quickly she had become fond of him.

That sort of liking led to hasty decisions and regrettable mistakes.

6

William woke in his hotel bedroom and stretched, the bright winter sunlight filtering through the drapery at his window. Throwing back the covers, he yawned, feeling inexplicably optimistic in mood and outlook. He strode to the window and whipped back the curtains.

From his vantage point on the third floor, he surveyed the busyness of the street, savouring the aspiration the comings and goings inspired in him. Whichever direction he looked, people toiled. Whether it be behind the rudimentary tables set out along the pavements selling fruit or flowers, or the smartly dressed businessmen, their top hats gleaming, their canes flinging out and returning to the pavement in purposeful gestures of authority.

It was a new day. A new beginning, and he would fully embrace it. Yesterday's failure to secure a much-wanted deal was now pushed to the back of his mind.

Turning from the window, he reached for his robe from the end of the bed and put it on, before walking to a small corner desk. Pulling a sheaf of papers towards him, William reread the details of the men he would see today and what exactly he wanted or needed from them. His positive mood could be due to his eternal embrace of test or obstacle, but he could not deny a definite amount could be credited to his unexpectedly enjoyable sojourn at Carson Street yesterday. Not to mention the delectable whore he'd met there.

Octavia had met his eye with such confidence, her wit and intelligence clear in her unabashed willingness to challenge almost everything and anything he said. Placing his pen in the wooden holder on the desk, William stared towards the window again as though he could somehow direct his mind's eye to the house on Carson Street.

She could have no inkling how her verve had affected and inspired him, but he gave her a nod of gratitude anyway. She held such observation and instinct and had managed to obtain a lot more information about him than he usually would have given. Yet he did not regret anything he had shared with her. Somehow, their connection had led to him speaking openly about his ridiculous marriage frustration, which was surprising in itself considering he never divulged anything of his business matters. Why would he when he always found a solution to any problem?

And Octavia had been incredibly easy to talk to, had made him wonder who she was past her work. Her conversation intrigued him enough that it incited him to contemplate her background and who she really was – so much so, he had been rather pleased when the time came for him to leave. The last thing he wanted was to become fond of a whore. Such a misstep would inevitably lead to an unfavourable situation, no matter how amiable the woman.

William returned to his papers and did his utmost to force Octavia from his thoughts as he picked up his pen and dipped it in the inkwell. He made note of some strategies, enquiries and goals he would endeavour to achieve by the day's end. That done, he opened his small pocket notebook, in which he logged appointments and important contacts. He had just two weeks remaining in Bath and he was determined to make the most of them. The man he was due to see later today could provide the investment and knowledge William needed to make some vital changes to the working conditions of his mills. This gentleman was not a mill owner but involved in Bath's workhouse and was trying to make a difference to the poorest, most deprived areas of city.

William stood and walked to his closet. He removed his suit and proceeded to dress, his mind whirling with the plausibility of his thinking that it was men like Francis Carlyle who could provide the help he needed. William's mills were not just about producing the best quality cotton, in the most ardent quantities, but also focused on eliciting the best and most contented workers possible. Surely if he learned whether the hardships and complaints of his workers, as they stood at the moment, were duplicated in other cities in the country, that would eventually lead to better work practices all over?

If he were to speak to people involved in charity in Bath, then Devon, even possibly travelling from Manchester to Liverpool in the New Year, surely then he would have a good grasp on what needed to be done and what should be avoided. Many, admittedly not all, of the mill owners he knew in the north showed little enthusiasm for improvement, only a bull-headed focus on profit. Could they not see that they had a duty to do something for the hardworking employees under their care if they had any chance of those workers remaining loyal?

And, God knew, William coveted loyalty above all else. With no interest in marrying – at least not until he was absolutely safe in the knowledge that financial insecurity would never worry his own family as it had his parents – he would continue to vehemently live out his commitment to his father, mother and sisters while amassing as much of a fortune as he could.

Deep inside, he harboured the fear that his carefully constructed identity and self-built wealth would disappear and everything he now knew would come tumbling down around him. But, like his love for his family, he could not – would not – forsake the people working for him. The very people he had once been himself and without whom he would have nothing now.

For the time being at least, his family were his priority, and he would ensure they continued to live the rest of their lives as abundantly as possible and not fret over the lack of income to buy even the most basic of food or fuel as they had in the past. His mother and father lived out their retirement in a home they loved, which William had purchased for them, and happily spent their days together in its garden or else inside discussing the rights and wrongs of the world.

As for his sisters, the eldest was newly married after a long courtship with a man the entire family had begun to suspect would never propose but, happily, he had surprised them all just last Christmas. A quick wedding had followed, with William paying for as much as Elsa's beau would allow.

Then there was Clementine, his youngest sister, who grew increasingly passionate and curious in her studies and reading. So much so that William had no doubt she aspired to join the growing number of female explorers in both Britain and abroad.

Family was what mattered more than anything else, with each generation ensuring the prosperity of the one before and the one after. William inhaled as pride filled him before he reached for his hat. He would not think too deeply about his fear of starting a family of his own. Of failing to be as good a husband and father as his own. To do so would mean admitting he held weakness, that he could not conquer all within and outside of him.

Once he'd made his way downstairs to the lobby, William approached the dining room and nodded at the smartly dressed man at the entrance. 'Good morning. Mr William Rose for breakfast.'

'Of course, sir. If you'd like to follow me?'

At the table, William ordered coffee and a full breakfast before reaching for the newspaper folded beside his plate. Shaking it out, he nodded at the couple sat on one side of him and the elderly businessman to his right. The dark-wood-panelled room was elegant in its grandeur, the gas lighting bathing the space in brightness despite the winter month, only further fuelling William's optimism for the day ahead.

He turned his concentration to the paper.

Great changes expected as Councillor Maurice Lane secures position on the board of governors

William's affability vanished as he gritted his teeth, scanning the copy. 'You snidey...'

It was abundantly clear that Maurice Lane had known that his position on the board of governors was secured before his meeting with William last night. How else could such an announcement be made in the morning's paper? The man had kept true to their meeting for one reason and one reason only: to gloat. To spew his power over William in a deluge of torment.

Well, the man had certainly succeeded in making William sick to his stomach. He folded the newspaper and slapped it none too gently on the table, barely managing to acknowledge the waiter who laid his breakfast before him.

Anger swirled inside of him as William stared blindly at the bacon and eggs, nausea coating his throat. Was this the way business was to become? Less honesty and more hoodwinking? Less taking a man on his business acumen and more on his marital status and position in society? Good God, had the world turned on its axis when he'd not been looking?

Muttering a curse, William snatched up his cutlery and attacked the rashers, his heart beating hard, his resentment building. With each bite his sense of injustice gathered strength. The way he conducted business would not be dictated by the likes of Maurice Lane or anybody else who felt social climbing came above honestly won profit and a sense of duty to one's workers.

Well, whether he had the misfortune of seeing Lane again or not, this afternoon he was meeting with a man both wealthier and more congenial. A man who had made his fortune respectfully and through hard work every single day of his adult life.

A man who had turned his attention to the workhouse and was beginning to provoke charitable whispers among the city's elite. If William secured Francis Carlyle's advice, maybe even his investment, then Lane's rejection would be all but forgotten.

William gripped his knife and fork. Yes, Mr Francis Carlyle would be the man for William to do business with. Maurice Lane could go hang.

7

'Thank you so much for holding this back for me.' Octavia beamed at Mrs Warburton, the bookstall holder. 'You have no idea how desperate I have been for market day to come around this week so I could collect it.'

'Oh, Miss Marshall.' The older woman laughed. 'I suspect you wait like a rabbit trapped in a cage for *every* market day. Tell me one week when I haven't seen you here eagerly looking for what new books I have for sale.'

Fondness for Mrs Warburton swelled inside Octavia and she smiled, passing her a cash note. 'Which is why I don't want any argument from you about accepting this as a thank you.'

Mrs Warburton's eyes widened as she pressed one hand to her breast, the other clutching the note. 'I couldn't possibly! This is far beyond the cost of—'

'I will not take no for an answer,' Octavia said, covering the woman's hand with her own. 'You are a such a darling for picking out the books you know I'll like. I have been searching for a copy of *Mansfield Park* forever. It sold out almost as soon as it was published and has remained sought after ever since. I was beginning to think even finding a second-hand copy was an impossibility. This is a rare find, Mrs Warburton, and I am in your debt.'

'But—'

'Now I must hurry. I'm paying a visit to Nancy and want to get her some flowers. I'll see you again next week.'

Octavia hurried away before the lovely Mrs Warburton could protest further. Joining the crowds that had gathered by the abbey for the market, Octavia weaved her way through the throng, selecting some beautiful pink roses from the flower stall and then, as a special treat, a small pouch of wrapped chocolates.

Humming happily to herself, Octavia tried her utmost to ignore the leering glances of some of the men she passed, their eyes roving over her from head to toe. Market day was *her* day and she, unlike Nancy, refused to flirt or engage with any male interest away from the house.

She finally emerged onto Queen Square and walked up the steps of Francis's grand townhouse and knocked on the door.

The door was opened by young Alice, who bobbed a semi-curtsey, her blonde curls spilling from her cap, her green eyes slightly lowered. 'Good morning, Miss Octavia.'

'Well, good morning to you, Alice.' Octavia smiled, her heart aching for this poor young girl and all she had endured at the city's workhouse before being adopted by Nancy and Francis. It was clear that it would take time and patience as Octavia's friends waited for Alice to trust them enough that she finally accepted there was no need for her to work for them out of gratitude or anything else. 'You seem to be more settled in every time I visit. Are you getting along all right?'

'Yes, miss.' The girl's gaze remained lowered as Octavia

entered, and Alice closed the door. 'Nancy is in the drawing room. Can I bring you some tea?'

'The drawing room?' Octavia glanced towards the stairs. 'Is she with someone?'

'Not right now, miss.' Alice smiled sheepishly. 'But she has got it into her head that she and Francis need to have some hobnobs over. To butter them up.'

'To do what exactly?'

'I don't know, but the longer I live here, the more I realise Nancy is always up to something.'

'Indeed, she is.' Octavia sighed. 'Then I'd better go up and tea would be lovely, thank you.'

The girl hurried away towards the kitchen, leaving Octavia staring after her as she removed her coat and scarf. She had no doubt Alice was the first of many workhouse children Nancy and Francis would find homes for, but Octavia was also acutely aware of the struggle they faced in their heartfelt mission. Placating opposition to their efforts for rousing public interest and support sometimes seemed impossible.

Not to mention the production Nancy and Francis had planned to show at the Theatre Royal. Francis might be a talented writer and had duly tweaked the script to explain Nancy's pregnancy, but the play was scheduled to start in February and Octavia remained more than a little alarmed that Nancy still intended playing the lead part so close to when her baby was due.

Not that there was any chance at all of her friend relenting.

Picking up her purse, the flowers and chocolates, Octavia approached the stairs. She knew all too well the fight her friends were up against in their bid to help as many children as possible. God knew, Louisa had been the one person keen to show Octavia kindness, as opposed to forty others who had turned away from her when she'd been hawking on the streets. Sometimes it was too much for people to look a person in desperate need in the eye, let alone offer a helping hand.

Yet Louisa had done both the day she had met Octavia...

Swallowing against the unexpected lump that rose in her throat, Octavia entered the drawing room. Nancy stood with her back to the window, a sheaf of papers in her hands as she surveyed the piano and then the sofa through narrowed eyes.

Octavia cleared her throat. 'It looks as though I am disturbing something of importance.'

'Importance? More like a pain in the frigging arse.' Nancy blew out a heavy breath, cursed and walked to a side table, unceremoniously flinging down the papers. She met Octavia's gaze and grinned. 'But I'm so glad you've come by. I no longer have the enthusiasm for entertaining that I did when I woke. Come and give me a hug.'

Placing the flowers and chocolates next to Nancy's papers, Octavia embraced her friend, happiness warming her for how well Nancy looked considering the stage of her pregnancy. 'I assume Lyme Regis did you good?' she asked, holding her at arm's length. 'They say it is quite the place for honeymooners these days.'

'It was lovely, but cold by the sea...' Nancy wiggled her eyebrows. 'Not that we spent a lot of time out of the hotel bedroom.'

'I have no need to know more. Here.' She thrust the roses and chocolates at Nancy. 'A small welcome-home present.'

'Oh, the flowers are lovely and...' She peered into the pouch and let out a little squeal. 'Chocolate! Well, these are entirely mine. My husband can go without.'

Alice entered carrying a tea tray. Octavia slid her gaze to

Nancy and smiled to see her friend looking at Alice with such love in her eyes, her longing for the girl's happiness palpable.

'Thank you, Alice,' Nancy said, as Alice laid the tray on the low table in front of the sofa. 'I'll let you know if we need anything else.'

Alice nodded and quickly left the room, closing the door behind her.

Nancy sighed. 'Oh, I wish she would relax a little more around Francis and me.' She shook her head, gesturing for Octavia to take a seat before sitting herself. 'She has been with us for almost three months but still insists on working as our maid and not just live here as our adoptive daughter.' Nancy's voice cracked. 'Which is exactly what she is.'

Octavia took her hand and squeezed, hating the pain in her friend's soft grey eyes. 'Give her time. She went through hell and back at the workhouse. She is proud, Nancy. She probably feels you are already doing more than enough by taking her in.' Octavia looked around the beautifully decorated gold and cream room. 'This house will be like a palace to her. Can you blame her for not yet considering herself anything more than a rescued orphan?'

Nancy wiped her fingers beneath her eyes. 'Trust you to speak about the situation as though it was a scene from one of your novels.'

'And yet, the picture I painted made you smile. Books provide escape, happiness, and I – for one – will continue to live through them for the rest of my life. Now...' Octavia removed her gloves and reached for the teapot. 'What are your plans now you're back?'

'Well, Francis and I hope to place at least four more children in good homes, or at least good employment, by Christmas. Francis is working hard to obtain more and more business associates who lean towards generosity rather than gain. It was important to him that Alice came to live with us, but he knows that's not possible for every child so he's determined to find people willing to employ or home children and treat them as well as he would.'

'He's quite amazing, you know.'

'Oh, I know.' Nancy beamed. 'That's why I made him mine.'

'The fact of the matter is, Nancy Carlyle, there is nothing or no one that you wouldn't make yours if that was what you wanted.'

'True.' Nancy accepted the cup of tea Octavia offered her. 'Francis is meeting with a gentleman this afternoon who sounds promising. Even if my husband suspects the man's interests will not lie in the welfare of Bath's lost children but rather those living further north.'

Octavia lowered her cup, a strange knot forming in her stomach as she was reminded of William. 'Northern businessmen... what a conundrum they are.'

'What?'

Octavia sipped her tea. 'I had a drink with a man at Carson Street last night. A Mr William Rose. He was quite full of himself but amusing, too. Had opinions about anything and everything that was raised between us. From business to marriage. I found him—'

'Marriage? Since when do culls discuss marr—'

The drawing room opened, and Francis entered, dressed in a black business suit, his dark blond hair neatly combed and lightly oiled. His gaze fell on Octavia and he smiled. 'Well, hello there. How are you?'

'I'm very well,' Octavia said, accepting the light kiss he brushed to her cheek. 'How are you?'

'Very well.' His gaze slid to Nancy and his eyes immediately darkened with blatant desire. 'Why wouldn't I be after a four-day honeymoon with this one?'

'This one?' Nancy feigned offence even though her eyes glittered with mischief and a blush leapt onto her cheeks. 'The man has no idea of courting whatsoever.'

'Courting?' Francis laughed as he sat down. 'You're mine now, woman. I have absolutely no need to court you.'

'Hmm, we'll see about that.' Nancy waved her hand. 'Now, enough of your silliness, I was just telling Octavia about your meeting this afternoon and our hope that it might lead to the gentleman employing children from the workhouse.'

'I'm afraid that won't be the outcome of today's meeting, my love.' Francis blew out a breath. 'The man owns a couple of textile mills and from what I can gather from friends who already know him, Mr Rose's interests lie in the—'

'Rose?' Octavia's heart gave a jolt. 'William Rose?'

Nancy raised her eyebrows. 'Isn't that the name of the man you spoke to?'

'Yes. It was him who came to the house last night.' Octavia faced Francis. 'I can't believe you are meeting him this afternoon.'

Francis frowned, his gaze concerned. 'Why? Did he upset you?'

'Upset me?' Octavia bristled, hating the heat that rose in her cheeks as William's face filled her mind's eye. 'As if anyone could upset me. William Rose included.'

'Good, because from what I have been told from some mutual associates, William Rose is a stand-up and trustworthy man. An astute and seasoned businessman who rarely takes no for an answer, yet he does have ideas that benefit his employees. Something I find both inspiring and full of humility. Of course, if there is another side to him I should be aware of, then I'd be glad to know before I meet with him.'

Octavia swallowed. Suddenly she had much to say about William. How much he had interested her and made her want to know more about him. How she had felt a certain, unidentifiable something between them that had made her believe he would undoubtedly match her, blow for blow, if they were to indulge in a war of words and wills.

She feigned nonchalance with a shrug and reached for her tea. 'There isn't. He just struck me as pleasant, that's all.'

'Are you sure?' Nancy narrowed her eyes. 'You seem more unsettled than you were a few moments ago.'

Octavia laughed. 'I am not unsettled. The man was perfectly fine.' She turned to Francis. 'Tell me more about your meeting.'

'Well, he wishes to consult me on my philanthropy rather than my work at the theatre. It seems he is invested in improving the working conditions at his mills.' Francis gave an approving nod, his eyes showing his pleasure. 'Which, of course, I heartily applaud. From what I've been told, William Rose has ideas that are not always backed by others. He is quite obviously a man who knows his own mind.'

Octavia sipped her tea, pleased that her opinion of Mr Rose had been seconded rather than disproved. 'And that is why you are meeting him? To discuss the welfare of the children working at his mills?'

'On the contrary, I think he wishes to gain information from me regarding children and their function in the workplace.' Francis shifted further back into his seat. 'But no matter how amiable the man might be, I will not be sending any child to work in one of his mills. Wretched places for children. For men and women, too, no doubt. No, I will advise him on anything philanthropic he might like to discuss, but there will be no possibility of me asking him to take one of my children.'

'*Your* children, my love?' Nancy smiled, her eyes teasing.

'Yes. *My* children.'

Octavia looked between her friends, the shock of the coincidence that Francis was meeting with William subsiding. It pleased her that Francis had been told of William's virtues. She so often relied on her intuition and it was satisfying to have her good instincts about William confirmed.

She had enjoyed sparring with him in jest as much as she had speaking with him. An idea began to form in her mind. Oh, it would be such fun to further her tormenting of the man! A little jesting between them would do no harm when he was leaving town in a couple of weeks. Besides, she softly smiled, she was entirely convinced William Rose would be delighted by her teasing and it would give him something to remember her by.

'Francis…' she murmured. 'Is there any chance you were thinking of investing in Mr Rose's businesses as well as offering him your advice?'

'No. None at all.' He brow creased again. 'Why?'

'Would you be willing to play a little jape on Mr Rose? For me?'

Francis glanced at Nancy. 'A jape?'

Nancy narrowed her eyes as she looked at Octavia. 'What are you up to?'

'Mr Rose, as nice as he is, is more than game for a laugh, I fancy. I think he would appreciate my joke…' She looked between her friends. 'Once he realises my plan was meant in jest and not malevolence.'

Francis frowned. 'What is it you want me to do exactly?'

'If he brings up the possibility of you investing, which I have no doubt he will, just answer him with a refusal as follows…'

Octavia slid a sly smile to each of her friends. 'Say you do not invest in businesses run by unmarried men.'

'What? But that's ridic—'

'Please, Francis. He was so riled that he had received rejection from investors for this singular reason. To have you further press the point will be hilarious. I appreciate you will have to eventually tell him the torment came from me, but please, I would so enjoy your retelling of his reaction.'

Nancy grinned. 'I love this, but do you think it a good idea? What if he takes offence rather than see the funny side?'

Octavia waved dismissively, the need to tease William too strong. 'It will be fine. He's leaving Bath soon to return to Manchester. Anyway, I'm entirely convinced he'll see the funny side.'

Francis sighed and rubbed his hand along his bearded jaw. 'Do you know something, Octavia? When you or Louisa are with Nancy, I feel thoroughly browbeaten.'

Octavia grinned. 'Is that a yes? You'll do it?'

'Fine, fine. I'll do it.'

Octavia put down her cup and clapped. 'Excellent.'

8

William checked his pocket watch for the second time in ten minutes before glancing towards the hotel's gilded front doors. Councillor Lane's dismissal of his business proposition yesterday evening and news of Lane's new role in government this morning, had stretched William's impatience to meet with Francis Carlyle to breaking point. Did the businessmen of Bath think him a fool? A man to be toyed with? First his damn marital status comes into question and then a second contact keeps him waiting.

He glanced at his watch again. Fine, so Carlyle had five more minutes before he was officially late, but still...

He looked towards the doors just as a smartly dressed man entered the lobby, his stature self-assured and commanding. From what William had heard about Carlyle's progressive work at both the theatre and Bath's workhouse, he had no doubt that this was the man he'd been waiting for.

William strode forward, his hand outstretched. 'Mr Carlyle? William Rose.'

'Ah, Mr Rose, it's good to meet you.' Carlyle shook William's hand before he glanced upwards at the hotel's fancy ceiling and enormous chandelier. 'And in the most extravagant of surroundings.'

William inwardly cursed his choice of venue. Francis Carlyle might be one of the wealthiest men in this city, but he was also a man who made no secret of the fact his priority was resolutely grounded in the benefit of those in dire need. Those who needed help not hindrance, care not criticism. He would undoubtedly consider this hotel and its patrons the epitome of all he disliked.

William gestured with a wave of his hand towards some small tables situated in the far corner of the lobby. 'Shall we take a seat? I have arranged for coffee to be brought over once you arrived.'

As Carlyle led the way, William's determination that this meeting would succeed where his last had failed only grew stronger. It might be proving a lot more difficult to obtain investment during this trip to Bath than he'd envisaged, but he would not give up his idea to learn more about southern business practices just yet. He harboured thoughts of venturing to Birmingham or Bristol and intended visiting them in due course.

Once they were seated and the coffee served, William settled in a wing-back chair. 'So, Mr Carlyle, tell me about your endeavours at the workhouse. I have heard many good things about you and your progress since I arrived in the city.'

'Considering I embarked on the work less than six months ago, things are going very well indeed.' Carlyle's blue eyes brightened with unmistakable pride. 'The best might be that my new wife and I have adopted a child of our own from the workhouse. Alice is wonderful...' his smile faltered, 'if not deeply affected by all that she has suffered. In time, I hope her trust in us will increase and her confidence grow.'

There was no doubting the man's sincerity and William greatly admired Carlyle's undertaking. 'You clearly have a profound need to help those less fortunate, as do I. My mills provide employment, of course, but I'm also aware of the responsibility – the morality – that comes with that.'

Carlyle carefully watched him, his eyes ever so slightly dimming with what looked to be scepticism. 'Maybe you do, Mr Rose, but I cannot say that I would ever place a child I was helping into one of your mills. Or any mill. I have not heard a single story that has led me to believe they are in any way suited to children working at them.'

William fought to keep his defences lowered. The man did not know his mills and he did not know him. 'That may be true of many mills around the country, sir, but I believe my mills are run differently. Run better.'

'But you employ children?'

'Not under the age of thirteen. I believe every child deserves to have some form of education. However, I also know the plight of many families and it is not always possible that they can give the luxury of schooling to their children. Instead, they are forced to send them out to work.'

'Of course, but there is a difference between acceptable work for children and barbaric child labour. I understand the mills can be harsher places than the workhouses, with some children labouring up to twelve hours a day.'

'In some maybe, but not mine.'

Carlyle cleared his throat and held William's gaze before he abruptly reached for his coffee. 'I hate to say this, Mr Rose, but I have heard the horror stories. Cotton fibres clinging to hair and clothes causing breathing problems; workers exhausted by heat, hunger and long hours. Not to mention the accidents where limbs are—'

'Mr Rose...' William struggled to hold his temper. How dare Carlyle presume him to be the same type of employer as some of the lowest in the industry? 'Let me make something clear. I run my mills as fairly and as considerately as possible. I do not employ children under the age of thirteen; the ratio of men and women is equal, thus giving each household the potential to double their weekly income. Not only that, I open the mills an hour later than most and close them an hour earlier.'

'Even if what you say is true—'

'It is true,' William said, firmly. 'I also allow twenty minutes for breakfast, an hour for lunch and thirty minutes for tea, providing all food and water. That alone means my workers are neither starving nor abnormally exhausted.'

Carlyle replaced his coffee cup on the table and when he spoke, the fiery accusation in his tone had somewhat lessened. 'And why would a man with such business expertise choose to do all those things when others do not?'

'Because...' William clenched his jaw. He would not tolerate the man belittling his professionalism, whether he needed Carlyle's progressive knowledge about environmental overhaul or not. 'Reduced hours mean my workers are less tired and, in turn, they produce more cloth. Time and again, my theory has been proven right.'

Slowly, Carlyle's mouth lifted into a smile. 'I do believe you speak sincerely, Mr Rose. It's possible my friend's summary of you was entirely misplaced.'

William frowned. 'What friend?'

'I believe you met her last night. Octavia Marshall.'

'Octa...' Words flailed on William's tongue as fleeting satisfaction whispered through him that Octavia had spoken of him... only to be quickly replaced with annoyance that her reference had clearly not been in admiration. 'She spoke to you about me?'

'She did.'

How in heaven's name could Carlyle be friends with a whore? 'I must say I'm surprised you know Miss Marshall. Excuse my impertinence, but I wouldn't have thought a man as happily married as you seem to be would have need to visit a brothel.'

Carlyle's smile vanished. 'You are impertinent indeed, sir.' His cheeks darkened, his eyes glinting dangerously. 'Even more so considering the woman Octavia worked with for well over a year and remains best friends with is now my wife.'

Shocked, William flinched. 'Your...'

'Wife, sir.'

William opened his mouth, tried to say something – anything – to make up for his faux pas and hide his embarrassment. Carlyle had married a whore? The notion seemed ludicrous.

At last, William found his voice. 'I apologise. You are, of course, free to marry whomever you choose. Whatever their vocation or station in life.'

'Indeed, sir, I am. More than that, I have married a spectacular woman whom I love with all my heart. Nancy is my life. The pride I want her to have in me is why I strive so fervently to make this world a better place. She is the woman I need standing beside me in everything. Always.'

Carlyle's passion was so palpable, a rare shame shrouded William as he sat back in his seat and tried to ignore the pang of envy that Carlyle had a wife whom he regarded as the light above all others. How would it be to feel that way about another person?

Carlyle stood. 'On that note, I think it best we call an end to our meeting, don't you?' He extended his hand. 'I wish you all the best, sir.'

Damnation. William abruptly stood. 'Sir, I apologise for my rudeness. Please, if you can forgive my presumption, I would appreciate just a little more of your time. I truly admire your work and it would be an honour if you would allow me to pick your brains about my future aspirations.'

Indecision warred in Carlyle's eyes before his tight jaw loosened and he slowly lowered his hand. He blew out a breath. 'Apology accepted. I do not like to go back on an agreement, and I did agree to advise you.' Carlyle resumed his seat. 'Despite your misplaced assumption about myself and my wife, I can see why Octavia would enjoy your company. I have the impression she takes kindly to people who have the ability to admit their mistakes... although you could certainly do with polishing up your manners a little.'

Duly chastised but grateful for Carlyle's quick forgiveness, William sat down and picked up his coffee. 'What did Octavia say about me exactly?'

'Not so much.' Carlyle sighed. 'But I must tell you that she and my wife are not backwards in coming forwards with their teasing, Mr Rose. Octavia was keen for me to tell you, for her amusement and possibly yours, that I do not invest in businesses owned by unmarried men, but I am no longer in the mood for my wife's and Octavia's fun and games.'

'She...' William stiffened. Well, of all the lowly, conniving... Yet laughter trembled in his stomach, his heart picking up speed. Did Octavia wish to continue their sparring? Interesting... 'I see. Maybe I need to make appointment to see Octavia again. Take a second chance to set things straight between us.'

'On your head be it, but if you go to the house, I recommend you tell Jacob you wish to make an appointment rather than arriving unannounced and demanding to see Octavia. Louisa runs a tight ship.' Carlyle raised his eyebrows, seemingly in warning. 'And I wouldn't want anything – or anyone – I have had associations with to upset that.'

'Message received, loud and clear, Mr Carlyle.'

Loud and clear, indeed. William took a sip of his coffee. One thing was for certain, he was far from finished in his association with Octavia Marshall.

9

'Obviously with a Christmas wedding we won't have a very wide choice of flowers, but I thought...'

Louisa's voice faded as Octavia stared at Carson Street's small back garden through her friend's study window. The barren trees bent and trembled in the cold autumnal wind, their branches long-reaching, gnarly fingers – very much like the talons that clawed at Octavia's conscience.

As much as she tried to join in the wedding preparations, as much as she smiled and nodded, her thoughts turned to herself and her own future whenever the subject of Louisa's wedding was raised. What sort of friend did that make her after every-thing Louisa had done for her? She could literally hear her father's voice in her head: *You are selfish. Assuming. Take, take, take...*

After all that had happened to her, both good and bad, she was still nothing more than the girl who had fled her home after her father's deterioration into violence and near-madness after her mother's untimely death. Too afraid, or too weak, Octavia had not known how to care for her father in his grief while she struggled with her own.

Her mother, the family lynchpin, was no more and her family and home had quickly become unhinged, breaking apart into pieces. Octavia closed her eyes as memories battered her, feeling equally as painful as her father's fists had upon her body. And now part of her wished to flee again, start over somewhere new where she could reinvent herself afresh.

'Octavia, are you even listening to me?'

Octavia jumped and snapped her gaze to Louisa. 'Of course, I am. Flowers. How about roses?'

'I finished talking about flowers a few moments ago. Are you all right?'

'I'm fine.' Octavia forced a smile. 'I was just thinking about something I read in the paper yesterday.'

'The paper?' Louisa's disbelief in Octavia's feeble claim was clear. 'You're thinking about a newspaper article now, when there is so much to organise?'

Feeling guilty that she was so distracted when Louisa needed her, Octavia sat straighter in her seat and gave her friend her full attention. 'I'm sorry. What did you say that I missed?'

Louisa put her hands on her hips and paced back and forth in front of her bureau. 'I asked you what you thought about inviting the neighbours? They have been good to turn a blind eye to our business here, but I'm not sure Mrs Brown or Mrs Dobbs would want to be seen at a whore's wedding.'

'Then if they don't, they don't deserve an invite,' Octavia said, firmly. 'Why even consider them when there is every possibility one of them might have alerted the papers about us? We still don't know who is stirring the pot about the brothels around town. It could well be someone we thought we could trust.'

'Hmm, you're right.'

'And anyway, just because you're getting married, that doesn't mean you have to invite the whole street.'

Louisa's violet eyes darkened with suspicion. 'Is it the claims in the paper that the brothels are being watched that has you so distracted? You know Jacob and I said to ignore it.'

'And I am, but I still think if Mrs Brown and Mrs Dobbs are too uppity to—'

'If the authorities turn up here, we'll deal with them then. Not before. Gossip and press speculation about the sex trade is nothing new. Anyway, it seems to me your agitation has nothing to do with the police. Is my talking about the wedding beginning to grate? Is that it?'

Octavia's cheeks heated as she huffed a laugh. 'Why would you ask me that?'

'Answer the question.' Louisa glared as she stepped closer. 'Does my getting married annoy you?'

Angry words danced on Octavia's tongue, her pulse beating in her temple as she grappled to trap all of her insecurities inside. She curled her fingers around the arms of her chair, trying to calm her suddenly racing heart.

'Well?' Louisa demanded, her cheeks now flushed, her eyes wide in expectation. 'Does it?'

'Of course not,' Octavia said quietly, holding Louisa's gaze and somewhat surprised by her vehemence. 'Does it bother you?'

Louisa flinched. 'What?'

'You are clearly more troubled by these arrangements than I could ever be.'

'Is that so? Well, let me say this. If you were more like Nancy, you'd at least have the honesty to tell me what you are thinking. After all, it was clear after we spoke at Nancy's wedding that you had reservations about me marrying, but I had hoped I'd allayed your fears. Clearly I failed.'

'And what about your fears, Louisa?' Octavia retorted, knowing full well she was hiding her selfishness in retaliation and hating herself for it. 'You are not full of love and laughter like a bride in waiting, looking forward to her special day!'

Tension permeated the room, pressing down on Octavia's chest. Somehow, despite the whoring, the streets, the hunger, she had managed to maintain a modicum of the manners and decorum with which she had been raised. Yet, in that moment, such horrible feelings swirled inside her, urging her to break free of her upper-middle-class breeding and embrace who she was now. A woman trapped within a life she had fallen into and now wished to escape. A woman who had lived and eaten with others on the streets, who had stolen bread so that she might eat, had turned a trick in a filthy alleyway so that she might rent a bed. But how was she to leave? What else did she know but long-ago privilege and whoring?

She closed her eyes and breathed deep before opening them again. God in heaven, were those tears in Louisa's eyes? 'Louisa, I'm sorr—'

'Don't be.' Louisa tightly crossed her arms, her gaze unhappy. 'You're right. I am more worried than joyful about Jacob and I marrying. I fear the change as much as you, if I'm honest.'

'You do?'

Louisa exhaled a shaky breath. 'He wants a family, but the thought of becoming a mother scares me senseless. I need to keep running this house, Octavia. I need all it represents of how far I've come. But how can I expect Jacob to agree to me remaining a brothel madam if I become pregnant with his child?'

'Oh, Louisa.' Octavia stood and gripped Louisa's elbows, her concerns for herself dissolving under the fear in Louisa's eyes. 'Jacob knows how passionate you are about your independence. Surely he will not push you to have a child if you are not ready?'

'I'm not so sure. He loves me so much and...' She shook her head, tears glistening on her lashes. 'And I don't want to lose him.'

'You won't.' Octavia brushed her fingers under her friend's eyes. 'He is here for the long term. Trust me.'

'Then at least tell me you will be here, too. I have a feeling I'm going to need your sensible head more than ever once Jacob and I are wed.'

Guilt pressed down on Octavia. How could she promise such a thing when her need to leave the Carson Street house grew stronger each day?

She walked to the window and stared into the street, lacking the courage to face her friend with what she was about to say. 'I can't promise that when I continue to feel it's time for me to move on. Things are changing with us, and they are changing in the community.' Taking a deep breath, Octavia turned. 'It feels as though the end to what I know and love living and working in this house is changing more than I can cope with.'

Louisa crossed her arms, her violet eyes gleaming with what looked suspiciously like tears. 'Surely, you know that I will never desert you? Will never give up on this house? For goodness' sake, we have been friends long enough—'

'That you should know how much this house means to me, too. But I can't stand by and do nothing when I suspect the life I've lived these past few years will come to an end... whether that be in a few months or even a year from now.' Octavia walked closer, praying Louisa heard and understood her. 'I have to start thinking where I go from here. No matter how much you and

Nancy continue to claim you are not changed, you are. Both of you. Nancy is already married or you soon will be, too. That changes everything.'

'Does it really fill you with dread that your closest friends have found love?'

'Not for you and Nancy, but for my own standing in life, yes.'

Pain and fear swirled behind Octavia's chest. How could she possibly confess to Louisa how scared she was of being alone and on the street again? Of having two more people she had come to love and trust slip away from her?

Her mother's passing and her father's enraged, grief-stricken deterioration already haunted her so deeply. The memory of her final altercation with her father – when he had pushed her to the floor, taken his belt and whipped her across the head and body as though she were a child he despised when he had once loved her so very much – was yet to leave her.

'Octavia? What is it?'

Octavia swallowed, blinked back her tears. 'I would love for you and Nancy to always be there for me, but marriage means commitment to your spouses. Not to friends or associates... and, in my experience, maybe not even to your children.'

'Do you really think Nancy or I would ever put Jacob and Francis above our children?'

Octavia suddenly felt entirely exhausted. 'I just need to find a path of my own, Louisa. Please don't think me selfish, but just that I am taking responsibility for my own life. Isn't that something you would normally applaud?'

Louisa stared before her shoulders dropped and she gave a small smile. 'You're right. I would. Come and sit down.'

They walked to the sofa and Octavia clasped her hands tightly in her lap.

'Tell me what you would like to happen,' Louisa said.

Octavia swallowed, unsure where to begin. Gathering her courage, she drew in a long breath. 'When my mother died, my father diminished in mind, body and feeling. His grief was poured onto me – into me – both in words and wrath. So much so that I was forced to accept how weak and unworthy I am.'

'What? Octavia, for the love of God, you are not—'

'No, Louisa, I am entirely convinced he would not have become the man he did had I been a better daughter. If I have paid more attention to him while I was growing, then he would not have collapsed so completely upon Mama's death.'

'But you could not have controlled the way your father's grief consumed him. His decline was not your fault.'

'Maybe not, but he made me believe I am selfish and maybe I am, but that won't stop me from protecting myself against a future where I have nothing. You and Nancy marrying has just made me think about my prospects past this house. If I am ever to live respectfully, to be proud of who I am and how I live... to make my mother proud, I need to find the fortitude to make that happen.'

'Your mother would be proud of who you are now.'

'Proud that I am a whore? That I once was destined for a good marriage and now sleep with men for money?' Octavia wiped her tears with the backs of her fingers. 'I don't think so and neither do you. Not really.'

She stared into Louisa's eyes, her thoughts returning to the passion she had seen in William Rose as he spoke of his business, of how it was clear he would do anything to make his mills succeed.

Pulling back her shoulders, Octavia took a long breath and tilted her chin. 'I think I would like to become a woman of business. Maybe buy a small shop or invest in someone's industry.'

Louisa smiled. 'A businesswoman... oh, yes, I can quite imagine that.'

Excitement simmered inside Octavia, certainty echoing in her mind.

'Well, then...' Louisa stood. 'If business is what your mind and heart is leading you to consider, I think you should start your research this very evening.'

Octavia's smile faltered. 'What? How?'

Louisa's eyes glistened with satisfaction before she walked behind her desk and pulled an open ledger towards her. 'Yes, it is as I remember.'

Octavia stared at her friend's bowed head. 'What is?'

'Mr Rose. He has an appointment with you tonight. You could ask him about investing in his mills.' She looked up. 'Or at least ask if he might be willing to share some details about his business. There is much I can teach you about figures and balancing, of course, but unlike me Mr Rose is a man who deals with people outside of a single enterprise. He will give you a much clearer impression of business than I could, I'm sure.'

'Possibly. But—'

'You liked Mr Rose, did you not? Felt a connection with him?' Louisa raised her eyebrows. 'The fact he is returning speaks volumes considering his supposed reluctance to come here the first time around. He clearly liked you, too.'

Octavia's cheeks warmed as her stomach knotted with hope. Could what Louisa implied be true? Had she nudged into William's thoughts since they last spoke, as he had hers? Might he be willing to teach her about a new, exciting future in commerce?

'You should get yourself ready,' Louisa said, firmly taking Octavia's elbow and steering her to the door. 'Mr Rose will be here at ten o'clock.'

Forcing herself to move, Octavia opened the study door. 'I'll... yes... get ready.'

She slowly walked into the hallway, barely hearing Louisa's study door click shut behind her.

Once Octavia reached the bottom of the stairs, she stopped. 'Oh, no.'

How could she have forgotten what she had asked of Francis? She had no idea how his meeting had fared with William earlier that day. Had he acted on her request to tease the man?

How in heaven's name was she to probe William when he had made it blatantly clear that women had no place in his future? When there was every chance he might have deemed her jesting as ridiculously juvenile?

What was more, she was a whore. He could easily laugh in her face at the suggestion she might become involved in business.

But then his wonderful, interested gaze filled her mind's eye and a soft smile pulled at Octavia's lips. No, he would not be so derogatory. His fairness to others seemed clear to her even if she knew little else about William Rose. She sensed his kindness, his willingness to listen, despite his often-hardened focus on life and ambition. He would help her, she was sure.

Her optimism ignited, Octavia climbed the stairs. All she needed to do was prove her sincerity and drive for change and success by way of enthusiasm, commitment and passion.

Or if all else failed, she could, of course, simply seduce the man...

10

William turned into Carson Street and strode towards the house. Having secured an appointment with Octavia this evening, he could not wait to see her. His desire to confront her about asking Carlyle to goad him and how she had mistakenly presumed William for a man who could be persecuted in such a way could not be suppressed a moment longer.

Not that he felt the least bit maltreated. Her continued attention was a definitive form of flattery, surely? If she felt the need to torment him, she wanted his attention. Otherwise, why involve Carlyle in her entertainments?

William smiled, anticipation of their reunion exciting him. Her blue, blue eyes appeared in his mind, the wonderful, teasing way she smiled. It was hard to deny that it wasn't his attraction to Octavia that had drawn him back to Carson Street as much as the need to level the playing field. Her attempt to provoke him had merely increased his interest in her.

Beautiful, intelligent and funny.

In another world, she might have been the kind of woman he would like to spend time with, but these days his focus was on business and the only woman he could afford to spend time with was one he might consider marrying. A woman who was strong, understanding of his work, stalwart enough to stomach the good and bad sides of the industry.

Unfortunately, no such woman had yet appeared.

'Mr Rose. Good evening.'

William had just reached the bottom step of the house when Jacob, the six foot three high and wide doorman, spoke. Purposefully holding Jacob's steady gaze, William mounted the steps and nodded. 'Jacob. How are you? It's good to see you again.'

'I'm very good, thank you, sir.' Jacob's breath puffed in plumes in the cold evening air. He rubbed his gloved hands together. 'Octavia is waiting with Louisa in the parlour if you'd like to join them.'

'Thank you. Is there any reason you cannot wait inside? Have clients knock on the door? The temperatures have noticeably dropped this evening.'

'I prefer to stand out here. There's been talk of possible trouble for houses such as ours. If I'm out here, I'll get no nasty surprises from the other side of a closed door.'

William was about to ask about the nature of the perceived trouble and what Jacob intended to do, but then thought better of it. It was sometimes wiser not to poke at a hornets' nest when they were built like Jacob Jackson. Not that William had any doubt he would handle himself well enough with Jacob, should the situation arise. But why tempt fate? Touching the brim of his hat, William entered the house.

He hung his coat and hat before smoothing the lapels of his suit jacket and walking into the parlour.

Octavia was sat on the sofa, her brow creased as she read a book, holding it aloft in one hand, while the other dipped into a small bowl of sugared almonds beside her. His impending arrival seemed not to be concerning her one whit.

'Mr Rose.' Louisa Hill smiled as she rose from the desk at the window, an unmistakable glint of amusement in her eyes. 'Welcome back.'

'Thank you.' He glanced at Octavia again as she slowly lowered her book and met his gaze. 'Octavia.'

'Mr Rose.' She laid the book on a side table and stood. Her smile was wide, her eyes bright and alert as she came towards him. 'You are here.'

You are here? What did that mean? Did she think he would change his mind? Did she hope he'd change his mind? 'I am. Our appointment was at ten, was it not?'

'Yes, but I wasn't sure...' She waved her hand dismissively. 'It does not matter. Can I pour you a drink before we go upstairs?'

Her gaze dropped to his mouth, her blue eyes glittering with clear intent, which had the unsettling effect of making him feel as though she had simultaneously cupped his groin. 'Um, yes, thank you. Brandy would be good.' He nodded at Louisa where she stood at the drinks cabinet, her gaze drifting back and forth between him and Octavia. 'If you don't mind, Mrs Hill.'

'Not at all. And, please, call me Louisa. We're not much for formality here, are we, Octavia?'

When Louisa turned away to pour the drinks, William forced himself to hold Octavia's unwavering stare. There was something wholly different about her tonight. The flirtation was still there, the underlying teasing, but also a harder, more determined look in her eyes that he could not decipher.

'You look lovely this evening,' he said, purposefully drawing his gaze over her décolletage and the tightened bodice of her emerald-green satin dress. 'The colour of your dress is beautiful on you.'

She opened her mouth slightly, but at first no words emerged. She stared at him, a slight blush creeping into her cheeks. 'Thank you.'

He winked and her colour deepened. William barely resisted the urge to punch the air in triumph. Whether she intended seducing him, talking her way out of her jest with Carlyle, or merely tormenting him, he had made it clear he was equally in the game as she.

Louisa approached and William accepted the drink she offered. 'Thank you.' He took a fortifying mouthful. 'Very nice.'

'I understand you are only in the city for a short time,' she said. 'Your business is in textiles, is that right?'

'Yes. I own a couple of Manchester mills. I am looking for investment and also advice from others of industry. It helps to speak to people from different parts of the country as well as locally if a man is to keep up with, or maybe even improve, current practices.'

Louisa's gaze lingered on his, something going on behind her violet eyes that he couldn't determine. She abruptly faced Octavia. 'Well, that sounds most interesting, doesn't it, Octavia?'

William lifted his glass and studied Octavia over the rim. There was a definite glimmer of nervousness beneath the perceived confidence in her gaze. Something was certainly going on between the women that somehow involved him, but what, he had no idea.

Octavia turned to him and smiled. 'It *is* interesting. I wonder how you feel about women investing or partaking in business, Mr Rose? Is that something you are averse to? Or do you encourage it?'

'Well, I'd encourage it, naturally. Although I haven't come across it in the textile industry yet.' He looked from Octavia to Louisa and back again. If this was some sort of test, he would pass with flying colours considering the strong females he had grown up with. 'Growing up with my mother and sisters taught me to never underestimate women. Ever.'

Octavia's eyes lit with satisfaction and she smiled. 'Well, that is most progressive of you, Mr Rose. Most progressive.'

William raised his glass and drank. The woman was bewildering. Articulate, clearly intelligent, and now discussing business in such a manner he could almost forget he was supposed to be here for sex. Not that he had any intention of indulging, of course. No, his intention was to call Octavia out on her attempted provocation by way of Carlyle, ensure their jousting was drawn to an end, pay for her time and then leave. Never to see her again.

Even if the notion felt decidedly less gratifying than he would like.

Louisa moved towards the door. 'Octavia, will you be taking William upstairs immediately? You know you are more than welcome to sit here awhile if you wish.' She laid her hand on the doorknob. 'I am going to my study. I have a lot of work to do.'

'No, we'll go upstairs now.' Octavia turned to William. 'If you are ready, Mr Rose?'

He studied her, trying in vain to fathom the thoughts in that attractive mind of hers. 'Of course.'

'Good, then if you'd like to follow me.'

As William left the parlour, his mind reeled. Part of him was keen to set the record straight and leave, yet another part was hesitant to do either, his body beginning to fail him. Seeing Octavia again, talking to her and trying to understand her had stirred an unwelcome and wholly disconcerting rekindling of his damnable attraction to her.

There was something beguiling about a woman who spoke so eloquently, who clearly knew much of the world and wasn't afraid to challenge and speak with a gentleman of wealth and standing. She was feisty, certainly. But it was more than that. Octavia Marshall had clear control of her emotions and an aptitude for conversation that challenged and intrigued him, that made him want to be a better man, to impress her with his strengths and play down any weaknesses.

He had never met a woman so mysterious yet open, so tormenting yet sombre. It was baffling, but entirely captivating and the combination made his body shift carnally.

Dangerous. That was what she was – very, very dangerous.

And he had to put a stop to her enchantment.

'Octavia.' He reached out as she stopped outside a closed bedroom door, gently but firmly grasping her elbow. 'We should talk.'

'And we will.'

She turned the door handle, but William tightened his grip. 'Wait.'

Her hand slipped from the door and concern darkened her eyes. 'Is everything all right?'

William looked deep into her eyes and, once again, felt as though he was teetering on the edge of something he couldn't explain. 'You... I...' He released her elbow and pushed his hand into his hair. 'I didn't come here to be alone with you this way.'

Her gaze drifted over his face before meeting his eyes once more. 'But now you've changed your mind?'

'What?'

'It's a simple question, William.' She dropped her study to his mouth again before slowing lifting her incredible lashes and pinning him to the floor with her brilliant blue gaze. 'Do you want to be alone with me now?'

'I can't make love to you when—'

'You won't be making love to me.' She lightly touched her

fingers to his jaw. 'This is a business arrangement. The same as any other.'

A spike of something that felt far too much like a blow hit the centre of his chest and he swallowed. What in God's name was happening to him? Since when did he react so uncertainly to anything... anyone?

He pulled back his shoulders. 'Octavia, I know.'

She dropped her hand from his face, amusement sparking in her eyes. 'Know what?'

'Know what you asked your friend, Francis Carlyle, to say to me when I met with him today. Why goad me that way? Why look to anger me?'

She stepped back as a smile twitched at her lips. '*Did* I anger you?'

Frustration of how impossible it was to be mad with her – to not push her against the wall and crush his lips to hers – pulsed through him. 'Yes,' he lied.

'Or did I entertain you?'

God, how did she evoke such battling, conflicting emotions inside him? Turn him around, make him doubt his sensibilities? His whole damn thought process! 'What?'

'Come...' She slipped her fingers into his and pulled him gently into the room. 'Let us at least be hidden from prying eyes and listening ears if we are to go into face-to-face battle.'

11

Somehow, Octavia managed to maintain her smile until William had walked past her towards the bed. She closed her eyes and took a moment to steady herself. She needed to focus, show him she was a woman in control of all she thought and did. The flirtation she so effortlessly embraced when entertaining culls faltered with William, her usual bravado nowhere near as strong and unyielding.

She sensed a deep integrity in him. A man who did not suffer fools gladly but was also interested in people. A man she would like to get to know better. A man who showed all the signs of being someone with whom she would like to collaborate on her very first business venture.

Although she had met several men of stature and influence within the walls of the Carson Street house, they were all local men, and she did not want her ideas laughed at or discouraged by a cull who knew her. William was a safer bet than any businessman she had met thus far. He did not live in the city, was unlikely to discuss her plans with anyone when his interests lay elsewhere than Bath and, moreover, she liked him.

And if it meant that in order to secure his help she must tell him as much, so be it.

'Octavia? Are you all right?'

Taking a deep breath, she turned. The truth was, William Rose had become the difference between her leaving Carson Street with something to hold on to and being forced to walk away with little more than an uncertain future.

She slowly walked forward and placed her drink on her bureau. 'Firstly, I apologise for asking Francis to say what he did to you. I—'

'You were merely continuing our battle, I believe.'

His smile surprised her and an alien sensation jolted through her as his hazel eyes bored into hers. She swallowed. Was his earlier annoyance feigned? Was he playing with her as she had played with him?

'Yes, I was.' She laughed. 'Am I forgiven?'

'Not yet, no. There are things we should discuss first.'

'Oh?'

He drained his glass and placed it on the bureau next to hers. He stood there for a moment, his gaze on the glass and his back turned. Octavia's heart quickened as a little of the authority she usually commandeered in her bedroom gave way. She really did like him far too much. Her power was wavering, his increasing.

Abruptly, he turned, his fingers tugging his necktie loose before he left it to hang either side of his collar. He moved his fingers to the buttons at the neck of his shirt. 'I didn't answer your question of whether I now wish to lie with you, despite having no intention of doing so when I came here.'

The intensity of his gaze was unnerving, erotic and entirely fascinating. Desire pulled low in her belly, and she tilted her chin. 'And?'

'Let us discuss your jape with Carlyle first,' he said, coming closer and lifting his hand to the fallen curl at her cheek. He twisted it around his finger, his gaze on hers. 'Telling him to say he'd not invest with an unmarried man was a canny shot at what some in this city consider my weakness. So much so, I could not possibly allow our association to end with you having the upper hand.'

Octavia rested her hand on his bicep; the contact he made with her would not be one-sided. She had witnessed him weakening outside on the landing, whether he realised it or not, and now he had regained his equilibrium, he clearly attempted to thwart hers.

That would never happen. Not here. Not in her domain.

'I would never assume I could gain the upper hand over a man like you,' she murmured. 'After all, I am no one in authority. I am merely a whore.'

'A whore with a brain. A brain and beauty and, if I'm not mistaken, a thirst for amusement. Often, it seems, at a man's expense. But you need to understand that I am not a man to be toyed with.'

'Oh, I am beginning to understand that very well. As I am sure you are coming to learn, I am not a woman who sits on her laurels but rather pushes herself forward. Who makes people notice her. Who can have a joke but also be serious when the need arises.'

He dropped her hair and put his thumb to her lower lip, brushed it back and forth. 'You are indeed a worthy opponent, Miss Marshall. One I find entirely bewitching yet wholly frustrating.'

She trapped his thumb between her teeth, kept him there with her eyes as much as her mouth. His gaze held hers until his cheeks mottled and the humour left his eyes, darkened into something far more dangerous.

Octavia's heart raced as she released his thumb.

She must ask him about his business. Put to him the idea of her learning from him before he left this room. Otherwise, she might never find the courage again. Yet the sexual tension between them was rife, her entire body alive with rare arousal...

She stepped back and took a few paces back and forth in front of him as her body battled their intimacy, and her mind battled with how best to raise the subject of investment. She must think of something to offer him in return for his education, but what did she have but her body? No. She would not offer him that. She could not when she wanted him to take her ambition seriously.

'Is there something you wish to ask me, Octavia?'

He had taken a seat on the bed, his brow furrowed, his shirt unbuttoned just enough that her eyes were drawn to the smattering of revealed chest hair. She snapped her gaze to his. 'Yes. Yes, there is.' She lifted her chin. 'I would like you to teach me about business. I have spent most of the afternoon poring over books in the library and have gained a much better understanding of the textile industry. But it is not necessarily textiles I need to learn about, but industry. If I am—'

'Wait. You've spent the afternoon doing what?' His eyes widened with disbelief and a hefty dose of confusion. 'Why would you... You want me to teach you about business?'

She pulled back her shoulders. 'Yes.'

The silence stretched, each second a beat of Octavia's heart and then... he laughed and laughed some more.

A jolt of anger shot through her, sudden and sharp, until heat rose hot at her chest and neck. 'Don't laugh at me. I am genuine in my wish. I want to better myself and make a living where I am not lying on my back. Please, do not mock me or I shall be forced to—'

'I am not mocking you,' he said, swiping his hand over his eyes. 'I am just surprised at such a turnaround. When I arrived here tonight, I thought I would say what I needed to say and then leave. Then I learn you echo my belief that we are equal sparring partners and now you say you wish to learn about business from me. Whereas I...'

She planted her hands on her hips and stared down at him. 'You what?'

'I, Octavia Marshall, have gone from being annoyed with you, wanting to best you, to wanting to lie with you.'

His admission was like an aphrodisiac as he clearly was not dismissing what she said out of hand but was instead seemingly impressed by it. His eyes drew her in but she fought back, held her ground. 'And that can most definitely happen, but first I need confirmation from you of whether or not you are willing to teach me. You are only in Bath for two weeks. Clearly, you must have a busy schedule, but I would appreciate any time you can spare me. Or maybe we could correspond with one another once you return north. I—'

He raised his hand, and she snapped her mouth closed.

'I cannot possibly give you an answer as easily as that.'

'Why not?'

'Well, firstly, I have never entered into any sort of business agreement with a woman before and secondly, I am hardly likely to agree to such an arrangement without seeing a clear benefit to me as well as you. Do you have any ideas about that, or have you only considered your own advantage?'

Octavia tried to gauge whether he teased her but only a quiet sobriety showed in his eyes. His tone had held no lecherousness or sexual suggestion, only interest and business. 'I can think of nothing yet, but I will.'

'Good. Then in the first instance, can I suggest we both think overnight about how this arrangement might benefit me as much as you and see what we come up with? After that, we'll reconvene.'

Excitement unfurled inside of her, and Octavia smiled. It was not an agreement, but neither was it a rejection. 'That would be most satisfactory.'

'Good, but for now...' He came closer and cupped her jaw, brushed his lips over hers. 'I wish to lie with you.'

Octavia closed her eyes as an overwhelming desire to have him swept through her. The fact he did not find the idea of her learning from him, of setting herself up in the world of business in any way impossible, bolstered her confidence immeasurably. She could not deny how his strength and charisma aroused her. An extraordinary feat considering her occupation, yet the sexual pull was there all the same. If she wanted him to help her to shape a new life, this desire for him could be a problem, but he would soon be away from Bath so she would not linger on that for the time being.

Yet, could she be sure it was her confidence that had stirred him as she hoped? With no way of obtaining that assurance, Octavia did the only thing she could in that moment and returned his kiss with equal fervour...

12

William stared at the ceiling, his arm relaxed beneath Octavia's neck as they lay in bed, both of them naked. He couldn't speak for Octavia, but for him, he could not remember the last time he had felt so entirely sated.

Yet still her request to learn from him managed to nudge into his thoughts. Her ambitions for a different future impressed him. The fact she was willing to learn about running a business from the ground up even more so. Hence the reason he hadn't dismissed the notion to teach her out of hand... even if he would have to be convinced that the union – not to mention the time he would have to commit to teaching her – would be of benefit to him, too.

Throughout his time in Bath, he had not procured the amount of investment or enthusiasm for his enterprise he would have liked... and that irked. He needed to do something radical to up his appeal to others in the south so that they might not only see the value in his growing business, but also that they automatically recommended Rose Textiles to those looking for work further north.

Could it really be that he needed to temporarily alter his marriage status? Jiggle his identity for a couple of weeks? Good God, find a woman who was willing to—

He turned his head on the pillow to find Octavia watching him and his heart stumbled. *Don't be so ridiculous, Rose...*

She gave a lazy smile. 'Happy?'

Temporarily pushing his business mind into submission, he protruded his bottom lip as though considering her question and hopefully concealing his growing fondness for her. 'I'm not sure. Maybe more content.'

She abruptly lifted onto her elbow, her blue eyes flashing with what was clearly feigned annoyance, her dark brown hair tumbling past her breasts. 'Content? I have never heard such an insult. Men leave my bed happy. Anything less is beneath my reputation.'

'Is that so? Well...' He jerked forward and pressed a quick kiss to her lips, before flinging back the covers. It would be wise for him to leave before his unexpected comfort at lying so idly with her grew stronger. Not to mention the outlandish notion bouncing around in his mind. Could he really suggest... would there be a possibility she might consider it? 'I will have to return again in order to give you another chance to prove your prowess.'

Walking about the room, he retrieved his hastily discarded clothes and dressed as Octavia watched him, now sitting up, her back against the pillows and the sheets pulled tight across her bosom. Her slight frown and somewhat distracted gaze led him to suspect her thoughts had returned to their prior discussions, too.

He could not leave without saying something to show he had been far from mocking at her wish to learn from him. His reflexive laughter before had been grounded in shock and then indisputable admiration. But what about the reciprocal idea he had that would benefit him? If she posed as his fiancée while he was here and investment success followed, he would know once and for all that it was his marital status that had been the encroachment on his usual achievement rather than lack of aptitude.

Something that was – of course – downright impossible!

'I want you to know the proposition you put to me earlier is not one I find entirely disagreeable, even if we are yet to discuss how we are to go about the teaching.' He faced the mirror and secured his necktie, before taking his hat from the bedpost. 'But it is never a good idea to jump into an arrangement with a relative stranger without your eyes being wide open, or at least getting to know a potential business associate as much as possible beforehand.'

'I agree.'

'All right, then. So why me? I imagine businessmen come through this house on a regular basis. Why have you selected me to teach you, when you know I will not be in the city for very long?'

'That is part of your appeal. I do not wish to open my desires and dreams to men who visit this house regularly, who could easily discuss my ambitions with others or, worse, mock them. If you and I can strike a mutually beneficial deal while you are here, one that suits us both, why not?' She shrugged. 'Plus, who knows, maybe if you tell me more about the north and I am impressed, you could become my escape from Bath, too.'

'Your escape?' Surprise shot through him. 'You wish to leave?'

'I don't know. I haven't decided yet.' A slight blush darkened her cheeks and she looked past him as though avoiding his gaze, or maybe because she had revealed more than she intended.

'But gaining the assistance of someone who does not live here suits my needs perfectly.' She met his gaze. 'Do you understand?'

He nodded. He did understand. He understood this was about more than business. Octavia Marshall was poised to flee. From her whole life or just Bath? More importantly, why?

Was he mad to entertain teaching her and have her pose as his fiancée in return? It was clear she was unlikely to be quiet or unopinionated. Yet would that necessarily be a bad thing? Could her intelligence, articulation and curiosity be to his advantage?

He rubbed his hand along his jaw. 'I have a rather unusual suggestion. Would you be willing to hear it?'

'By all means.'

He inhaled a long breath, praying she saw the advantages to both of them if his notion worked. 'As you know, I've missed out on profitable deals and associations because being unmarried at my age seems to provoke suspicion. Because I am singularly ambitious, rather than desiring a wife and children, that somehow makes me an untrustworthy businessman.'

'Which is madness.' She tutted and dropped her arms, her gaze annoyed. 'Why do people think they have the right to judge and demand how others choose to live their lives? Women in my occupation have to deal with such verdicts and sentencing as a matter of course, myself included. More fool me for assuming it easier for a man in this world.'

William smiled, relieved by her reaction. 'Well, that response encourages me further in my proposition. I think you could be perfect for what I have in mind.'

'Which is?'

'To pose as my fiancée.'

She flinched, her eyes wide. 'What?'

'Just while I'm in Bath. It would give us an opportunity to see how we work together. To see if business is something you actually want to be involved in. I have several more deals and consul-tatory meetings lined up and I can introduce you as my fiancée, say you have a love of the business and wish to sit in. Tell them that I value your input.' He lifted his shoulders. 'It will give you the opportunity to learn more about me and my enterprise. Plus, allow me the chance to secure more support, without having to further explain my lack of desire for a wife.'

'Are you playing a joke on me?' She grinned, her eyes delighted. 'You are incorrigible.'

'I'm serious. I am asking you to pose as my fiancée in return for me teaching you all I can while I am here and after I return to Manchester. What do you say?'

Her smile dissolved as she stared at him, before she rose from the bed and walked naked and beautiful to her closet. William failed to drag his gaze from her perfect backside, his groin twitching awake again. He quickly looked to the floor and counted to ten.

When he raised his eyes to her, she was knotting and tight-ening the sash of a satin robe around her with such vigour William wasn't sure if his suggestion had upset her or inspired her.

Her blue eyes burned with suspicion as she looked at him. 'And if I agree to this, can I trust that this arrangement will not weaken your promise to teach me? I will be angrier than you can know if I suspect you regard me as little more than a woman you can use.'

'I would never think anything of the sort. I only wish for us to get to know one another better. Give you the opportunity to see how I conduct business before we get any further into this.'

'Good, because it is important to me that I start making some steps towards building a future beyond Carson Street. Beyond prostitution. As long as you promise me that my acting as your fiancée will not affect what I want, then I will think about what you have proposed.'

'Excellent.' He stepped closer. 'Because I want you to be sure I am the right man to help you in your aspirations.' Suddenly he needed to hear that she trusted and liked him. That he was not the same as the other clients she had lain with... but he was also reluctant to cast himself in the role of her saviour when he would soon be leaving the city with no plans of when he might return. He cleared his throat 'I am also concerned you think me the answer to assuring all that you want.'

The colour in her cheeks paled and she pursed her lips as though trapping her words. Octavia did not strike him as a woman who needed saving, so why did he suddenly feel as though that was what she expected of him? He couldn't remember ever meeting a stronger, more confident female, yet as he looked into her eyes he sensed a deep underlying vulnerability in her that was wholly disconcerting.

He wished to high heaven that he did not sense her weakness, but William also knew it was not up to him to bolster it. They were most assuredly businesspeople – both of them – and, whether Octavia believed it or not, she would manage her future well enough, with or without him.

'I like you, William,' she said firmly, her chin high. 'I regard you as someone who will stride forward in his vision regardless of what others might say or think. That interests me and strengthens my wish to learn from you.'

Even though she had skilfully avoided confirming his concern one way or the other, he smiled, not having the heart to press her.

'But I do have one concern,' she said quietly.

'Which is?'

'There is every possibility I could be recognised in certain circles in Bath. What will we to do if someone at one of your meetings recognises me as a whore?'

He stepped back from her and rubbed his hand back and forth along his jaw. Why had he not thought of that? Because he had forgotten for a moment what she was... what she did. 'I see.'

'So, maybe your idea is not such a good one, after all.'

William's mind raced. He wanted her to be his fake fiancée. Felt she would play the part with the utmost excellence and professionalism. 'I will return tomorrow with a list of the men I am meeting. It's possible some might recognise you but unless they are sat at a table with us, I cannot imagine a man worth his salt interrupting our lunch or dinner to announce your occupation to the world.'

'You are willing to take the risk?'

'Are you?'

She smiled. 'Yes.'

He winked. 'Then so am I.'

'Good. Then I will discuss it with Louisa.' She walked to the door. 'And have an answer for you tomorrow. I will leave a message at your hotel.'

William put on his hat and walked downstairs with her. It had been an eventful and entirely enjoyable evening in more ways than he could have predicted. And he very much looked forward to seeing Octavia tomorrow.

13

The following day, Octavia walked into the Pump Room ahead of Louisa, Nancy and Jacob, her nerves jumping. She had called them together for this impromptu lunch gathering but if, as she suspected, her friends thought William's fake engagement proposal preposterous, it did not matter, for she had already decided to agree to it. However, it was important that she was open and honest with the people who meant so much to her.

There had never been lies, deceit or subterfuge between them in the time the four of them had lived together, and Octavia refused to be the one who broke the bond she hoped would be everlasting. No matter where their future lives might take them...

'Good afternoon, madam.' The maître d' bowed his head. 'Welcome to the Pump Room. Do you have a reservation?'

'We do.' Octavia returned his smile. 'A table for four under the name of Octavia Marshall.'

He looked at the ledger in front of him. 'Ah, yes. If you'd like to follow me?'

Once they were seated at the grandly dressed table, Octavia rested her folded hands in her lap. Despite the grey November afternoon beyond the floor-to-ceiling windows, the chandelier above them glinted beautifully, the silver cutlery shining against the pure white tablecloth. Everything was wonderful – and quite possibly provided an entirely contradictory setting for what might be a deeply shadowed conversation.

Her friends' chatter quieted, and Octavia turned from the window, not in the least bit surprised that Louisa, Nancy and Jacob all stared at her with identical expressions of expectation.

'Why are we here, Octavia?' Louisa asked.

Octavia cleared her throat, determined to battle against any insinuation of madness her friends might throw at her for even entertaining William's proposition. 'I have something I need to discuss with you. Something important.'

Nancy fiddled with the cutlery that was laid out just so, her grey eyes carefully watching Octavia. 'Considering this last-minute summons to lunch, I thought as much. What's wrong?'

'Nothing's wrong.'

'No?' Nancy raised her eyebrows. 'Spontaneity is not your thing. Never has been.'

'Well, then, that's how little you know me.' Octavia smiled, a frisson of bravado rippling through her. She might have leapt into her and William's union impulsively, but she had also done so with certainty, and her agreement became an even better prospect if it meant stunning Nancy with her plans. Her friend would no doubt bluster and complain, eyes bulging and cheeks red. 'Because what I have to say could be considered extremely spontaneous.' She looked around the table. 'I have made a decision about something but, as you are all my very dear friends, I want to be upfront with you. Even though the choice is mine, I am more than happy to listen to any reservations you might have.'

Louisa laid her napkin on her lap, her brow creased. 'You haven't been yourself for a few weeks now and your growing unhappiness bothers me. Does this have something to do with Mr Rose?'

'It does, yes.'

A waiter came to the table with a bottle of claret, immediately walking to Jacob's side for his approval. Octavia stifled her smile. The day Jacob preferred a glass of wine over a pint of ale was the day Octavia became entirely free of her father's long-reaching acrimony.

As the wine was poured, Octavia stared around the opulent, high-ceilinged room, surveying the silks and satins of the wealthy patrons, the suited pianist playing on the dais and the ease of the chatter and laughter that rang from every corner. There had been a time when she had thought she would never again enter a dining room of such sumptuous luxury, but Louisa had made it possible that Octavia could eat in establishments such as this whenever she might wish it. But it was important that she not sit on such good fortune lightly and looked to secure her future without her friends' constant help and support.

The sex trade was fickle, based on youth and looks. The Carson Street house could not expect the current frequency of business to last forever. Even if Octavia's friends were not married or soon to be married, the older she, Nancy and Louisa became, the less appeal they would hold. A simple fact of life, which none of them could afford to ignore.

Neither could Octavia ignore the question of whether sleeping with William had been a sound decision. He had paid her, and the transaction was properly executed, but she struggled with the realisation that he might wish to take her to bed as a paid whore again. If he did, she very much doubted he would take her seriously in her business endeavours.

She must make it clear to him they would no longer continue to have sex.

No matter the sexual tension between them.

With the waiter gone, Octavia lifted her glass and sipped before carefully lowering it to the table, forcing her mind to the here and now rather than her imminent conversation with William. 'During my time with Mr Rose last night, he proposed an arrangement to me. An arrangement I have decided to enter into as I believe it will be a step towards my new future.'

Louisa frowned, concern filling her eyes. 'I thought you were going to ask him to teach you about business. There is no need for any arrangement past his helping you.' Comprehension lit behind her gaze. 'Ah, he wants something in return.'

'Of course. He is a businessman, after all.'

Louisa shook out her napkin and placed it on her lap, her movements stiff. 'You do not have to enter into anything you are uncomfortable with. I have told you I have no intention of closing the house. Yes, Jacob and I are to be married, but as for children and my interest wavering from the brothel, that is not going to happen.'

'Louisa, you cannot possibly guarantee that but, for now, your plans have nothing to do with—'

'Wait.' Nancy raised her hand and looked around the table, her eyes narrowed. 'Why is the prospect of the house closing a part of this discussion?' She looked at Louisa. 'Is the business suffering because I am no longer there? Are you struggling?'

Louisa clutched Nancy's hand, no doubt halting an imminent outburst. 'We are not struggling and the house is not clos-ing. Our finances are not as high as they have been but I will adjust things accordingly. Now...' She faced Octavia. 'Before you go any further, I need your absolute assurance that Mr Rose can be trusted not to go back on the part of the bargain that benefits you.'

Octavia opened her mouth to respond, but Jacob spoke first.

He leaned back in his chair, his face grave. 'You know, Octavia has made a good point. She is right to be concerned that her circumstances at the house could one day change.'

Louisa snapped her gaze to her lover and Octavia's heart sank. Another disagreement between Louisa and Jacob was the last thing she wanted. She hated that her concerns might rouse agitation between them. Her anxieties were not theirs. She needed to remember that and not waver from her path. The self-ishness her father accused her of once more reared in her memory, but Octavia fought back.

Selfish or not, she had looked after herself ever since she left his care and would continue to do so. 'There is no need for you two to arg—'

'What do you mean by that, Jacob?' Louisa demanded. 'The house is not closing.'

'Maybe not anytime soon, but once we start a family, a brothel is hardly the place—'

Louisa laughed, colour rising in her cheeks as she glanced at Octavia and Nancy. 'Children are far down my agenda. We—'

'*Your* agenda?' Jacob's jaw tightened as he reached for his glass. 'We are to be married, Louisa. It is *our* agenda that matters now.'

With the possibility of her selfishness causing trouble between two of her dearest friends, Octavia closed her eyes and inhaled a strengthening breath. 'Please, don't argue.' She opened her eyes. 'I asked you to lunch to share my news, not cause tension between you.'

Nancy sniffed. 'Since when can the passion between those two ever be curtailed, Octavia? They'll argue now and then fight it out some more in the bedroom once we're done.'

Louisa lifted her glass and glowered at Jacob. 'The house is my security... *our* security. You know I need that after what happened before.'

Octavia inwardly groaned, berating herself that she had made Louisa think of her first husband. His suicide had affected her in every possible way. Emotionally, financially and mentally. After pulling herself from the most unimaginable circumstances, Louisa had built a new life filled with wealth, friends and a man as strong and good as Jacob. Something Octavia could only dream of achieving.

But maybe Louisa had unwittingly become the motivation behind all that Octavia set out to achieve now. Maybe Louisa was the one whose approval and blessing she needed more than anyone else sat around the table.

She lifted her wine glass. 'You two can sort out your differences later. I called you all here to discuss something and I'd prefer that you allow me to do that.' Octavia looked at each of them in turn. 'As I said before, I have decided to accept a proposal Mr Rose put to me.'

Nancy sipped her wine. 'And what is the proposal exactly?'

Octavia smiled, her stomach knotting with a flurry of excitement. 'An engagement. A betrothal... of sorts.'

'What?' Nancy's eyes widened. 'He proposed marriage? But I was under the impression you've only just met the man!'

'He would like me to *act* as his fiancée. Just for the short time he is in Bath.' She turned to Louisa. 'I asked him if he would be willing to teach me what he could about business, and this was his request in return.'

'But his fiancée, Octavia? Why, for goodness' sake? He does know people will ask questions? That there is a good chance you could be recognised?'

'And we've discussed that, but we are willing to take the first step and see what happens. He's a good and fair man. He said that he would prefer I had the opportunity to find out for myself whether business interests me before I begin my studies. Joining him on his meetings will help make up my mind.'

The waiter returned with another behind him. 'Your main courses, sir and madams.'

Octavia tapped her foot upon the marble floor as their dishes were laid out and condiments placed in the centre of the table.

Once the waiters retreated, she seized the moment to press her determination. 'William is not up to anything other than expanding his business opportunities. It seems his single status has had a bearing on the investment decisions of the great and wealthy to such an extent that some deem him less capable or trustworthy than they would if he was married.' She shook her head and picked up her cutlery. 'Complete nonsense, of course, but there we are.'

Nancy gave a firm nod. 'Well, I think it's in the man's favour that he is happy for you to meet his associates. If you trust that the arrangement will be beneficial to you as well as Mr Rose, I don't see a problem. He obviously thinks you capable of holding your own in front of these uppity fools, so who are we to stop you from proving that?'

Relief eased a little of the tension in Octavia's shoulders. She had Nancy's support, but it seemed Louisa and Jacob were a different matter entirely. Due to past circumstances and the hardships they had endured, Louisa and Jacob tended to fight for what was theirs... whether side by side or individually. The trouble was, protectiveness of their own prosperity sometimes spilled over to consume their hopes for Nancy and Octavia, too.

She very much doubted her union with William would be accepted easily by either of them, but she would not sway in her decision.

'I know this is seems a little rash,' she said. 'But I have given it due thought and I will be joining Mr Rose in his plan. Now...' She reached for her wine. 'Shall we raise a glass to my schooling and future success as an independent businesswoman?'

'And how does Carson Street fit into this plan?' Jacob glanced at Louisa, whose gaze remained fixed to her plate, her jaw set as though her heated words with Jacob had far from guttered. 'Do you plan seeing your regular culls? Or are we to share them out between Adelaide and Eliza?'

His tone dripped with irony and Octavia glared, lowering her glass to the table. 'There is no reason why I cannot conduct business as usual at the house *and* accompany Mr Rose. It's entirely possible his meetings will take place in the daytime, leaving me free to work in the evenings.'

'Are you absolutely sure Mr Rose can be trusted?' Louisa asked quietly, her gaze sceptical. 'That he is not using you for his own gain?'

'I am intelligent enough not to be duped by him. He is a businessman to his core, and I have no doubt he suggested this arrangement for money and advantage. But the same can be said of me, can it not? So, to that end, I am an equal partner in this plan.'

Her friend's gaze bored into hers before Louisa abruptly nodded and looked to her food. 'Then do what you must. Just be careful.'

Octavia smiled and looked at her own plate, Nancy's stare burning into her temple and the atmosphere tense. Yet triumph and excitement unfurled inside Octavia.

She would be a woman of business. Who knew where that would lead? A deep sense of rightness – of destiny – filled her heart. She would send a message to William the moment she returned home.

14

William paced the lobby of his hotel as he waited for Octavia to arrive. They had exchanged letters back and forth from Carson Street ending with William suggesting she join him for a business meeting with some associates that evening. If she was so inclined, he asked that she arrive half an hour before the others so that they might talk a little first, giving him the chance to share his desired objective for the meeting.

The trouble was, the invitation was so last minute, he'd received no answering response and thus had no idea whether or not she would arrive. Considering the nature of her occupation, he very much doubted evenings spent away from Carson Street were possible.

He drew out his pocket watch. Another five minutes and he would be forced to accept she would not be joining him and make his way into the hotel bar to wait for his associates.

Then he glanced towards the hotel's revolving door and Octavia emerged.

His heart stuttered as she spoke to the doorman, her gaze calm as she surveyed the grand lobby, her natural elegance further accentuated by her smart green and black skirt and jacket, her dark curls tumbling from beneath a black hat edged with green flowers.

William inhaled a slow breath, barely resisting the urge to release a quiet whistle of appreciation. She radiated confidence and grace, a coolness that belied the passion he knew her capable of behind closed doors. Anticipation of the night ahead quivered low in his gut, the prospect of her joining this evening's meeting heightening his need to impress her.

Her coat was taken, and the moment the doorman dipped his head in a gesture of deference, William strode forward to greet her. 'Octavia, you came.'

She turned and laughed as she laid her hand on his arm. 'Oh, William, you startled me.'

'I'm so pleased you are here.'

'You were lucky it is a Monday evening. The only night the brothel remains closed.' She lifted her gaze towards the ornate ceiling, the enormous crystal chandelier suspended above them sending prisms of light in every direction. 'Gosh, this hotel is wonderful.'

He stared at her profile, once more marvelling at her beauty and wondering how she came to work as a prostitute. 'Shall we find a table in the bar?' He held out his arm. 'I thought we could have a drink before my associates arrive.'

'Lovely.'

As they walked, William stood a little taller, immensely pleased by the admiring glances that came their way. He completely understood the interest. The fabric of her outfit shimmered beneath the gaslights, her chocolate brown hair gleaming. He glanced at her and smiled as she looked about her in clear wonderment as though absorbing every detail of the hotel. It gratified William to think she might tell Louisa Hill about it once she returned to Carson Street.

They entered the wood-panelled bar and William spoke to the steward standing to attention at the door. They were directed to a small booth in a far corner of the room, which had been reserved for William's meeting.

Once seated, William raised his hand to a nearby waiter and ordered a glass of brandy for himself and the glass of the sweet white wine Octavia had asked for.

'How many gentlemen are you expecting?' she asked once the waiter had disappeared. 'Only, I was hoping it won't be too many for my first covert operation.'

'Just two and you'll be absolutely fine. Generally, businessmen don't bite. Besides, don't think I'm fooled that you aren't used to dealing with gentlemen of every type.'

She grinned sheepishly, the irresistible teasing he enjoyed so much sparkling in her eyes. 'Then tell me what I can expect. How well do you know these gentlemen?'

'Very well. We have done business for the past couple of years. I'm sure you'll find them as amiable as I do. Their names are Ernest and Matthew Mayhew. They are astute investors interested in the proposed building work being mapped out by local government for Bath's city centre.'

'And you hope they extend their interest to your mills tonight?'

'Yes.' He sat forward again as his ambition rose. 'I have been working towards better ventilation, more space between looms and additional wash areas in my mills for a while now. If I want to take my working conditions into a higher sphere, improve the reputation of Rose Textiles and the textile industry in general, it's going to take more money than I can spare right now.'

'Does Rose Textiles not already boast a good reputation?'

'Well, yes, of course...' William hesitated, as he fought to curb the immediate defensiveness that laced his voice. Octavia was just beginning her exploration of industry and still had so very much to learn, both good and bad. If he was to teach her anything, he must teach himself deeper patience. 'But the cotton industry is tough. Sometimes cruel and dangerous. Yet, it is also vital to the prosperity of Great Britain and fundamental in supplying work for thousands of people up and down the country.'

'I see.' She tucked a curl behind her ear. 'And the wider you can spread your costs, the better chance you have of speeding up the improvements and making the profits the investors will expect.' The interest in her gaze was genuine as she nodded. 'Then I look forward to hearing you explain all tonight so that I might learn about your plans, too.'

William shifted closer, the passion he held for his enterprise filling him. 'My business has grown in profit year on year, but when I started concentrating on my workers, their environment and conditions, I saw a huge rise in productivity resulting in higher income for both them and me. I believe it is time for every industry in this country to review their working practices. I want to make others see that we need to invest in people as much as we do manufacturing and industry.'

'And I admire that very much. So, my role in tonight's proceedings will be what exactly, bearing in mind my main objective is to learn all I can? I might have agreed to act as your fiancée, but I don't want you to lose sight of why I am really here.'

He was tempted to take her hand, to bolster her trust in him that he did not take people for granted, Octavia included, but he refrained. The business-like aura emanating from her now could not be mistaken and he sensed one wrong move from him would bring their arrangement to an abrupt end.

'The most important thing tonight is that you gain an insight into the way I work, my ethics and values. Only then can you decide if I am the right person from whom to learn.'

'What do you mean?'

'As I said before, there are plenty of businessmen in the city you could learn from, but the first rule of business is to do your utmost to ensure you work with people you respect. You need to be certain that you respect me, Octavia, that you like me enough that you trust me to be a decent man. A businessman, yes, but a moral one too.'

Her brow furrowed as she studied him, her gaze momentarily dropping to his mouth before she raised her eyes to his. 'I understand.'

'Good.' William inhaled. It was suddenly his absolute wish that they took their association further, that she believed in him as he realised he believed in her. 'Let me ask you this. Do you care about the futures of women and children? Do you hope that their rights might one day be as close as humanly possible to men's? That the poor are given enough inspiration that they aspire and dream as the wealthy do?'

She smiled, her eyes lighting with pleasure. 'Well, of course.'

'Then you will be so much more than a pretend fiancée if you can articulate to Ernest and Matthew that your wish to see more equality for all mirrors mine. Coming from a strong, intelligent woman who has known the world from both sides – albeit they won't know that – I really think they will listen to you and tonight will be more successful for you being here.'

'Do you really mean that?'

'I do.'

She smiled softly. 'Then I think this could be the start of a wonderful partnership.'

An almost overwhelming urge to kiss her whispered through him. The need to take her in his arms, not as a whore but as a woman – *his* woman – was as foolish as it was dangerous. 'Octavia...'

The waiter returned with their drinks, halting William's possibly catastrophic mistake of saying something reckless.

Their drinks were placed on the table in front of them and when they were alone, William raised his glass in a show of nonchalance that he hoped disguised his ever-growing fondness of her. 'A toast. To our new and possible future.'

She clinked her glass to his and sipped, her gaze locked on his with cool intensity, before she looked away.

William studied her profile as she stared towards the bar's doors. *My God, she is so beautiful...*

She snapped her gaze to his, her smile wide. 'I believe your associates have just walked through the door,' she said as she slowly rose to her feet. 'We will continue our discussion another time. For now, we have business to conduct, do we not?'

He quickly looked over his shoulder and stood, extending his hand in welcome to the Messrs Mayhew as they approached the table. 'Gentlemen, I am so glad to see you again. Ernest, Matthew, this is my fiancée, Octavia Marshall. Octavia, Messrs Ernest and Matthew Mayhew.'

15

'What a success! You are an asset indeed, Octavia. I could kiss you!'

Although secretly thrilled by William's declaration of how well the evening had progressed, Octavia bit back her smile as they walked from the bar into the hotel's opulent lobby. 'But you will do no such thing. I am happy that you secured the investment you were looking for, but I really think the Mayhew brothers would have been keen to work with you, with or without me.'

'I beg to differ.'

William gently grasped her elbow and Octavia stopped, met his warm hazel gaze, nonplussed that the frisson of excitement in her belly heated to something that held absolutely no connection to business.

It must be her renewed confidence making her feel so utterly desirous of him rather than drawing a firm line through their intimacy as far as the bedroom was concerned. From the impressed admiration she'd seen in every set of male eyes around the table whenever she asked a question or offered an opinion, to the rush of power she'd felt as William had shaken hands with the Messrs Mayhew, having secured not just the investment he'd wanted but also a large amount more. Every aspect of the evening had been so incredibly empowering, only further supporting Octavia's theory that securing a business of her own was the right path.

'You spoke to the Mayhew brothers as though you were a seasoned lady of business.' William smiled, his satisfied gaze lingering on hers. 'I had no idea you would charm them quite so easily.'

She laughed. 'Neither did I but I thoroughly enjoyed myself.'

Despite her modest protestations, Octavia wanted to laugh with the joy of feeling that she had embodied or discovered a new part of herself she never knew existed. It was exhilarating, liberating... as though she stood on the precipice of a new, infinitely more abundant and exciting life. It was as frightening as it was thrilling, but she would not turn away.

'So, you haven't been put off?' William asked. 'My mentoring you is still on the table? Because it most certainly is for me.'

The excited determination in his eyes sped her heart but now was the time to lay down a few ground rules. She had to be sure William understood her interest went past the monetary. She wanted to learn and grow, make her mark in the world in a way that was respected and brave.

'It is, but...' She glanced around her as people milled to and fro throughout the hotel lobby. 'You must understand the depth of my ambition. I want to become a part of the business world. To be respected and successful. I have to know I can trust you beyond your time in Bath. It could be I never hear from you again once you return to Manchester.'

He took her gloved hand and raised it to his lips before pressing a firm kiss to her knuckles, his gaze sombre. 'I promise you, I will not renege on our agreement.' His fingers squeezed hers. 'I am a businessman through and through. I neither make promises I cannot keep nor retreat when the fight gets hard. I am in this because you have shown me – in your manner, with your eyes and with your words – how much you want to succeed, and I want to help you to do just that.'

'Yet all that you need from me will be taken in the next two weeks, whereas my part in the deal might not come at all.'

'Octavia, please.' His jaw tightened, his gaze boring into hers. 'You must trust that I will not forsake you.'

Octavia breathed deep, her gaze drawn treacherously to his mouth before she looked into his eyes. 'I believe you...' She shakily exhaled and smiled. 'I trust you.'

He smiled, relief showing in his eyes. 'Good. Now how about you join me for another meeting tomorrow? I have a lunch date at the Palm Hotel. The men I wish to make a deal with represent the difference between me having the immediate resources to be able to make a difference to my workers or making little difference at all.' His smile dissolved and he exhaled. 'I suspect you've known what it is to struggle and will understand just how important it is that changes are made wherever possible. Life is hard when you are living hand to mouth. Living with the fear of how or when your next meal might come or whether you will have enough fuel to see you through the winter.'

Tears pricked the backs of her eyes to witness his passion and determination. 'I understand only too well.'

The sudden dryness in her throat made it difficult to swallow. His earnestness was dangerous, tempting her to share her past with him. Not with shame but pride. To confess that she, like the people walking about them, had once known luxury, coaches and horses, fine dining and society, yet she had ended up alone and surviving on Bath's streets. But even Louisa, Nancy and Jacob knew little of her life before she came to Carson Street, how she came to flee from her home or why. To tell William, to allow someone else to learn of her heartbreak, fears and losses was too much. She couldn't possibly confess a word to him.

'The types of people who stay in hotels like this,' he continued, his cheeks mottled as he glared around the lobby again, 'people who have money and security, are the people I need to invest in my mills. I might not always agree with the way they live, so ignorant of others less fortunate, but their wealth is a way to forge forwards in my plans. I want Rose Textiles to be a place where generation after generation toil happily and proudly.'

She frowned. His passion was so tangible, it made no sense that he would not do anything and everything to bring his ideas to fruition. 'Then considering marriage appears a sticking point to some, maybe it is time for you to genuinely marry.'

'What?'

'I'm serious, William. If being married elevates your ambitions, why not just find a woman to marry? You are successful, handsome and, from what I've learned so far, kind and considerate. Any woman of standing would happily become Mrs William Rose.'

'Maybe they would, but I am not ready. Not yet.'

'Why not?'

'Because it will take a special kind of woman willing to stand alongside me, Octavia. A very special woman, indeed.'

The intensity in his gaze sent a shiver along her spine. Tension filled the air around them, but Octavia held her ground. Sometimes the brooding, determined look in his eyes stirred her desire wide awake. Other times, his brooding was decidedly darker, more dangerous, but already she felt herself strong enough not to falter under his gravity whenever it appeared.

His shoulders lowered and he smiled, but it did not quite reach his eyes. 'Maybe you want me to confess what happened in my life to make me so resistant to marrying? If you do, it is only fair you tell me your story, too.'

Octavia tensed. He had caught her in what felt far too much like a trap. Her defences rose and she stepped back. 'Is this what working with you brings, William? Deflection? Argument?'

His smile vanished, his cheeks mottling with clear annoyance. 'A match of equals is what you are looking for, is it not? Well, here I am.' He opened his arms. 'I cannot promise I will be amiable all the time, but I very much doubt you can promise me that either.'

Her heart beat faster that their conversation had so quickly turned into a quarrel, but Octavia tilted her chin, determined not to be intimidated. 'All I'm saying is that if your agreement to teach me comes with the condition I act as your fake fiancée *and* bear my soul to you, then maybe the stakes are a little too high.'

Fear twisted and turned inside of her. The haunting shadow of her father suddenly shrouded her as though he laughed at her attempt to better herself, to reinvent herself as a woman of merit, as someone who had a good and honest place in this world.

Hating her vulnerability, Octavia steeled her heart against her growing fondness for William and stepped back. 'I think it best we say goodbye for now. I will see you tomorrow.'

He pushed some fallen hair from his brow and muttered a curse. 'I have no wish for us to part like—'

But she was already marching towards the doors, her legs ever so slightly trembling as she desperately sought the attendant who had taken her coat. Where was he? She needed to leave. Claustrophobia threatened as footsteps sounded behind her. Octavia closed her eyes, praying the steps did not belong to William.

'Octavia.'

She spun around. 'William, please. I'm tired. Can we not just say our goodbyes?'

'As you wish.' He raised his hand to the concierge. 'The lady's coat, please.'

'Yes, sir.'

Octavia watched the man walk towards the cloakroom, grateful for a diversion from William's intense stare. 'I enjoy our time together,' she said quietly, turning to look at him. 'But securing my future means everything to me right now and that will inevitably make me quick-tempered from time to time. I cannot afford to go along with this facade of an engagement only for you to walk away with all you wanted, and me with nothing more of what I want.'

'I told you that will not happen. You have my word. I want us to work together... side by side.'

The attendant returned with her coat and she slipped her arms into the sleeves. 'Thank you.'

Once the concierge had retreated, Octavia forced her gaze to William's. 'Until tomorrow then.'

'Until tomorrow.' He reached into his inside pocket and withdrew a money clip, counting off some notes before holding them out to her. 'Here, your payment.'

Octavia froze. 'What?'

'For your time.'

Heat leapt into her cheeks, her heart racing. 'You... you still think...'

Swiftly turning, she strode to the door, her head held high, but humiliation clenched like a fist deep in her stomach. For just a fleeting time, it had felt as though William saw past the whore, past a woman who gave paid favours, to the lady she had once been.

But it seemed his interest in her was only skin-deep. He, like every other man she'd met in this city, saw nothing more than what she had become. Well, that was fine. She held no shame in her survival. No regret in her path.

William Rose would undoubtedly regret that his actions could very well mean he had just let her slip right through his fingers.

16

Two nights later, William walked a little unsteadily down the steps of Tanners gentlemen's club, his head already beginning to ache from his overindulgence. Not that he regretted his consumption. He damn well deserved it considering he had only managed to secure half the investment he needed again today.

He'd had four meetings since he had last seen Octavia. Meetings she had not attended. After her failure to arrive at the Palm Hotel as arranged, William's gut had churned with self-reproach. Her lack of contact sent him a clear message that she had no wish to see him again.

Why in God's name had he offered her money? It was a damn foolish thing to do and his shame was the reason behind his apprehension to return to Carson Street so that he might speak with her.

He was making mistake after mistake. A fake engagement. Misplaced confidence he could travel south in the hope of further investment and inside intelligence of how he could expand his enterprise. He should never have convinced himself – or let others convince him, namely Nicholas Fairham – that his lack of success was entirely enveloped in his status as a single gentleman closing in on his thirty-third birthday.

His meeting had gone well when Octavia had been present, but her attendance had by no means been the sole reason for its victory. The truth was, the businessmen here seemed to have only a passing interest in a northern company or putting the needs of their workers higher on their professional agendas. Which was a mistake, of course. The north was fast becoming the epicentre of British industry with Manchester as its cornerstone.

Had he not taken on apprentices from the south? Youngsters, both male and female, who had been sent north by parents desperate for their children's working income. A sad truth, but a truth all the same.

The idea of returning home having not achieved all that he had planned grated on his self-worth. William was not a man who gave up easily on anything. He had just eight days left in Bath; he had to see his commitment through. He had thought long and hard, planned his strategy late into the night before coming here and he would not fail to take more money and knowledge back to Manchester.

It seemed all that mattered to the elite in this damn city was where you came from, whether your family were moneyed and your bloody marriage prospects. Each of which had been alluded to in one form or another during William's last meetings.

Britain was overflowing with snobbery. Superiority and revolutionary blindness. And, although William wanted the privileges of wealth and success, nothing about the darker strategies and motivation of accomplishment appealed.

A young and happy couple, arm in arm and laughing into one another's eyes, brushed past him and he quickly stepped back. The woman looked at him with wide, shocked eyes while her lover gripped her a little closer to him, steering her forwards.

'You are quite safe, sir,' William shouted after them. 'I am rich, live in a grand house and know that is more than enough to make me acceptable to you people!'

Ignoring the stares of others along the street, William marched towards his hotel, hating the stirring of loneliness and melancholy that shrouded him.

He glowered, cursing as the skies opened and great drops of rain spattered his face and clothes. Why had he allowed Octavia to walk away with their business unfinished? Yes, he had made a mistake offering her money, but she should have immediately turned her anger on him, called him a few choice names, whatever she needed to do. Why had she bloody well walked away?

Swiftly changing direction, William headed for Carson Street.

This time the door of the house was closed, no sign of Jacob standing sentry on the top step. Maybe the house was closed for further business this evening, although considering the late hour, the door was probably closed because it was filled to capacity.

William clenched his jaw. He would not allow his mind to wander to what Octavia might or might not be doing in that moment. He had to see her.

After climbing the steps, he rapped on the door.

It was immediately opened by Jacob, whose reasonably relaxed expression promptly became a scowl as he assessed William from head to toe. 'Mr Rose.'

Initially unperturbed by the doorman's less than friendly greeting, William nodded. 'Good evening, Jacob,' he said, belatedly realising that Octavia could have easily relayed details of his blunder to the entire household. Christ, there was every chance Jacob could land him a punch at any moment. William braced, feet planted – not an easy feat considering his current state of intoxication. 'I would like to see Octavia, if I may.'

'You may not. You're drunk and she's busy.'

'Then I would ask to see Mrs Hill so that I might make an appointment with Octavia for tomorrow evening.'

Irritation darkened Jacob's gaze. 'Come back tomorrow and I'll consider it.'

'I'm going nowhere. You either allow me access or remove me.'

Jacob grinned and dropped his folded arms. 'The latter will be my pleasure, sir.'

Just as William tensed, ready for what would undoubtedly be the brawl of his life, female laughter and a deep male voice sounded from inside the house.

Jacob turned as William stared past him into the hallway.

Octavia descended the staircase ahead of a finely dressed man whose eyes hungrily roamed over Octavia's back as though he wished to devour her, despite quite clearly already having had the pleasure of her company, judging by his mussed hair and tieless, open shirt. A shot of something that felt far too much like jealousy assaulted William in the very centre of his chest, and he dropped his gaze to his feet, trying his hardest to maintain a nonchalant expression.

Octavia's laughter came to an abrupt halt. 'Mr Rose, what are you doing here?'

William met her dark blue gaze. 'I wished to speak with you but as Jacob has informed me that is not possible this evening, I intend making an appointment for tomorrow.'

'I see.' A faint blush coloured her cheeks as she glanced at Jacob and then turned to the gentleman standing beside her, her smile immediate. 'Well, it's been a pleasure as always, Mr Compton. If you would leave your payment with Jacob, I would be grateful. I need to speak with Mr Rose. If you'll excuse me?'

'You are under no obligation, Octavia.' Jacob growled, his unflinching gaze on William's. 'If Mr Rose keeps turning up here unannounced, he should expect to be disappointed.'

Annoyance simmered inside William as he held Jacob's gaze. The man might be built like a stone wall, but there was no way in hell William was leaving here now that Octavia had said she would speak to him.

'We won't be long. Good evening, Mr Compton.' Octavia nodded at the gentleman and then looked at William, her forced amiability not quite reaching the depths of her eyes as she held out her arm towards the stairs at the end of the hallway. 'Mr Rose? If you'd like to follow me.'

With a sneer at Jacob, William stepped after Octavia, cursing when he stumbled on the corner of the hallway rug before straightening. He could practically feel the doorman's amusement following him along the hallway.

Octavia, dressed in a silk robe and seemingly very little else beneath the fine fabric – God help him – led him down some steps into the kitchen. 'Take a seat, William.'

He walked to the table and sat, flinching as she closed the door behind him with unnecessary force.

She planted her hands on her hips, her eyes flashing with anger. 'What on earth do you think you are doing turning up here half-drunk? I can smell the liquor on you, William. Your eyes are bloodshot, and your skin is glistening with perspiration.' She glared. 'This is a high-class establishment. You are lucky Louisa did not see you in this state. I am beyond surprised Jacob didn't throw you down the front steps.'

'I had to see you.'

'Why?'

'Our business is not finished.'

Her eyes widened and then she huffed a laugh. 'Well, it seems I have cause to enlighten you. Our business, William, was finished the moment you offered me money at the hotel.'

He slumped back in the seat, a headache throbbing at his temple. 'I didn't want you to think I was taking your time for granted. I meant no insult by it.'

She crossed her arms, her cheeks red. 'Well, it confirmed you still see me as a whore, no matter how much I might have helped you that night. But I am grateful for your derision because now I know your words about us working together were little more than puffs of air.'

'For the love of God, I made a mistake.' He leaned his elbow on the table and dropped his forehead against his hand. 'Am I not entitled to forgiveness since I came here and risked a beating from Jacob and a dressing-down from you?'

He lifted his head.

Hesitation warred with the anger in her eyes before she gripped the back of the chair in front of her. 'Even if I were to believe you now see that offering me payment was a mistake—'

'I do.'

'Pretending to be your fiancée adds nothing to my business aspirations and certainly does not bring me any closer to my goals. So, we are finished in our association, William. Now, if you would please leave, I am very—'

'Tell me your goals. Your *real* goals, not your business goals.' William ran his gaze over her face, suddenly desperate to know all that was in her heart and how he could magically produce what it was she wanted, because over his dead body was their association finished. 'Maybe if I understand them, we can agree to a new set of rules, here and now.'

She smirked and pushed away from the table. 'You're drunk. There is little point in me talking to you at the moment.'

The tension between them grew and William pinned her with an unwavering stare. 'I suspect you want to learn about running a business because you want to leave this house. Start something of your own making. I want to help you, Octavia. I have no wish to use you. I want you to be as happy in any agreement between us as I am.'

The wall clock ticked out the seconds as she considered him, her shoulders so high they almost reached her ears. 'There are plenty of other businessmen I can approach in this city. I don't need you, William, but it seems, as you are here again tonight, you have concluded that you need me.'

'I do need you, and not just as a fiancée,' William said, firmly. 'I think we go along well together. We fit. I will teach you, you will succeed, and that will be a feather in my cap as well as yours. I need my worth proved as much as the next man.'

'Is that so?'

'Yes. I became who I am by taking one step at a time, one day at a time. If I can do that, there is no reason you cannot achieve the same success the same way. If you forgive my offering you money, I promise you I will not stop helping you until it is clear to both of us that you no longer need me.'

'And what if that takes longer than you bargained for? What then?'

'Then that will be entirely my own fault, but a deal is a deal.'

Suspicion shadowed her gaze. 'Why would you do that for me?'

Even though the true reason immediately leapt onto his tongue, William's deep-seated vulnerability rose quickly. He had no choice but to be honest with her. How could he be anything else when he so badly wanted her forgiveness? She was smart and she was canny. He was also starting to believe she knew whenever he even considered telling an untruth, let alone uttering one.

He held her gaze, his heart beating a little faster. 'Because you are the only woman I have ever met who has come even close to being what I could desire in a fiancée, that's why.'

Two spots of colour leapt into her cheeks as she stepped back. 'What is that supposed to mean?'

He laughed, somewhat pleased, but also slightly offended by her look of undisguised horror. He raised his hand, flapped it in front of him in such a manner that he was reminded of just how drunk he was. 'It means, Octavia Marshall, you are the only woman on God's earth capable of convincing my business associates that you hold the power to capture my heart.'

'William, you have no idea what you are say—'

'Oh, but I do.' He grinned, leaned back in his seat. 'You are strong and quick-minded. Have as much of a temper as me and can stand in front of me, head held high even when I am acting like a complete arse.' He slapped the table. 'That is the sort of woman I want beside me... one day.'

She studied him before she huffed a laugh and walked to the stove. She lifted the kettle. 'It's late and you're intoxicated. Anyway, what you want no longer has any bearing on anything.'

She filled the kettle with water from an earthenware jug on the counter. William's mind raced. He had to offer something that would persuade Octavia to continue their charade, convince her that their pretend betrothal would ultimately help her towards her goals as it would his. She might think the suggestion entirely grounded in his own benefit, but it wasn't. He liked her. Would happily work with her, but he believed she needed to spend time with him at work in order for her to be absolutely certain business was really the direction she wanted to take and how big a commitment she would need to make in order to reap any benefits.

He leaned forward. 'What else do you want? Do you wish to see my mills? Come to Manchester? Learn all that is happening in the north?'

She stilled, the match between her fingers lingering over the stove, her back rigid.

'If that is the case,' William continued, 'all I am asking is that you continue for these next few days as my fiancée and then if you wish to return to Manchester with me, so be it.'

The silence stretched as she slowly turned, her gaze glazing as her thoughts took over. The longer she stared at him, the brighter her eyes shone with something hardened – and entirely confusing. Until...

She lifted her chin. 'Fine. I will continue as your fiancée for the remainder of your time in the city.'

He exhaled. 'Excellent. You will see that I—'

'And when that time comes to an end, I will go with you to Manchester.'

Words stuck in his throat as he slowly leaned back in his seat. He might have made the suggestion but no part of him had really expected her to agree...

God above, what had he done now?

17

Absolute resolve thundered through Octavia as she held William's stare.

She had spent the time since she last saw him poring over books and example business ledgers, sat with Louisa and discussed business dealings and processes. She had educated herself, and the thought of having a business of her own one day evoked a passion in her like nothing had before.

But although she still had much to learn and carried a certain amount of trepidation, it felt more right than ever that William be the one to teach her. With his throwaway offer of her coming to Manchester, Octavia now saw that moving away from Bath, away from Carson Street, could be the way to accelerate her wish to start again even sooner than she'd thought.

No one would know her in the north. She could hide her past and forge her future without presumption or judgement. It was the opportunity she had been waiting for – one she would never have considered had William not come into her life and unwittingly become the portal to her creating a new beginning.

She needed to flee north and become the woman she

genuinely wanted to be. She might not be entirely certain who that woman was yet, but the adventure to discovery was waiting for her regardless.

The boiling kettle pealed through the silence, both her and William flinching out of their paralysis.

She strode towards the stove. 'You are clearly stunned that I have so readily agreed to your suggestion to return north.'

'How can I not be? You can't possibly leave here in a matter of days as though you have no commitments to this house. To your friends.'

Octavia closed her eyes, her fingers tightened on the cloth covering the kettle's handle. 'I will deal with all of that,' she said, cursing the ache that beat in her heart. Opening her eyes, she poured water into the teapot to warm it before returning the kettle to the stove. 'All you need to concern yourself with is whether or not you can deliver on your side of the bargain. To teach me all that I need to know so that I might be able to start a business of my own.'

'You don't mean in Manchester?'

'Why not?' She carried the pot to the table before walking to the dresser and retrieving cups and saucers. 'Once there, I will find lodgings close to your home or your mills and we shall go along in our learning well enough, I'm sure,' she said, determined not to be intimidated by her somewhat ludicrous sense of simplicity or the disbelief on William's handsome face. 'While you are here, I will help you. When we go north, you will help me.'

'Just like that?' He huffed a laugh before swiping his hand over his face, his eyes no longer glazed but meeting hers without impairment. 'People in the north are different to here. Our ways and culture will be completely foreign to you. What then?'

'Then I will persevere,' Octavia said firmly, as she poured

milk into the cups. 'Surely by now you know I am neither a coward nor someone who gives up easily. I am a survivor, William. There is little that fazes me.'

'And what if you do not like the man I am in Manchester?'

She turned, the first flutters of uncertainty taking flight in her stomach. 'What is that supposed to mean?'

His jaw tightened, his gaze growing steely. 'I am a hard-working businessman, Octavia. My work is unforgiving, difficult and pressurised. I am often stressed and short with people, including my parents and sisters. Here in Bath, you are surrounded by people who love you. In Manchester, you will know only me.'

Octavia swallowed as his hardened stare bored into her. She could not falter. She had to take this chance, had to prove to him and herself that she could do anything. 'And while I am learning, you will be enough... bad-tempered and unsavoury company or not.'

'You're really determined to come back with me?'

She finished pouring their tea and sat, pushing a cup towards him. 'Yes.'

His hazel eyes flitted over her face before his voice softened. 'Are you running away, Octavia?'

She held his gaze, hating the way he had said *running away* as though it branded her a coward. But she wasn't afraid, she wanted to leave Bath in order to run to something more, something that would fill her – heart, body and soul. Something that had nothing to do with escape...

'Maybe I am running, but to a better future, to one day having something real and profitable of my own. Besides, I have no intention of waiting for the time when I am forced to leave this house. I will walk out of my own volition. You know I am capable of embarking on this dream. Otherwise, you would not be here.'

He sipped his tea, his eyes gauging her above the rim before he lowered the cup. 'Maybe, but I also suspect you coming to Manchester is madness and, I think deep down, you do, too.'

'But that madness is causing a knot of excitement in my belly.' She smiled. 'I was raised to be sensible, well-behaved and courteous, yet...' How much did she tell him? How much should she share in order to secure his agreement? 'When I was forced to flee my home after my mother's death, all that I had thought paved out for me was stolen and I became foolhardy, badly behaved and, sometimes, downright rude.'

He smiled softly, his gaze amused. 'Is that so? Well, maybe you will fit into my life well enough after all.'

She returned his smile, unable to resist the light dancing in his eyes. 'But today, I am a combination of the girl I once was and the woman I am now.' Instinctively, she reached for his hand where it lay on the table. 'I want to use all I have learned to get back to the security and respect I once knew and, hopefully one day, the love and protection of a good and kindly man, which was also promised to me. It's important I do all I can to shape the life I want and I'm asking you to help me to do that.'

Something flickered in his gaze she couldn't decipher and he slowly eased her hand from his. 'Love and protection?'

'Yes. Why does that...' She laughed, cursing the heat that rose in her cheeks. 'Oh, I see. I did not mean I need those things from you. Do not worry. But I would like to think that one day I will have a life free of the fear of abandonment and this horrible resentment towards my father. Even if I have to make it so by my own means and mettle.'

This time he reached for her hand, his gaze dropping to their fingers as he passed his thumb back and forth across her skin.

'My adolescence was clearly different from yours,' he said quietly, lifting his eyes to hers. 'My parents loved me and my sisters a lot more than they did themselves. They gave us their last morsels of food and went cold if it meant our hunger was kept at bay or we needed an extra blanket.' His grip tightened on her fingers. 'That sense of undisputed security and love is what I wish for my own family one day.'

The earnestness in his words and eyes clawed at Octavia's heart. He looked so afraid, yet passionate too. 'I have no doubt you could create that now if you had to,' she said quietly. 'Why do you look as though you imagine such a thing impossible?'

He slipped his hand from hers as he leaned heavily back in his chair. 'I'm not convinced. Not yet. First, I need to know my business is strong and will survive me intact for my children. That they will never go hungry. I need to be sure all I have built will remain standing before I can even think of marrying and starting a family.'

Empathy swelled in Octavia's heart, and she nodded. 'I understand. You are a good man, William.'

He stared at her. 'What if you hate Manchester? Hate the time you are alone? Hate my mills? Then what? If I suspect you are unhappy...' His gaze turned tender. 'You are a brilliant lady and I won't risk it being me who extinguishes your light. You have a brightness that's as rare as it is beautiful.'

Her heart fluttered. When he was like this, so lovely and kind, she could almost imagine herself walking on his arm in society, have him whirl her around a ballroom or make love to her on crisp, white sheets... but none of that was in their future. She was not a young, privileged girl anymore, she was a woman who lived in reality, not in one of her novels as Nancy so often accused her of doing.

She inhaled a long breath. 'Everything will be fine. I want to make my life worth something, William. To mean something to others. But even the possibility of it meaning something to just one person is enough for now.'

His brow furrowed. 'Surely your life means a lot to your friends here?'

Shame flooded through her and she closed her eyes. 'Yes. Yes, of course it does.'

'Then—'

'As you fear being unable to give your family security, I live in fear of my father finding me living as I am,' she said, hating that she suddenly felt so shallow, so needy. 'I want to prove to him, to myself, that I am more than he predicted. After my mother's death, he went from the most loving father a girl could ask for to a monster. It was as though his grief sparked a whole other side of him. His violent outbursts, coarse language and unpredictability drove our once devoted staff to leave one by one until it was just me, him, his dutiful valet and our cook, Mrs Wells.' She smiled wryly, swiping a tear that had treacherously rolled onto her cheek. 'He never would have scared Mrs Wells. She was a force of nature. But once he began to strike me—'

Anger leapt into his eyes. 'God, I'm so sorry you had to live with a father who raised his hand to you.'

'Thank you. Once it grew too much to bear I fled, but the damage had been done. I tried to stay with friends of the family, but my father came bursting into their homes, ranting and raving and then took me home again.'

His jaw tightened, his hazel eyes dangerously dark. 'And in the end you had no choice but to leave with no idea where you might end up?'

'I packed as many valuables as I could, a little money and the clothes on my back. I eventually arrived in Bath.'

'So your father is wealthy? Your eloquence and obvious intelligence speak of you having a good education.'

She nodded. 'He is a landowner with a fairly vast estate, tenants and an income that many would envy.'

'But he has never looked for you?'

'Not as far as I know, and I hope he never finds me. Not now, anyway.'

Not now I'm a whore...

She looked towards the window. 'The last of my friends is to be married at Christmas and that has pushed me into action. I need to forget I am a whore and start again.' She met his gaze, her heart aching to see such sympathy in his eyes. 'Learning from you could be my chance to do that.'

He didn't speak for such a long time that Octavia's cheeks warmed as her humiliation grew.

He slowly stood and held out his hand. 'Will you stand for me?'

She pushed to her feet and slid her hand into his. With gentle fingers, he brushed a curl from her cheek, stared deep into her eyes and then lowered his lips to hers.

Every ounce of strength slowly seeped from her body and Octavia leaned into him, deepening their kiss and connection. He pulled her closer, her breasts, naked beneath her robe, pressed hard to his chest.

Adrenaline and arousal washed through her, a certainness of spirit that told her William would keep her safe for as long as he could, that he would not hurt or harm her. Maybe her thoughts were based on nothing but her fear of a future she couldn't predict, but as he drew his mouth from hers to press feather-light kisses upon her cheeks, Octavia had never felt so safe in a man's arms.

He dropped his forehead to hers. 'We will spend as much

time as we can together over the next few days and if you still wish to return with me to Manchester... then, yes, I will teach you all I know.'

'Thank you.'

'We will work out how to explain to people who you are and why you are in Manchester as the time draws closer. I fear there will be many questions and much curiosity from both my staff and my family.'

'Maybe it would be simpler to continue our charade of being engaged.' Octavia laughed.

'Maybe we should... It would be one way of explaining things.'

'William, no.' Octavia took a step back. 'I couldn't possibly deceive your family and nor should you. They love you and trust you. Haven't you just said as much?'

'And nothing would make my parents happier than me bringing home a sweetheart, believe me. It will just be for the time you are learning. So that people accept we are betrothed and their curiosity is satisfied.'

'But they will ask questions, surely? Your family will want to know about my family, where I am from—'

He brushed his lips over hers again, his gaze happy. 'Leave everything to me. All will be well. You trust me, don't you?'

'Well, yes, but...' She closed her eyes, once again fearful that he did not truly understand the will burning inside of her. It meant so much to her that she might one day be looked at as a lady rather than a whore. Maybe a marriage of mutual convenience was the way forward. After all, true love was something she could never hope for – was something she wasn't sure she even wanted after her father, who claimed to love her, had come to think nothing of beating her until her body was bruised and her heart destroyed.

'Fine. We will do what you think best,' she said, looking deep into his eyes. 'I won't make the same mistakes I did with my father, and you will not be disappointed in me.'

'You made no mistake with your father. He should have cared for you as my parents always have for me.'

She laid her head on his chest, not wanting her bitterness to give him cause to doubt his decision. 'You're right. Of course you're right.'

18

William nodded his thanks to the waiter as a steaming cup of coffee was set down in front of him in the lounge of the George Hotel. He stared through the leaded window beside him at the people, carriages and carts that passed by along the cobbled street.

The sun shone hazily through a blanket of thin grey cloud on this chilly November morning, which only further provoked William to consider his imminent return north. Since Octavia had pleaded her case for returning with him to Manchester, his liability to her, how he'd kissed her, had harangued his conscience more and more.

He could not deny his feelings continued to grow for her, but it was *why* they were growing and what it meant for their union that bothered him. What had started out as a chance meeting had gathered momentum until he had asked a beautiful woman, a whore no less, to pose as his fiancée. Octavia had not only proved her worth in that role but had also convinced him that he could help her change her life for the better.

And he most likely could, but he couldn't help feeling his

reasons for doing so were less than honourable. He had no doubt that she would learn his business quickly and competently, that her intelligence and zeal for a better life would ensure her success. But what about all the hours in between when they were not working? What of his associates' questions of how he and his fiancée had met? His family's questions about Octavia and how well William knew her? His workers' curiosity when they saw him spending more and more time with this new woman who looked like a goddess and spoke like she belonged in Buckingham Palace?

Would people start digging into her past? Would his senior workers ask one too many questions? Would his parents?

But despite these reservations, William did not want to let her go, refuse her, or return to Manchester without her... and the fact that it was his heart leading those assertions rather than his head was more terrifying than any obstacle that might arise once they arrived there. Was he falling in love? Lust? Or was he trying to act the hero for someone less fortunate, as his mother so often accused him of doing? Was his care for Octavia genuine, or founded in his own conceit, his own carnal desire?

He no longer saw her as a prostitute but as a woman, vivacious and beautiful. One he desired, one he wanted to lie with and possess between the sheets. Yet she had made no indication that sex between them would ever occur again now that their teacher–pupil deal had been struck. Why would she want to muddy the waters between them? Risk the physical overtaking her dreams of becoming financially secure?

These were the thoughts that had ravaged his mind throughout the night and now, as he waited for Octavia and his associates to arrive for their meeting, the notion that William was losing his mind seemed entirely plausible.

He drew a folded letter from his inside pocket, his uncertainties only made stronger by his mother's familiar penmanship. Yet her report about her and his father's continuing home life brought a smile to his lips as she explained she had dropped by William's house and the staff were doing well. That his father was being kept busy with his latest invention, despite his mother's despair at the banging and clanging coming from the outhouse her husband used as a workshop.

William lifted his gaze once again to the window.

For the last two years, his mother had pleaded and beseeched him to wed. Now, as William approached his thirty-third birthday, his mother would be delighted that he was engaged and most likely bury her curiosity and any reservations she might have, preferring to wholeheartedly embrace his future wife and the grandchildren she could give her.

William stilled.

What if he and Octavia were to truly marry before returning to Manchester? Wouldn't that halt any words of warning from onlookers and give Octavia the security she craved? He could still teach her what she wanted to know about business, and she would arrive in Manchester respectably married. People's questions would surely be less probing if William had made a clear declaration of his love and commitment to her?

He returned his mother's letter to his pocket, his heart beating fast.

He was deeply fond of Octavia, respected her. She made him smile and relax. She was more different than any woman he had ever met. He needed to marry one day. He needed children to whom he could pass on the enterprise he had so carefully built. The thought of Rose Textiles falling into the hands of someone outside of his own kin was a scenario he could not contemplate.

Why not bite the bullet right now and marry the woman

who made him forget about work for more than an hour or two, who made him think of a future beyond profit and progression to personal happiness? That had to be a positive sign that things could work out between them, surely?

Hadn't she herself mentioned marrying one day? Of finding a good and wealthy man as she had been once promised by her family?

'Ah, William. It's good to see you again.'

He started and immediately stood, his heart still racing as he offered his hand to one of the two men who had approached his table. 'Malcolm, it's good to see you too.' He forced a smile at the older of the two before turning to his friend's young protégé, praying his greeting did not sound as strained as it felt. 'Joseph, how are you?'

'Good, thank you, sir.'

The gentlemen sat, and William raised his hand to a nearby attendant for more coffee as he tried his hardest to turn his mind to business. But how was he to do that when Octavia had not yet arrived? Concern unfurled inside him as he glanced towards the hotel's gilded doors. What was keeping her? She had said she would arrive as early as possible before his associates.

'So...' Malcolm Winston settled back in his seat and extracted a cigar from a silver case, his grey whiskers lifting as he smiled. 'You are looking well, my friend.'

William dragged his gaze from the front of the hotel. 'As are you.'

'Can't complain, can't complain.' Malcolm cut the tip of his cigar, his shrewd gaze showing his mind was forever on his next deal. 'As you are here seeking investment, I assume you are ready to expand Rose Textiles?'

'I am.' William crossed his legs and tried to calm his nerves about how to introduce Octavia once she arrived. 'Business is good, I can't deny that but, as always, it could be better. The three of us have worked well together in the past and I thought you might consider deepening our association.'

As an attendant brought a silver coffee pot and china cups and saucers to the table, William glanced again towards the hotel's doors, willing Octavia's arrival.

Once the waiter had retreated, Joseph cleared his throat and addressed William. 'Our freights are increasing every day and we will be exporting overseas by early next year. The quality of your textiles is undisputed, so Malcolm and I are very interested in what you have to say.'

The sharp tap of court shoes across the tiles turned William's head and his heart stumbled as Octavia hurried towards them looking beautiful, if not marginally harassed.

She smiled, her bright blue eyes clear and happy. 'Oh, William. I am so sorry I am late.' She nodded to Malcolm and Joseph, now on their feet and their eyes filled with undisguised admiration. 'Gentlemen.'

Malcolm was the first to hold out his hand. 'A pleasure, Miss...'

'Oh, I do apologise, I am Miss Marshall. William's fiancée.'

William froze, his smile so wide his cheeks ached. He'd been dithering how to raise his engagement and Octavia simply announced it as though their pretence was of little consequence. She was wonderful.

He cleared his throat. 'She is indeed. Darling, this is Malcolm Winston and his colleague, Joseph Harwood.'

Pleasantries were exchanged before William pulled out a seat for Octavia, and Joseph left the table to order the tea she had requested.

Octavia placed her purse on the floor by her chair. 'I hope I haven't missed anything of importance?' She smiled at Malcolm. 'As William and I are to be married, I want to learn as much about his mills as possible. He has told me you conduct a lot of business in Bath?'

'I do, but Bath is more Joseph's domain than mine, Miss Marshall.' Malcolm smiled. 'I am only here on a short visit and then I will be returning north. Have you and William been engaged very long?'

'We—'

'A couple of months,' William interrupted. 'We were introduced during the summer ball at the Assembly Rooms. I was quick to ask Miss Marshall if I could write to her but, before long, letters were not enough and I have been visiting back and forth from Manchester for several months now.'

Octavia squeezed his fingers. 'William is quite the romantic scribe. I just couldn't resist him.'

As they laughed, Joseph returned to the table. 'Your tea, Miss...' He stared at Octavia, wide-eyed. 'Why, do you know, you are awfully familiar. Are we acquainted?'

Dread dropped like a stone into William's stomach and he snapped his gaze to Octavia. Her cheeks held a faint blush, but her hand was steady as she accepted the cup and saucer from Joseph. 'Oh, I'm sure you are mistaken, Mr...'

'Harwood.' Joseph frowned as he intensely stared at Octavia. 'No, no. I'm most certain I have seen you before somewhere.'

'Maybe you had the same pleasure as William and have danced with Miss Marshall at the Assembly Rooms.' Winston reached for his coffee and laughed. 'However, you missed the mark, my boy, so you can put your eyes back in their sockets. William and Miss Marshall are engaged to be married.'

William clenched his jaw and thought fast. There was no

way in hell Octavia would be in any way embarrassed or humiliated while he was around.

Joseph continued to stare at Octavia, and William quickly stood, firmly grasping Joseph's elbow. 'Why don't we go and hurry along our table? We should have been seated for luncheon by now.'

'But—'

Propelling Joseph away from the table, William inwardly cursed. Had Joseph been to Carson Street? He was never one to stand on ceremony and if he knew Octavia to be a prostitute...

'Just hold on a second.' Joseph pulled his arm from William's grip and pinned him with a disbelieving stare. 'I've just remembered where I've seen Miss Marshall. Have you taken leave of your senses? Do you know who she is? Or rather, *what* she is?'

'She is a woman.' William's anger rose, his protectiveness for Octavia immediate. 'One I intend to marry.'

'Are you mad?'

William glanced towards Octavia as she chatted with Malcolm, seemingly entirely relaxed judging by her smile and gestures. She clearly had the mettle to deal with whatever situation arose, as did he and over his dead body would he allow Joseph to cause a scene.

Bloody hell, had he slept with her?

William looked at his associate. 'I don't know what you think you know about her, but she is my fiancée, and I advise you to think very carefully about what you say to me next. She will be leaving for Manchester with me and we are to be married.'

'For the love of God, man.' Joseph shot his gaze across the room before facing William again, his cheeks mottled. 'She's a whore.'

William curled his hand into a fist at his side. 'I'm warning you, Joseph.'

Their eyes locked and William's heart beat hard as he fought to keep hold of his need to punch the man.

'Fine.' Joseph lowered his shoulders, took a step back. 'It's your funeral. But it's just as well for both of us that it is Miss Bloom I prefer. Can you imagine if I had bedded Miss Marshall, if that is even her real name? Where would that have left us?'

'That part of her life is over. Now, be a gentleman and keep your mouth buttoned. I intend giving Octavia a new and better life away from here and if doing that makes me happy, it should you, too. Now, promise me, not a word of this to Malcolm.'

'But you can't possibly marry the girl,' Joseph protested. 'If I recognised her, others will too.'

'Which is why I intend taking her to Manchester.'

'You are playing with fire. Don't be a fool.'

William lowered his voice further and spoke his next words through clenched teeth. 'One man's foolishness is another man's wisdom. Just promise me you will keep who she is to yourself. This is nobody's business but mine and Octavia's.'

Joseph stared at him for a long moment and then raised his hand in surrender. 'Clearly there are changes afoot at the Carson Street house. Miss Bloom recently wed and now it seems Miss Marshall is jumping ship.'

'And did you object to Miss Bloom marrying?'

'Of course not, but the man who married Miss Bloom is not someone I do business with, is he?'

'Do I have your word you will not breathe a word about Octavia to Malcolm or anyone else?'

'Fine, you have my word.'

'And will this affect our business dealings going forward?'

Joseph laid his hand on William's shoulder. 'Clearly your choices about women are questionable, my friend, but in business, there is no one better. Come, let's return to the table before your fiancée thinks I have upset the apples in her wedding carriage.'

William followed Joseph across the lobby, praying the man kept his word. It was quite obvious now that if he and Octavia were to go ahead with their arrangement, they needed to leave Bath sooner rather than later.

19

Octavia left the hotel on William's arm, desperate to ask him what had been said to change the atmosphere so noticeably after he had disappeared for a while with Mr Harwood. The meeting had gone well, but the lunch had felt rather rushed at both Mr Harwood's and William's instigation.

A horrible, gnawing feeling had remained in Octavia's stomach for the remainder of their time together. The recognition on Mr Harwood's face had been clear for all to see and soon she was half convinced he'd been a client of Nancy's once or maybe even twice before.

She glanced at William as he stared straight ahead, his jaw tight. If her suspicions were right and Mr Harwood had recognised her, that could be enough for William to bring a halt to all that they had agreed upon. He might have said before it happened that he was willing to take the risk of her being recognised, but the reality was a different matter entirely.

'I thought we might take a walk to the park,' he said, interrupting her thoughts. 'We can take a carriage ride once we're there.'

Octavia studied him, trying to read his thoughts. 'Now?'

'If you don't mind?' He laid his hand over hers on his forearm and continued to stare ahead, seemingly to avoid having to look at her. 'We need to talk. Preferably alone where there is little chance of eavesdroppers.'

So, this was it. Her concerns were justified, and William had changed his mind about her leaving for Manchester with him. She had spent the entirety of last night considering and reconsidering her choice to flee Bath and start again in the north. Not once had the decision felt wrong or even rash.

The prospect excited her as much as she suspected it would alarm Louisa and Nancy.

She glanced at him. 'Is this about Mr Harwood?'

A muscle flickered in his jaw. 'Yes.'

Octavia stopped and slipped her hand from his arm. 'What is it? Neither of you succeeded in hiding something was amiss. I'm sure Mr Winston felt the tension too, even if he did still agree to the business you proposed.'

He drew in a long breath and looked along the busy street. 'Harwood remembered how he knew you. He's been to Carson Street.'

'I see,' Octavia said quietly, hating that she might have caused William embarrassment. 'I thought that might be the truth of it. Did he say when he visited the house? How often?'

'No, but it seems he only ever paid for time with Nancy and, from what he inferred, that didn't happen very often.' William held out his arm. 'Come. Let us go to the park. I'd rather not discuss this in the middle of the street.'

As they walked, questions danced on Octavia's tongue and trepidation lay heavy across her heart. She desperately wanted to embark on their working relationship, elated that she had a plan in place for her future. One that would not involve Louisa having to make the hard decision to one day tell Octavia that she had to leave.

It felt liberating to take charge of her own destiny. To do something that went some way to proving not everything she did was founded in selfishness. With each modicum of pain or distress she eliminated for Louisa, Nancy or Jacob, Octavia could begin to believe she could atone for the anger her self-involvement had provoked in her father and how it had led to him so cruelly revealing his loathing of her. His cruelty had stripped away all she once was and had. Now it was time to create something true and long-standing.

She glanced again at William. It was clear his thoughts continued to consume him and it seemed more and more likely he was about to call an end to their arrangement.

Victoria Park glistened under the low winter sun, frost dripping from the trees' overhanging branches onto the hats of walkers and the bridles of horses. Colours abounded, from the women's hats and fitted coats, to the gentlemen's shiny top hats and silver- and ivory-topped canes, all adding a welcome flash of optimism against the austere backdrop of barren trees and empty flower beds.

Yet Octavia felt nothing but a growing despair as William led her through the throng to a trio of black and gold carriages awaiting employment, the horses pawing the gritty road, their breath pluming white in the slowly dropping temperatures.

Octavia stood back and tried her best to control her anxiety as he approached the driver of the one in front. If William had changed his mind, then she would just have to concoct another way of seeking the freedom and respect she craved. Her life at the brothel no longer felt secure. No longer silenced the tormenting belief that her existence would be abhorrent to the mother who had wanted so much for her.

Sadness threatened and she turned her attention to a group of children playing catch with their mothers, the small ball hitting the ground so often that it was impossible not to smile at the children's tenacity and the mothers' patience.

'Octavia?'

William held out his hand to help her into the open carriage, the seats a deep green velvet. Once aboard and seated side by side, William covered their laps and legs with the thick wool blanket he'd been given by the driver.

They jolted forward and began at a trot along the shrub-lined pathways.

Unable to bear William's contemplative silence any longer, she faced him. 'You look troubled.'

'I am.' His brow furrowed as his serious hazel gaze bored into hers. 'Are you quite certain you still wish to return with me to Manchester? The transition will not be easy or without problems. Both here and there.'

'I know.' She exhaled a shaky breath, holding on to the hope he had not entirely dismissed the idea. 'I am yet to tell Louisa and Nancy as I'm sure they will have more advice than I can bear. Are you deeply upset that Mr Harwood recognised me?'

'Upset? No, not at all. That's not to say my reaction, my need to thump the man, did not come as a surprise. It did, but I was foolish to believe you would not be recognised.'

Octavia placed her hand on his arm, shamefully flattered that he felt so protective of her. 'Well, I'm glad you did not strike Mr Harwood. I fear that would have made the whole thing worse. Besides, if anyone has been foolish about not taking more care, it's me.' Octavia fought to maintain her pride in having found her own way by whatever means. 'If you can't work side by side with a whore trying to change her life, then say so, William. I am hardly going to condemn you for it.'

'You don't understand.' Determination burned in his eyes. 'It isn't what people might say about me. It's the judgement I felt from Joseph that you are not good enough for me to be associated with.' He shook his head. 'He looked at me as though I had entirely lost my mind by being with you.'

'People judge. Surely you know that?'

'But coming from him, his words were nothing more than hypocrisy. How can he so vehemently present his disapproval when he has been to Carson Street for his own gratification? He has no care for how Nancy might feel. Or why she is doing the work she is doing. The man annoyed me beyond measure.'

'But that is the attitude of most men. Women are objects to use and dismiss at their whim.' She squeezed his fingers. 'But you are different. I came to that conclusion in much the same way as Louisa and Nancy did about Jacob and Francis.'

'But am I so different really?' He looked across the park, his jaw tight. 'I'm not so sure.'

Disappointment that she failed to rouse him whispered through her. 'You are different, William. You are willing to give me an opportunity in full knowledge of what I do. Don't you see how different that makes you?'

'Maybe, but...' He turned. 'My business is everything to me, my life's work. I can't afford for my reputation to be tarnished.'

Humiliation stung hot at her cheeks. 'Tarnished? By me?'

'I'm just being realistic. If we are to go ahead with our arrangement, I think it best we leave Bath as soon as possible.' He inhaled a long breath, his hazel eyes roaming over her face to linger at her lips. 'I don't want people to look at or think of you as a prostitute and I want to give you all that you want. All that will make you happy. But...'

'But what?'

'I don't know.' He stared at her mouth before meeting her

eyes. 'It's just that you are far too beautiful, far too kind and quick-witted, far too astute and rational to be classed as a... working woman. Whether that is what you are or not.'

She smiled, pleased by his words. 'There are hundreds of prostitutes who are beautiful, kind and quick-witted and are living the same existence as me. Many far worse. It's the way of the world. No one sells their body out of choice. Or if they do, I am yet to meet them.'

He tightly gripped her fingers, his gaze shadowing with a deep solemnity. 'I need you to be absolutely sure about Manchester before we go any further. Are you really prepared for the judgement we are sure to face?'

'I have a very thick skin. There is no need for you to worry about me.'

'Then there is something I want to ask you. It's a possible solution I think will make the transition from Bath to Manchester easier for us both.'

'Yes?'

He inhaled a long breath, shakily released it. 'How about we marry?'

'What?' Octavia's heart leapt into her throat before she huffed a laugh. 'Don't be absurd. We couldn't possibly.'

'I know it sounds ridiculous, but I want to do all I can to protect you, Octavia. To avoid as many awkward questions and presumptions as possible once we reach Manchester. I need to keep you safe.' His gaze flitted over her face, to her hair, and he offered her a strained smile. 'Believe me, my mother will be over the moon I have married, regardless of having never met you.'

Octavia stared at him, wondering if he had lost his mind or at least maybe a piece of his brain had slipped from his head and was rolling around the footwell of the carriage. 'You are serious.'

'Yes, yes, I am. It will be advantageous to us both. I will have a wife and your reputation will be intact once you arrive to start your brand-new life in the north.'

'And you believe your parents and family will just accept me as your wife?'

'Well, there will be questions, of course, but you are well-spoken, educated and worldly. They will be impressed by you. Never in a hundred years will they suspect your occupation while you were in Bath.'

Octavia shook her head. 'I think you are somewhat delusional, William. I cannot believe things will be as simple as that.'

'They will if we make them so.'

A slow annoyance began to build inside Octavia, and she slipped her hand from his. 'So you believe everything will be sunlight and flowers if we marry?'

'Well, no...' He carefully watched her. 'But I do think—'

'You haven't considered how my money will immediately become yours? How I will lose every ounce of my independence in a single vow while you have so much to gain?' She curled her hands together in her lap, her anger simmering hot in her stomach. 'No, William, my answer to your romantic proposal is no. I will come to Manchester as your fiancée only or not at all. Once I have learned all that I need to we will find a reason to break off our engagement and go our separate ways.'

It was as though the shouts and laughter of the people they passed, the chirping of the birds and the clop of the horses' hooves completely stilled. All Octavia could hear was her racing pulse. How could he assume she would agree to a marriage arrangement when she had not benefited an ounce from their agreement thus far? He really must think her a fool.

He leaned back against the seat. 'You're right.'

Something shifted in her chest to see what she believed to be disappointment in his eyes. Was he disappointed that he'd failed to dupe her? Or disappointed that she had so quickly refused him?

Now was not the time to contemplate such things. Emotion could not seep into a situation that could lead to her risking everything and he nothing. 'I will not be taken for a fool,' Octavia said firmly. 'Not by you or anyone else. This is a business arrangement and pretending to be your fiancée in Manchester works for me as it has worked for you in Bath. Marriage is out of the question.'

'You're right. It was an idiotic suggestion. I apologise.'

His apology was said in a monotone, leaving her no way of deciphering his true thoughts or feelings. Her resolve began to weaken but she had to stand firm.

She looked across the park. 'Good, then let us say no more about it. I will tell Louisa and Jacob of our plans as soon as I return home.'

20

Octavia resisted glancing over her shoulder at William as they parted ways on Pulteney Bridge, he to return to his hotel and she to Carson Street.

Her mind raced with the conflicts that lay ahead of her at the house and in her future but, more than that, she had become undeniably and unexpectedly afraid for her heart. The disappointment she was convinced she had seen in William's eyes had sent a dangerous jolt through her entire body.

The very real possibility that – in time – she could come to love him. To care for him. His passion for his work and family combined with the tenderness and care he had shown towards her were having a wholly unnerving effect on her. He was good, kind, hardworking, even progressive and forward-thinking, and the longer she spent with him, the more she wanted to be with him for longer than she had anticipated.

And now he had introduced the possibility of marriage. How was she to steel her heart against him – to protect herself and her money – if he continued to treat her so well?

The only man she had ever truly loved was her father and

she had not come close to loving anyone else since their estrangement. She had steadfastly guarded her heart, feelings and intimacy like a goaler guarding a prisoner. No freedom and absolute retention.

She had never got over the fear that, sooner or later, anyone she came to love, or who came to love her, would eventually banish her, turn violent or resentful. After all, she had believed her father loved her unconditionally. She had been wrong, and he had only loved her as a by-product of her mother.

Octavia stopped at the wall that lined the gushing waters of the River Avon and stared blindly into its depths as a horrible feeling of foreboding whispered through her. The prospect of becoming William's wife had immediately slammed her defences into place, rousing a deeply rooted terror of having to explain herself to someone forever. That was what marriage would mean and she could not do it when it risked being a union of convenience for him and possibly something deeper for her.

Yet, for so long, she had harboured a secret hankering for this kind of security. To one day meet a man who loved and respected her, who wanted to build a life with her. Their home, dreams and aspirations bound as one. But even with William she could not surrender her self-imposed protection and take a leap of faith. Not even for a man who held such a pot of property and wealth that she might never fret over food and warmth for the rest of her days.

And what of William? At first, he had proposed a temporary engagement, had deemed her someone to charm and beguile investors into doing business with him. What need could he have for a permanent wife plucked from a brothel in Bath? A woman he barely knew? Unless of course, he viewed her as a brood mare. Someone to supply him with an heir. After all, his parents and sisters could not guarantee the legacy he had built remained. But to choose her – a whore – when he could surely have the pick of any woman in Manchester? It made no sense.

Octavia swallowed against the sudden dryness in her throat and continued along the cobbled road, her head bent to the winter wind and not giving a fig about the knowing looks sent her way by some of the men and ladies who smirked unkindly as she passed them. Whenever she, Nancy or Louisa was in the vicinity of Carson Street, recognition was more likely, the derision often palpable.

It hadn't bothered Octavia for the longest time. She had been happy to have a roof over her head, food in her belly and company in front of a fire where the lack of coal was never contemplated.

But with her friends' marriages came her need for complete security.

She let herself into the house and started to unbutton her coat when there was a burst of female laughter from the kitchen. A little of her worry lifted as Louisa's and Nancy's teasing of one another grew in volume. With Jacob nowhere to be seen or heard, Octavia was glad of the opportunity to speak with her friends alone. As she rid herself of her coat, hat and scarf, Octavia pushed aside the trepidation that unfurled inside of her and walked towards the steps leading to the downstairs kitchen.

Considering she and William had brought their departure to Manchester forward by several days, the option to delay talking to Louisa and Nancy was impossible. She owed them too much to conceal anything, let alone something as consummate as her leaving Bath... possibly for good.

Louisa and Nancy sat at the kitchen table, cutting and chopping vegetables for dinner, a half-drunk glass of wine within reaching distance of Louisa and a small glass of ale by Nancy.

'Well…' Octavia forced joviality into her voice as she strolled into the room, her eyebrows raised. 'I see we are arduous in our duties, ladies.'

Nancy grinned, her pretty grey eyes twinkling mischievously. 'I might be with child, but I've not lost all sense of myself. Even Francis agrees the odd drink with friends won't hurt if it makes me happy.'

'That's true enough,' Louisa added, raising her glass. 'There's nothing a glass of wine won't help. Octavia? Will you join us?'

She glanced at the clock. It was barely five o'clock but if her friends weren't concerned, then neither would she be. A glass of Dutch courage would certainly be welcome. 'Why not? It might make what I have to tell you both a little easier.'

The jolly atmosphere subtly shifted as Octavia took a glass from one of the cupboards, her friends' gazes burning into her as she poured herself some wine. She took a hearty sip and sat at the table. 'So, things have moved on with regards to my arrangement with William.' She willed her heart to slow lest it burst clean out of her chest. 'He has agreed that I can return with him to Manchester.'

Silence fell like a heavy curtain, but Octavia held fast, refusing to yield to her friends' unspoken judgement.

Nancy smirked and dropped her gaze to the potatoes she was peeling. '"Course he has, and I'm going to give birth on stage, stark naked and my legs akimbo in front of Prince Albert himself.'

Louisa nudged her, her gaze steely and pinned on Octavia. 'What are you talking about?'

'When I agreed to pose as his fiancée, William agreed to teach me about business,' Octavia said. 'But the more time we spend together, the more I realise that this venture deserves a whole new beginning and—'

'You propose that beginning to be in Manchester,' Louisa finished, her voice unusually quiet.

'With William Rose,' Nancy added. 'Whom you barely know.'

'I may barely know him, Nance, but I trust him. He respects my opinion and supports me in my business aspirations. For now, that is all I need from him and... from you.' Octavia looked between her friends, her shoulders back, confident in her decision to go to Manchester, if not in the safety of her emotions. Whatever her friends might say, Louisa and Nancy had absolutely no possibility of dissuading her. If she didn't take this opportunity now, it could be months, maybe years, before she had severed the obligation Louisa must feel she held for her. 'We will be leaving in the next couple of days. There is nothing for you to worry about. I know what I'm doing.'

The clang of Nancy's knife as she tossed it onto the metal plate in front of her sent a jolt through Octavia's stretched nerves. 'Since when are you the foolish whore in this house? You're the sensible one. The one who tries to keep me on the straight and narrow as much as possible. The one who does nothing without careful thought and consideration.'

'Exactly.' Octavia sipped her wine and lowered it to the table, pleased that the ruby liquid did not tremble. 'Then trust this is the right path for me. Whether or not you agree.'

She turned to Louisa, who had put down her knife and now stared at her hands, pressed flat on the table as though she was holding herself steady. Octavia's heart beat faster. She had not been prepared for the sudden paleness of Louisa's face, the scar along her cheek standing out and almost taunting Octavia with the memory of its infliction. They had been through so much together.

She swallowed past the lump in her throat. 'Louisa—'

'If I had thought for one moment that my marrying Jacob and Nancy marrying Francis would turn you into a woman who thought she should grab the first man she thinks worthy—'

'That is *not* what I am doing.'

'—I would have refused Jacob and held Nancy captive,' Louisa finished. She sipped her wine and put the glass down so heavily, claret leapt onto the table. 'What you propose is dangerous. I respect your instincts and maybe Mr Rose is trustworthy, but don't you think it is a little perilous to travel halfway across the country with him? You won't know for sure he is all he seems until you return north with him. See him at home, with the people he knows, at work. What if it comes that he is not the man you thought him to be?'

Octavia tightened her fingers around her glass and lifted her chin. 'I will deal with any problems as they arise. For now, though, I believe William to be my avenue to a fresh start and nothing you say will deter me from taking this opportunity.' Resolute, she held each of her friends' gazes in turn. 'William and I have told each other of our wants and wishes and what we foresee as the outcome. He knows I am not a woman to be coddled or misled and I have no romantic or naïve dreams of a guaranteed happy ever after. What will be, will be.'

'I'm sorry, Octavia, but Louisa is right,' Nancy said. 'You have not spent enough time together for either of you to truly know the other. Why are you really doing this? Apart from the fact you clearly think you're going to be left on the slag heap.'

Octavia looked at each of them, inwardly pleading her dearest friends and confidantes let her go without unnecessary heartache. 'I've had enough of being nothing more than a whore. I never would have contemplated moving away with anyone before now, but William has proven with his words, his care for me and others, that he will not forsake me. Things have moved on between us.'

'Moved on?' Nancy's eyes widened, her cheeks flushing with agitation. 'Migrating birds move on, Octavia. Not friends. Not whores who have a lot to be thankful for in this house and in this city.' Nancy's voice cracked before she snatched her up her glass and drained it. 'You belong here. With us.'

Octavia stared as Nancy looked away from her, swiped her fingers over her cheek. Octavia reached for her friend's hand where it lay on the table. 'Things are no longer the same, Nance. You are *married*. You will be starring in a play next year. *You* have moved on. Don't you see that?'

'Yet, here I am, still sitting around the table.'

'You know what I mean.' Octavia squeezed her fingers. 'Why can you embrace a different life but I can't?'

'No one is saying that.' Louisa sighed as she pushed to her feet before walking to the window. She tossed the remainder of her wine into the sink and turned, her face still pale, her violet eyes shadowed with worry. 'But Nancy is right about one thing. We are meant to be here for each other. Everything between us secure and trustworthy. That was my vision when I decided to open this house and it is what we stand for now. One of us moving halfway across the country was not the plan.'

'According to whom?' Octavia asked, quietly. 'Since when have we had a claim over each other? Written it down that we must stay within a mile or two of each other for the rest of our lives?'

'God above, Octavia,' Nancy snapped. 'You know perfectly well what Louisa is saying.'

'Do I? Because if you both expect me to stay in Bath against my wishes then you are being utterly unfair.' Octavia stood. 'Our lives are different now. *We're* different and there's nothing wrong with that. In fact, it's something to be celebrated, is it not?' She paced the kitchen, her arms flung wide as though she could encompass the whole house. 'When your first husband left you this house, Louisa, you had nothing else yet made it work for you. You and Nancy stepped back into a life you thought over because you did not see any other option. Despite that, you were determined to build a future on your own terms.'

'But this house was *mine*, Octavia,' Louisa said. 'And Nancy was here, right beside me, and I knew she would be whatever might have happened. And then I met you and brought you here to live with us in safety and with love. What you are doing is nothing like that. You will be alone in a strange city. What if you need us? What if you find yourself in trouble and have no way of contacting us? What then?' She shook her head. 'God only knows what Jacob will feel about this. You say we are being unfair caring about you and wanting you close by to ensure you are all right, but I don't see that as a bad thing, Octavia. Not at all.'

Octavia's heart beat hard at the insinuation of her selfishness, the tears glistening in Louisa's eyes sending a slash across her heart. She could hardly deny her leaving was not another act of self-interest. She was grabbing this opportunity to better herself, not for the benefit of her friends and not for the benefit of the Carson Street house.

She dropped her chin to her chest, counting the seconds to stem the tears pricking her eyes. If she cried, they would think her weak, unsure – or worse, incapable of such a bold step.

Inhaling a strengthening breath, Octavia walked back to the table. 'Please, let us not fall out,' she said quietly as she sat and reached across the table for Nancy's hand. 'Both of you know that I came from a different life, that I was once destined for a good marriage, a wealthy husband and children at my feet. Part of me still wants that, but I also need to see what I am capable of alone. Just as both of you do.'

Louisa joined them at the table and her gaze lingered on Nancy's as Nancy looked back at her, a silent concern passing between them.

Octavia frowned. 'What?'

Louisa faced her. 'Why mention marriage? Are you so certain about William that you have thoughts of marrying him one day?'

Suddenly, Octavia felt incredibly exposed. She might have rejected William's proposal today, but who knew if she would in the future, should their lives remain intertwined?

She looked at Louisa and then Nancy, desperate that her friends release her without resentment or fear. That they allow her to make a mistake or a success of her decision. Allow her to come out of this with a happier, more beautiful life, or a broken heart and dream. Either way, she would have taken her own life in her hands, been responsible for her future in a way she never had before.

'Who knows? But for now it will not happen and I have told him so.'

'You have told him so?' Nancy's eyes widened. 'He has asked you?'

'In a roundabout way, yes.'

'What does that mean? He either did or he didn't.'

'He inferred we marry before going to Manchester so that my reputation would be protected. For his part, he knows his remaining unmarried is distressing his family and even affecting his business. It would have been a marriage—'

'Of convenience,' Louisa interrupted, her violet eyes flashing with irritation. 'Well, thank God you refused. You deserve love as much as Nancy and me, Octavia. A fake engagement is one thing, but marriage...' She shook her head, her jaw tight. 'Absolutely not.'

'Which is why I refused,' Octavia said firmly. 'Please, just trust that I am in control of this plan as much as William. We are a partnership, equals. I have made that blatantly clear.'

'And if you're wrong?' Nancy asked, her eyebrows raised. 'What if Louisa's concern is justified and William comes to be someone different than you thought?'

'Then I will leave Manchester and start again somewhere else, or even come back to Bath. I have no fear of failure, but I do fear being a burden, a tie to you both and to this house for the rest of my days.'

Louisa shook her head, hurt showing in her eyes. 'We are not supposed to be a tie to one another, but we are supposed to be bonded. There's a huge difference.' She walked to the counter and gripped its edge, her gaze flitting from Octavia to Nancy and back again. 'The rumours about the authorities cracking down on the brothels is gathering traction. Jacob is out right now trying to find out who is behind the action and what they have planned. It might come that we need each other more than ever.' She held Octavia's gaze. 'What if we need you and you are hundreds of miles away?'

Sickness coated Octavia's throat. Just the thought of not being here if her friends faced outside danger made her want to throw her plans with William to the side, but how could she when she felt so strongly that it was the right time to leave her whoring and all its perils and jeopardies behind?

She forced her gaze to Louisa's. 'You will get a message to me somehow and I will come back immediately. I would not forsake you if the occasion arose, but I need to chase my dream of one day working alongside a good and worthy husband and building a good life for him, for me and the people we care about.' She swiped the tear that rolled over her cheek. 'Please, give me your blessing.' She turned to Nancy. 'Both of you. We will never stop writing to one another. We can send letters back and forth as much as we wish. This is a shift, that's all. We will be friends forever.'

Nancy looked at Louisa and Octavia waited. It did not matter what they said. William needed her right now and she needed him. Their reasons were very different, but Octavia felt deep in her heart that they would find a way to make it work for both of them.

'Fine.' Louisa sighed. 'You have our blessing on one condition.'

'Which is?'

She smiled. 'You return for my wedding at Christmas.'

Nancy coughed. 'Two conditions, actually.'

Octavia bit back her smile as relief unfurled inside her. Clearly something had passed between them for Louisa and Nancy to give in to her. 'Two?'

'You return again for my stage debut.'

Octavia's smile broke. 'Agreed.'

'Actually...' Nancy grimaced. 'Three conditions. You need to come home when the baby is born, too.'

Octavia laughed. 'Well, of course. You both truly give me your blessing?'

'Yes.' Louisa nodded, tears glinting in her eyes. 'We are going to miss you so much but it's clear you have to do this... But that doesn't mean we aren't going to worry about you, day and night.'

Octavia smiled. 'I love you, you know.' She faced Nancy. 'And you... to a certain degree.'

Nancy picked up half a carrot and threw it half-heartedly in Octavia's direction. 'Funny. Very funny.'

Octavia and Louisa laughed as Nancy rose to her feet,

drained her glass of ale and swiped her hand across her lips. 'Right, well, I can't stay any longer or my husband will be moaning about the absence of my delectable company today.' She took her coat from the back of the chair and shrugged it on, taking her hat from the seat next to her. 'I'll see you—'

The front door slammed and then heavy footsteps sounded outside the kitchen door before Jacob stepped into the room, his brow furrowed. 'What's going on here then? Tea at the Pump Room?'

'I'm just leaving,' Nancy said, walking towards him and standing on tiptoes to press a kiss to his cheek. 'Don't miss me too much, you lot. Ta-ta, for now.'

Octavia shook her head as Nancy vanished from the kitchen, her heels clicking along the hallway tiles towards the front door. 'That woman.'

Louisa, still smiling, slipped her arms around Jacob's waist. 'Octavia will soon be leaving us too, my love. Although her absence will be a lot more permanent than Nancy's.'

Jacob met Octavia's gaze, his blue eyes wary. 'What is she talking about?'

'It's nothing for you to worry about.' Octavia sighed, wishing Louisa had given her a little more time to prepare for Jacob's reaction, which would undoubtedly be worse than Louisa's or Nancy's. 'I am leaving Bath for Manchester—'

The abrupt pounding on the front door followed by coarse hollering and shouting forced Octavia's words to stick in her throat. She looked at her friends and they looked at her and then each other.

'Stay here,' demanded Jacob, pointing at the women in turn. 'No doubt this has something to do with my asking around this morning. I'll see what's going on.'

He made for the door and so did Octavia and Louisa...

21

Just as Octavia, Louisa and Jacob entered the hallway, Adelaide and Eliza came rushing downstairs dressed in nothing but towels, their eyes wide.

'What's going on?' Eliza cried. 'Are we being raided like they said in the paper?'

'The paper?' Octavia glanced towards the door as it was pounded on again. 'They are reporting raids now?'

'Yes.' Adelaide nodded frantically. 'They made six or seven arrests in a single house on Gay Street yesterday.'

Panic simmered inside Octavia. 'Go upstairs and get dressed. Thank God we don't have any culls due for an hour or more. Do as I say. Go!'

The girls scrambled upstairs and Octavia joined Louisa where she stood slightly behind Jacob. He glanced over his shoulder at them, nodded and then pulled open the front door.

A man stood on the top step, dressed in an open black wool coat, his intricately patterned waistcoat and gold pocket watch displaying his obvious wealth.

Dread knotted Octavia's stomach as she looked at the three

constables on the steps behind him and the further four hatted gentlemen waiting on the pavement, their expressions alight with unsettling eagerness.

Like a circling pack of wolves waiting to pounce on their prey.

Louisa's hand slipped into hers and Octavia glanced at her. Her friend stared resolutely ahead, her chin high and her back ramrod straight. Octavia followed suit, turning her glare on the man in front of Jacob.

'What do you want?' Jacob growled. 'We don't want no trouble.'

The man merely smiled. 'I'm sure you don't, Mr Jackson, but I'm afraid trouble has arrived at your door whether you like it or not.' He raised a piece of paper. 'My name is Alexander Middleton, I am an alderman working for the city and intend turning the public's attention on houses such as this one. So, with the law's support, I am here with a warrant for the proprietor's arrest... in the first instance.' His smile widened as he leaned slightly to Jacob's side and stared directly at Octavia and Louisa. 'But, of course, the warrant applies to whomever else I might find at the property.'

Jacob stepped forward, his hands clenched into fists at his sides. 'Let me tell you something—'

'Jacob!' Louisa gripped her fiancé's elbow. 'Don't.'

Spurring herself into action, Octavia drew on every survival instinct she utilised on the street and marched past Jacob and Louisa.

She stood in front of them, feet apart, hands planted on her hips and faced Middleton. 'How long have you been watching this house, sir? Have you received complaints from our neighbours?'

'Oh, no, there is no need for me to be in receipt of a complaint, Miss...'

Octavia stared at him, determined she would not reveal her name until absolutely necessary.

He smiled as he looked left along the street before facing her again. 'I am under no obligation to answer your questions. Officers? Arrest them.'

Gritting her teeth, Octavia resisted the officers and the gentlemen as best she could as they rushed the steps, the three officers and two of the four gentlemen striding past her into the house. As she grappled with the two men who had her firmly in their grip, forcing her hands behind her, dread and helplessness stormed inside her as Louisa's yells resounded from the walls. Cursing and threats filled the air as the three officers finally managed to wrestle Jacob to the hallway floor, the side of his face mashed against the tiles.

With the three of them handcuffed, two officers ran upstairs and soon brought Adelaide and Eliza to join the others in the hallway. Louisa continued to shout, her cursing almost as bad as anything Nancy might have said had she been here and arrested along with her friends.

Pain ripped through Octavia's shoulder blades and she surrendered, sending up silent gratitude that Nancy was free and, God willing, she would be able to do something to help while they were incarcerated.

Once Jacob had been unceremoniously restrained and yanked to his feet, he, Octavia and the others were marched down the house's steps into Carson Street and the waiting carriage parked out of view of the house.

People had gathered along the pavement, neighbours standing in their open doorways. Defiant and proud, Octavia met their eyes and nodded at the few who smiled and raised their hands in support, and promptly stared down any judge-mental looks sent her and her friends' way.

One by one, she and the others were pushed into the back of the carriage, rough hands to their heads and backs as they sat down heavily on the wooden benches.

Octavia flinched as the doors were slammed shut and bolted.

'For Christ's sake...' Jacob muttered, his cheeks mottled and his eyes bulging with anger. 'What a frigging mess this is going to be to sort out.'

Louisa looked at him, her face pale. 'It will be all right. As soon as Nancy gets wind of our arrest she and Francis will summon help, one way or another.' She winced as the carriage jolted into motion and they started along the cobbled street. 'Were you due to see William Rose tomorrow, Octavia?'

Octavia nodded. 'Yes, he'll soon begin to worry where I am. We were going to meet for breakfast at his hotel.'

'Breakfast?' Jacob sniffed. 'Fancy. Well, let's hope Mr "Fancy Pants" Rose uses his money and his smarts to get you out from behind bars, shall we?' He shot a glare at Eliza and Adelaide. 'Stop your crying, you two. You know we'll make sure you're all right.'

'If I know William at all,' Octavia said, 'he will do all he can to help. But considering we know Nancy as we do, there is every chance she will have us out and free by the morning if the constable in charge accepts what's good for him.'

Jacob scowled. 'Yeah, well, we'll see.'

Octavia met Louisa's gaze, her friend's face expressionless, leaving Octavia with no idea what her friend thought or felt. A status more worrying than if Louisa had been ranting and raving or even quietly weeping.

What in God's name were they going to do now?

22

William touched his hat and nodded a sombre hello to the people he passed as he walked through Bath's streets towards the post office. Although he had spent yesterday evening writing a list of goals he had in mind to achieve once he and Octavia returned to Manchester, his thoughts had still been very much attached to the rapidity with which she had refused the idea of marrying him.

To be hurt by her rebuff was downright ridiculous when her reasoning had been so entirely valid, yet it had indeed hurt. He had thought – hoped – that she was coming to care for him as he was her. Clearly, that was not the case.

Their relationship was one of business to Octavia – nothing more, nothing less.

And overnight, he had forced himself to accept that with gentlemanly honour. Who could blame her for not wanting to establish an attachment to him – to any man?

William forced his shoulders down and a smile to his face. Well, he was excited for her future regardless. Octavia might not wish to marry him, but she did wish to come north and the prospect of showing her his home and mills was exhilarating. She was so interested, so keen to learn.

No one should sit still in their God-given life. People should embrace what miracle they have been given, take risks and try new things. Neither he nor Octavia knew if what they were embarking on was madness, but hell, they were doing it anyway.

He glanced at the two letters he held, one for his mother and the other for Foley, his butler. What he wouldn't give to see the shock on their faces when each read his words. He suspected his mother would rush into the workshop looking for her husband, waving the parchment above her head and exclaiming the news of William's betrothal as though he was the first man on the planet to fall in love.

He had no doubt her delight would sate his mother enough that she would not ask too many questions. His smile faltered. At least, not to begin with.

As for Foley, he was a man of few words and stern countenance. He would categorically disapprove of Octavia staying at the house when she and William were not yet married, and it would be all he could do to contain his objections. But contain them he would because Foley was nothing if not professional and William had made it clear that the rooms on the opposite side of the upper floor to his should be made ready for Octavia's arrival. All properly above board and decent in view of propriety... even if he secretly longed for Octavia in his bed. She, on the other hand, would no doubt be immeasurably satisfied with the placement.

William stared about him at the people rushing to and fro, women carrying packages and men hauling cartloads of produce. It was nearly the 1st of December, and the mania of an approaching Christmas could already be felt in the air. A lingering discomfort for how Octavia might feel being away from her friends and all she knew at Carson Street badgered his conscience.

The last thing he wanted was for her to become lonely within a few weeks of her arriving in Manchester. He must ensure the festive season was celebrated at his home with more zeal than ever before. He would ensure Foley, Mrs Gaskell, his housekeeper, and the other house and garden staff came together to erect the very best decorations inside and outside of the house and ensure the most extravagant feasts were planned.

His optimism reignited, William picked up his pace and soon arrived at the post office. His letters duly posted, he decided to head to a nearby restaurant he had discovered that served the most delectable fish dishes.

As he passed a paperboy on the street corner, the headline of the newspaper stuck to the billboard beside the young lad made William's heart leap into his throat.

He halted.

Trouble for the ladies of Carson Street?

It screamed.

News of arrests!

'Boy, a copy of that paper, if you will,' William demanded, digging into his coat pocket for his wallet.

'Yes, sir.' The boy folded a paper and handed it to him. 'You know Carson Street then, sir?'

The gleam in the boy's eye would have been visible from the moon.

William scowled. 'Yes, I do. Not that you or anyone else has the right to stand in judgement of the women who live there.

They are all decent ladies, so you can wipe that smirk from your face.'

The boy grinned and turned to a gentleman waiting with his custom beside William. Quickly moving away, William walked a few yards before ducking into a deserted alleyway. He looked at the newspaper's front page.

It seemed there had been some sort of raid on the house the previous evening. Some righteous do-gooder by the name of Alexander Middleton had taken up the mantle of closing down houses of ill repute, regardless of the individuals residing inside of them. Slanderous accusations of debauchery and disorder peppered the report along with insinuations of far worse being found than could be printed in the newspaper's pages.

'Damnation.'

William slapped the paper closed and glared blindly ahead, trying to control the spark of temper that caught inside him. He reopened the paper and continued to read. Octavia and the others were being held in Bath police station? William trembled with outrage. Octavia was in a cell? He read that Louisa, Octavia and two other women at the house, as well as Jacob, had all been hauled in by armed bailiffs and the constabulary, and now awaited trial. Should they be found guilty, they would be transferred to prisons in London.

Roughly folding the paper, William looked skyward as though the gathering clouds might provide answers to what he could do to help. There would be little to gain from storming into the police station. He was hardly of distinguished enough standing in Bath, or even Manchester, to influence the retainment of prisoners.

He racked his brain and then thought of his friend and solicitor Thomas Marks. A man who joined William and Nicholas on their socialising from time to time whenever they were in Bath on business.

Yes, Thomas would help. The man fought daily for those trying their hardest to change the circumstances of the poor souls trapped within the squalidness of Bath's slums. Surely, the man would have sympathy with regards to prostitution and the women forced to undertake such occupation? Thomas certainly would not have the limited imagination of many who felt these women chose their course in life and only had themselves to blame.

Hurrying across town, William's mind raced, his heart in turmoil over what Octavia would be going through. Once he arrived at Thomas's offices, located on the ground floor of a townhouse on Milsom Street, he glanced at the small brass plaque bearing his associate's name and lifted the knocker.

A young clerk answered, his dark blond hair ruffled as though he spent much of his day running his fingers through it, his small eyes squinting at William from behind wire-rimmed spectacles. 'Can I help you, sir?'

'Yes.' William stood tall. 'I urgently need to speak with Mr Marks.'

'I'm sorry, sir, Mr Marks does not see anyone without an appointment.'

'I understand, and ordinarily I would not presume otherwise, but this is about a matter most grave. Please, I am more than willing to wait here while you speak to him. Can you tell him William Rose would very much appreciate a few minutes of his time?'

The clerk flicked his gaze over William's face before sighing heavily. 'Fine. Why don't you come in and wait? It's so cold today.'

'Thank you.'

William followed the young man inside and was directed to some wooden chairs lined up in the hallway adjacent to a closed door. Sitting down, William released a shaky breath as the clerk opened the door and disappeared inside. Murmured conversation filtered through the open doorway and then Thomas Marks emerged, his smile welcoming and his hand outstretched.

'William, this is a surprise!' he exclaimed, clasping William's hand. 'What the devil brings you here? I had no idea you were in town.'

'Thomas, it's good to see you,' William said, shaking his hand. 'Unfortunately, I am not here with glad tidings. There is an urgent matter that I would really appreciate your help with.'

'Of course, of course. Come into my office.'

Once they were seated at Thomas's desk, William took off his hat and placed it on the vacant chair beside him. 'This is rather a delicate matter and I appreciate you will have questions, but I'm afraid time cannot be wasted filling you in on every detail as I only know what I've garnered from this morning's paper.'

'Sounds intriguing.' Thomas leaned his forearms on his desk and laced his fingers. 'What seems to be the problem?'

William laid the newspaper in front of Thomas, the headline bold and black. 'I need you to do all you possibly can to get these people released. The Carson Street house may be a brothel, but these are decent people who conduct their business in the most discreet way possible. It is a good establishment, well-kept, and the women living and working there could easily be taken for ladies. They do not deserve this.'

Thomas lifted his attention from the paper, his brows raised. 'I see. Clearly, you are familiar with the house and the women?'

'I am.' William held his gaze as pride swelled inside of him. 'In fact, before this, one of the women was to return with me to Manchester. Now I fear our plans have been well and truly—'

'What?' Thomas's eyes widened and he slumped back in his seat. 'You're romantically involved with her?'

'No.' *Regrettably*. 'But I have agreed to help her in her quest to better herself through business. I gave her my word and I'll be damned if I won't do all I can to honour that. Please, Thomas, will you help me? Help her?'

The lawyer leaned back in his chair, his careful study filled with the very scepticism William had hoped not to witness.

23

Octavia stood from the hard wooden bench at the back of the police cell and tried her best not to breathe too deeply. The stench was rife with stale sweat, the rancid aroma of rotting teeth and days-old urine. She had mistakenly assumed her time on the streets had made her resistant to such filth but, judging by her constant urge to gag, clearly residing at Carson Street had somewhat softened her former robustness.

She glanced at Louisa who continued to stare at the wall opposite her, her face set before she walked to the bars at the front of the cell and peered at the sergeant sitting at a nearby desk, the papers in front of him ignored as he picked something from his teeth with a matchstick.

Disgusted, Octavia turned just as Louisa joined her at the front of the cell.

'Are you all right?' her friend asked, her violet gaze lingering on the constable. 'Us being here is little more than another challenge for us to conquer. I hope you know we'll get through this as we have a hundred other things.'

'*We* might, but I'm not so sure about them.' Octavia nodded towards Adelaide and Eliza where they sat huddled together in the corner, steadfastly avoiding the stares of the surrounding street whores and child pickpockets. 'They are too young to cope with this.'

'They will be fine. At least we persuaded the sergeant that we are entitled to let someone know where we are. I'm sure Nancy and Francis will have already set wheels in motion to get us out of here. Nancy will be incandescent with rage, believe me.'

'I agree, but if she is angry, she will get things done.' Octavia gave a wry smile. 'There is very little anyone can do to resist Nancy's charms when she puts her mind to it.'

'Exactly. I've asked that she employ a lawyer and try to gather the support of as many of our influential clients as possible,' Louisa murmured. 'I'm sure a few will come forward and try their best to make some inducement for our release. After all, Nancy knows enough about them to use as leverage.' Louisa took a deep breath, released it. 'Not that I want her to do that unless forced.'

'We were foolish to ignore the rumours that the do-gooders were gathering. We should have prepared ourselves by finding out more about Alexander Middleton and the groups he was involved with.'

'Well, we certainly won't sit on our laurels after we are released. There will have to be changes made in the future and not just at Carson Street.'

Octavia frowned. 'What do you mean?'

'I mean the sex trade is coming under scrutiny more and more often.' Louisa nodded towards the slothful sergeant. 'The police and their ilk will eventually crawl all over the trade looking to shut it down.'

Octavia stared at her friend as a shameful relief that she had already started making plans for a life away from prostitution calmed her. She had been right to think of her future after Carson Street and if – when – she was liberated from this godforsaken police cell she would grab William's hand and run. Louisa and Nancy both had good men who would look after them their entire lives, but it was clear Octavia could not afford to sit still and hope for a safe future.

'How do you think Jacob is faring?' she asked.

'He'll be fine,' Louisa said, despite the concern that immediately darkened her eyes. 'He will want us to concentrate on freeing ourselves and then worry about him later.'

'And what of his temper? It will be well and truly stoked knowing you are in here. If he doesn't control his outrage, he could find himself in front of the judge quicker than any of us.'

Louisa's gaze settled on Adelaide and Eliza, who both stared back at her and Octavia, their eyes wide with fear, their faces pale and drawn. 'He'll behave, I'm sure. He knows the strength of his fists as well as any boxer – or ex-boxer, as Jacob is. He won't risk being separated from us and the house for any longer than necessary. Carson Street and its future mean too much to him.'

'The house is bricks and mortar. It's *you* who means everything to him.'

'Maybe.'

'Maybe?' Concerned once again about her friends' relationship, Octavia gently touched Louisa's arm. 'You still want to marry him, don't you?'

Louisa huffed a laugh. 'You're thinking about that now?'

Octavia looked into her friend's eyes, trying to gauge her inner feelings. 'You don't seem as eager or as excited about it as you once were, that's all. Lately, the pair of you argue at the slightest provocation. I'm just concerned... especially now I'm leaving.' She glanced at the idle officer. 'If we get out of here, of course.'

'There is no doubt of us getting out of here, and Jacob and I are fine.' Louisa looked away, her shoulders stiffening. 'We will be married at Christmas as planned. Our arrests are a mere delay. Just wait and see.' She crossed her arms. 'Jacob and I have a difference of opinion about how our futures will look, that's all.'

'And you are confident those differences can be sorted out?'

'I am. I'm not ready to give up the brothel, so any plans for children and a home somewhere else will have to wait. I like giving girls a safe place to work and I think I always will. Jacob will have to accept my work is not yet done.'

'And if he doesn't?'

Louisa tilted her chin and looked again at Adelaide and Eliza. 'Then I will be forced to be alone as I've been before.' She turned, her cheeks slightly flushed. 'Which scares me to death, but I will prevail if it comes to that.'

'But—'

'Enough chatter about me and Jacob,' Louisa interrupted, placing her hand on Octavia's. 'We have more important things to worry about. Although I'm confident we will not dwell in here long.'

The certainty in her friend's tone cast the topic of Louisa and Jacob's marital bliss to the wayside. 'I don't see how, when Alexander Middleton seems so set on his mission. He was damning us to hell and back when he was at the house.'

'And what of it?' A smile played on Louisa's lips. 'Our clients will not want the house to close and will soon band together once they hear of our arrest. All will be well.'

Octavia squeezed her hand, praying she was right. Louisa was her saviour and always would be. Her friend's confidence and commitment to others was humbling when Octavia could only think of herself, but what else was she to do? She had gone from being a privileged child born to wealthy parents to whoring – an occupation that held an unavoidable termination date.

And, whether Louisa accepted it or not, no matter how young they might be now, that date edged ever closer.

The hacking coughs and quiet weeping melted into nothingness as Octavia pondered the new life that awaited her in Manchester. It neither shamed nor embarrassed her that she was leaving with William, carrying hope in her heart for a life moulded by her own desires. She had no idea if she would take to business as she hoped, but she would never forget the importance of stability, of coin over care. There was every chance that if she thrived under William's tutelage and they worked well together, the two of them could go on to be business associates.

Octavia dropped her gaze to the flagstones, a funny sensation passing through her heart. Thinking of her and William never being connected through anything more than business suddenly saddened her far more than it should, yet what could she do but remain steadfast against her personal feelings for him? If she wavered, everything she had already put into place risked disintegrating.

If she acted on the desire to see him, kiss him – or, God help her, lie with him again – he would know that his proposal of marriage had not been quite as absurd as she had feigned.

The heavy stomp of a constable's boots approached the cell door. Octavia tensed as she stared hard at the officer.

'So...' He grinned, his eyes flashing with superiority and malice. 'How are you lovely ladies of Carson Street faring? Have all you need? Or shall I put some male prisoners in here so you feel more at home?'

Octavia curled her hands into fists at her sides. 'I beg your pardon?'

'Officer...' Louisa smiled and gripped Octavia's elbow keeping her still. 'I'm sorry, might I know your name or rank?'

The officer bristled and puffed his chest. 'Police Constable Ferris, ma'am.'

'Well, Constable Ferris,' Louisa continued. 'We don't deal with prisoners at Carson Street. In fact, we don't deal with officers of the law or even those without considerable wealth and influence. A fact I would bear in mind if I were you. After all, these are the types of men who run this city, who make decisions about where government assistance will be allocated.'

Octavia stepped closer to the cell's bars. 'Absolutely, and when we are released, it would be such a shame if we could not whisper our praises and requests for more support of Bath's police into the ears of those who could make that happen.' She raised her eyebrows. 'You know, the promotion of constables and suchlike.'

The man's eyes flitted between Octavia and Louisa, his cheeks mottled. 'You're whores, you don't know people like that.'

'Don't we?' Octavia smiled. 'Well, you'll have to wait and see, won't you? For better or worse, at least we know your name now and can use it in any way we see fit.'

Constable Ferris's eyes bulged, a vein protruding at his temple as he opened and closed his mouth like a blabbering fish. He muttered a curse, threw her and Louisa a glare and marched away.

Octavia turned to Louisa and they erupted into laughter.

24

William tapped his foot on the carpet in Thomas Marks's office as the lawyer stood in front of a floor-to-ceiling bookshelf crammed full of thick leather-bound books. What in God's name was the man looking for? Did legislation even exist with regards to extricating prostitutes from police custody?

He very much doubted it.

Thomas put an open book on the desk, the weight of it so vast, it landed with a thud. 'Well, as far as I can surmise in this short amount of time, we could have a fight on our hands,' he said as he continued to peruse the pages. 'I think the best way forward would be to gain an audience with the gentleman mentioned in the paper or maybe visit the city council. It would be helpful if you can gather an idea of the scope of opposition against the brothels and boarding houses. There's every possibility the authorities intend using Miss Marshall and the others as an example.'

Anger ignited inside William and he leaned forward. 'As an example? Over my dead body. Octavia – Miss Marshall – is the perfect example of a hardworking, aspirational woman. She is not someone to name and shame, drag down and use to further someone's political career.'

'Maybe not, but that is the way things often work in government. They take one aspect of society and attack it with brute force. All in the name of progress.' Thomas removed his spectacles and stuck one arm of the glasses between his teeth, his brow furrowed. His eyes glazed in thought before he pointed his spectacles at William. 'If this brothel is a better calibre than others, I assume successful men such as yourself, professionals and so forth, are these women's customers?'

'They are.'

'Then I would think they are the women's best hope for their release. There may well be a few who have come to care for them as you have Miss Marshall.'

All too aware that his care for Octavia had deepened tenfold since learning of her imprisonment, William fisted his hands as if in doing so he could stem his emotions. 'I would cite Nicholas Fairham as a possibility.'

Thomas raised his eyebrows. 'Nicholas? I had no idea he visited brothels.'

'It's not something gentlemen tend to advertise, Thomas.' William stood and paced back and forth. 'But that doesn't mean he wouldn't be willing to come forward in the ladies' defence. Vouch for their characters et cetera.'

'And what of the doorman? Jacob Jackson? Do you know if he might have friends in high places? I understand some politicians employ people like Jackson for protection.'

William gripped the back of his vacated chair. 'Jacob's a different kettle of fish altogether. He's an ex-fighter. Strong and proud. It's not beyond the realms of possibility that he has been held by the constabulary before, possibly even been in front of a judge.'

'Hmm. Well, let's concentrate on the ladies first and we'll see what can be done about Mr Jackson afterwards.' Thomas sat at his desk and pulled some writing paper towards him before lifting a pen from a marble inkwell. 'If I leave speaking to Nicholas to you, I will send a message to my friend who is a newspaper editor of a rival paper to the one that published this article. He might take up the cause and consider a counter-piece for tomorrow's edition.'

William reached for his hat. 'You are a friend indeed, Thomas.'

'Not at all.' The lawyer looked up from his writing, his brown eyes dark with resentment. 'In my experience half of these do-gooders who persecute prostitutes, tavern owners and the like are there to cause trouble more than they are to make change for the better. Get their names in the paper, shout about vice and debauchery, yet they do little else towards improving anything.'

'Whereas lawyers like you will come to instigate change *and* improvement, fairness in judgement,' William said, his hand on the door. 'Mark my words. Eventually, people in positions of authority will take up the mantle with as much determination as the people who have nothing to their names are willing to do.'

'I hope you're right. Come back tomorrow and we'll reconvene with what we've managed to do.'

William stepped through the door.

'Oh, and William?'

He turned back to the office. 'Yes?'

'How long are you staying in Bath? If we start along this path—'

'I will be here for as long as it takes to see Miss Marshall freed. I will not leave for Manchester without her.'

* * *

As it was lunch time, William headed for Tanner's in the hope of finding Nicholas and hopefully some of his associates who also frequented Carson Street. If he wasn't there, then William would go to Nicholas's office close to Queen Square.

Taking the steps into the club two at a time, William was greeted by the maître d' standing just inside. 'Can I help you, sir?'

'I wish to know if Mr Fairham is lunching today?'

'He is, sir. Is he expecting you?'

'No, but I am often a guest of his while I am in the city. I'm sure if you let him know I am here, he will—' There was a firm slap to William's shoulder, and he spun around. 'Nicholas, just the man I came here to see!'

'Well, then, I'm glad you found me... even if I was just coming from the washroom.' He laughed and turned to the maître d'. 'Would you be so kind as to set another plate at my table for Mr Rose?'

The maître d' nodded. 'Of course, sir.'

Once the maître d' had retreated, William stood directly in front of Nicholas to ensure he had his attention. 'I need to speak to you about something. Something important.'

'And you will while we eat. I'm famished,' Nicholas said, clutching William by the elbow and propelling him through the busy restaurant.

The room was noisy with male laughter and jovial camaraderie, the smell of roasted meat mixing with the lingering scent of cigar smoke that hovered in the air. The dark-panelled walls and even darker oriental carpet brought a conspiratorial intimacy to the space. William was almost surprised there wasn't a banner above the dais where a string quartet played, shouting, 'No Women Allowed'.

Nicholas stopped at a table by the window. 'I'll introduce you to some friends.'

William took a vacant seat at the table, the other three gentlemen already seated regarding him with varying looks of welcome and expectation. What William had to say would have been a lot easier if he could have spoken with Nicholas alone for a minute or two, but Nicholas was such a passionate, live-in-the-moment kind of man that William was just relieved he'd managed to ambush a modicum of his friend's attention.

Introductions were made as plates and cutlery, glasses and napkins were set in front of William, his mind whirling with how he was to tell Nicholas about the challenge he faced.

'So, out with it.' Nicholas grinned, lifting his brandy glass. 'What can I do for you?'

Glancing around the table, William inhaled a long breath. Speaking to Nicholas about Octavia would not be the same as speaking about her with Joseph, the associate who had so earnestly disapproved of William's supposed choice of fiancée. Joseph had been filled with judgement, whereas Nicholas was forever open-minded. Yet, what of the others around the table? No, he could not linger on that. Whatever they decreed, it did not matter. All William cared about was preventing Octavia from having to languish in a police cell any longer than necessary.

He pulled back his shoulders and lowered his voice. 'It's about the ladies of Carson Street.'

Nicholas's gaze bored into William's before he slowly lowered his glass to the table, seeming to purposefully avoid the curious gazes of his associates. 'What about them?'

'They're in trouble.' William nodded his thanks to the waiter who had approached and put his ordered glass of brandy in front of him. 'They need our help. More than that, they need assistance from every corner. Including influential men who would passionately disagree with them being detained by the constabulary.'

Shock leapt into Nicholas's eyes before he quickly looked to the others around the table. 'Will you excuse us for just a moment?'

William rose from the table and he and Nicholas walked through the restaurant and into the lobby where they stood almost toe to toe in a discreet corner.

'The women have been arrested?' Nicholas's cheeks reddened. 'How do you know this? After I took you to Carson Street, you acted as though you had no interest in returning.' He stopped, his agitation turning to amusement so typical of Nicholas. 'You old dog! You went back there, didn't you?'

'For God's sake,' William snapped, his impatience rising as he pushed his hand into his hair. 'This is serious. If we don't act quickly there is every chance the women and Jacob Jackson will be transferred to a prison in London.'

Nicholas's smile vanished. 'What?'

'Precisely. Now listen to me...'

William told Nicholas about his returning to Carson Street, his developing relationship with Octavia, and her returning to Manchester with him. Once his friend's curses and disbelief about those facts dissipated, William then told him about the newspaper report, the circumstances around Octavia's arrest and the help he had secured from Thomas Marks.

'So, your role is to speak to as many men as you can think of who visit Carson Street in the hope they will come forward as character witnesses.'

Nicholas's jaw tightened as he stared around the lobby. 'You're asking a lot of me, William. You're asking a lot of anyone who visits Carson Street. Those women might not deserve this maltreatment, but...' He turned. 'You cannot expect me or anyone else to expose our extramarital activities to the police. Good God, if the press printed our names our families' lives would be shattered.'

William's heart picked up speed. 'Are you refusing me? Saying you won't help Octavia and the others.'

'I'm sorry, my friend, but that's exactly what I'm saying.' Nicholas shook his head, his gaze firm on William's. 'My family life and career are at stake here – you've got to understand that. I won't do it.'

'God damn you, Nicholas,' William hissed. 'Then don't, but I'll tell you this for nothing, you are no friend. Not by a long shot.'

William turned on his heel before heading for the door, lunch forgotten along with his appetite.

Early morning light filtered through the small window at the top of the police cell wall and Octavia stared at the clouds as they inched across the sky. Judging by how they had changed from the palest pink to milky white, the city would be wide awake by now, people going freely about their business.

Yet the ladies of Carson Street were beginning their third day in what might as well be prison. Yesterday, she and Louisa had tried their best to allay Adelaide's and Eliza's fears by telling them all would be well but, in truth, Octavia had no idea what was happening or how long they would be held here. She was beginning to smell; the pins had long ago fallen from her hair; her hands were grimy and tainted with dust and dirt.

The only saving grace was that she and Louisa had received word from the officer guarding them that Nancy had managed to secure them legal representation and a lawyer would see them that morning. Maybe then, she and Louisa would know where they stood realistically because, until now, Octavia had been repeating hopes and possibly pipe dreams of imminent release over and over in her heart and mind.

Closing her eyes, she fought to stem the threat of tears – of weakness – but, once again, as it had through the night, images of her last day at her family home in Oxfordshire flitted behind her closed lids. What would her father think if he could see her now? If this had happened before her mother died, Octavia could imagine his horror and care that his daughter had been incarcerated, his arms outstretched to embrace her, promising he would do everything humanly possible to ensure her release. Yet the man she pictured *after* her mother's death only sneered, his eyes glittering with satisfaction that she had fallen so low.

Snapping her eyes open, Octavia raised her hand to her mouth to trap her sob, hating that every spiteful prediction her father had yelled at her, every insult and degradation he'd spat, continued to taunt her. In the years since she'd left him, she had turned those words into her motivation for survival. Now, as she sat in this filthy, stagnant cell, they felt like affirmations.

She looked down at Louisa's head in her lap and, with trembling fingers, gently smoothed the hair back from her brow.

'We won't be here much longer,' Louisa muttered.

Grateful for her friend's company, Octavia softly smiled. 'I didn't realise you were awake.'

'I've barely slept.' Swinging her booted feet to the floor, Louisa sat up and glanced towards the corner where Adelaide and Eliza slept, both women's eyelids flickering with dreams or nightmares. 'Surely we will find out a little more about our fate today. They cannot keep us here indefinitely.'

Octavia swiped her fingers beneath her eyes and rolled her shoulders, trying to alleviate some of her body's stiffness. 'I swear Constable Ferris is enjoying every moment of us being here.'

'His glee is founded in resentment,' Louisa said with a sniff.

'The man knows he could not afford to be in our company if we were not imprisoned by him.'

'True.'

'I've given some thought to our conversation about me and Jacob,' Louisa said quietly. 'And you are right to be concerned.'

Care for Louisa immediately hitched Octavia's heart. 'I am?'

'Yes.' Louisa's violet gaze saddened. 'Things have become strained between us and I was wrong to allow it to become so. If... *when*, we get out of here, I am going to take Jacob in my arms and tell him how much I love him. He deserves so much more than my ambition. He deserves my commitment to him, too.'

Octavia squeezed Louisa's fingers. 'He knows you love him, but it won't hurt to ensure he never forgets. Lord knows, if William walked in here right now...' She stopped, her cheeks warming. 'Not that I love him, but I would grab his hand and tell him we are heading to the train station and Manchester right away.'

'What?'

'I said, if William—'

'I heard what you said.' Louisa stood and planted her hands on her hips, her gaze suddenly angry. 'But surely you will not be leaving now?' She waved her arm. 'After this?'

Octavia tensed, ready for a fight. She was tired and hungry, her survival instinct rising. 'Of course I will be leaving.' She leaned back against the damp wall and crossed her arms, refusing to allow Louisa to corner her. 'Our arrest has proven to me more than ever that I need to change my life. Start making steps for a future far away from the streets, far away from vice and dirty backstreet taverns. Whether you like it or not, Louisa, our incarceration has only deepened my motivation to leave Bath.'

'Not only Bath, but clearly Nancy and me, too.' Louisa's

cheeks reddened as others around them, Adelaide and Eliza included, were roused from their slumber. 'If we get out of here, do you not think I will need you at the house? Have you even thought how much this will change things? That nothing will be the same at Carson Street now?'

Octavia abruptly stood, forcing Louisa to take a step back. She glared at her friend. 'If we are released, you and Jacob can return home and do what you will with the house. You own it, Louisa. It's yours. You can try to keep working from it or you could choose to make it a home. As for me, I will be left—'

'The newspapers will not be finished with us. Don't you see? Every do-gooder in the city will band together to persecute and harangue us.'

'Of course they won't.'

'They will, and in the midst of all that, you are just going to walk away? Leave me to rebuild the business, our reputation? Nancy is married and expecting a baby. I need you now more than ever.'

Guilt writhed inside Octavia but so did her need for survival and she tilted her chin in defiance. She would not falter. Would not forsake the biggest chance she'd ever had of bettering her life, bettering herself.

'You are not being fair,' she retorted, her irritation rising. 'Neither you nor Nancy are whoring anymore, yet it seems you cannot fathom why I would wish to stop. What do you think I'm supposed to surmise from that other than you and Nancy think yourselves better than me?'

Louisa sucked in a breath as she pressed her hand to her breast as though Octavia had struck her there. 'I think no such thing. Us three stand together as equals.'

'Then prove it, Louisa. You always told Nancy and I that our lives are our own. That you will never make us do anything we don't want to do.'

Louisa closed her eyes and tipped her head back.

Quiet settled in the cell as every set of eyes locked on her and Louisa. Adelaide and Eliza rose to their feet, their gazes flitting between Octavia and Louisa as though gauging whose side to take.

'And I meant it,' Louisa said quietly, as she opened her eyes. 'But I had not expected you to turn your back on me if the house or I were in trouble. Clearly, I was wrong.'

Tears burned the backs of Octavia's eyes as she tried to speak past the lump in her throat. 'I—'

The clang of Constable Ferris's baton against the railing made Octavia jump.

'Morning, ladies.' He grinned, his few white teeth gleaming among the darker ones in the half-light. 'Breakfast will be given to the rest of you shortly, but, Mrs Hill, you are to come with me.'

His key clattered in the lock before he opened the door, his malicious gaze firmly on Louisa.

Octavia reached for her friend, but Louisa lifted her arm away. And, with a single withering look, her friend left the cell and walked out of sight as Constable Ferris relocked the door.

Sickness coated Octavia's throat, her heart pounding as Adelaide and Eliza each came to her, muttering words of comfort. Octavia stared ahead, terrified that she had just severed one of only two friendships that meant everything to her.

Would Louisa ever speak to her again? Would she ever *see* her again?

There was no doubt that when Nancy found out about the argument, Octavia would certainly lose her love if she hadn't Louisa's. Nancy's entire being was centred around loyalty.

Loyalty to Louisa most of all. Tears trickled down Octavia's cheeks as she walked to the hard wooden seat. Would her selfish ways never abate?

26

Octavia would not have been surprised if she had worn the stone slabs beneath her feet to a shine with her pacing. Louisa had been gone from the police cell for what seemed like hours but was more likely one. Between comforting Adelaide and Eliza, and maintaining her own growing anxiety, Octavia's nerves were stretched to breaking.

She looked at window at the back of the cell, the clouds now a heavy grey indicating snowfall was imminent. The world continued to turn and the weather to change. If everything had been normal right now, she and her friends would most likely be making preparations for Louisa and Jacob's wedding, not to mention Christmas shopping. But nothing was the same, and now, after her altercation with Louisa, Octavia doubted things ever would be again.

An older, smartly uniformed constable approached Constable Ferris's desk and murmured something to him before standing back and looking towards the cell, his face sombre.

Dread unfurled inside Octavia as Ferris rose and

approached. Adelaide and Eliza came beside her and slipped their hands into hers.

'You three are to go with Sergeant Richardson,' Ferris said as he unlocked the cell door. 'He wants to ask you some questions.'

'All of us?' Octavia asked, surprised that she wasn't to be singled out above Adelaide and Eliza, considering her close association with Louisa. 'But my friends barely have anything to do with the house, Constable. They have no reason—'

'Less chit-chat.' Ferris glared. 'Come on, let's be having you.'

Octavia led Adelaide and Eliza out of the cell, and each received a brief nod from Sergeant Richardson before he stepped forward, leaving them to follow.

They walked along the dull, grey corridor until they reached a room containing a steel desk, three chairs on one side and two on the other. One of the seats was occupied by a suited, dark-haired gentleman, his kindly blue eyes meeting Octavia's from behind the lenses of his wire-rimmed glasses. He immediately stood and smiled but trepidation whispered through Octavia and she could not return his solicitous greeting.

'Please take a seat, ladies.' The sergeant's deep voice came from behind her as he closed the door. 'This is Mr Emmett Holloway, a lawyer here on your behalf, employed by a friend of yours, I believe, Miss Marshall. A Mrs Nancy Carlyle.'

Octavia bit back a smile as she pictured Nancy's expression when she introduced herself using her married name in the police station lobby. She would have ensured she was dressed immaculately, her language clipped and free of its usual cursing.

'I see,' Octavia said, returning her focus to the room and taking a seat at the table. 'Well, Mrs Carlyle is a good friend indeed and was no doubt beyond distressed upon learning of mine and my friends' incarceration.'

If Mr Holloway was here to help her, Adelaide and Eliza, had he already seen Louisa and Jacob? Could her friends be free, and it was only a matter of time before they were all reunited at Carson Street and able to laugh about these past days over a glass or two of wine?

'So, ladies, it seems you have a substantial amount of support in the outside world,' the sergeant said as he took a seat beside Mr Holloway. 'A number of gentlemen have come forward willing to vouch for your characters, saying they had the impression upon meeting you that your participation in what goes on in the house owned by Louisa Hill was not altogether voluntary.'

Octavia stiffened. 'What?'

Mr Holloway leaned his arms on the table, widening his eyes as though trying to relay an unspoken message to her. He cleared his throat. 'As it has been stated by several individuals that the three of you were not entirely enthusiastic in your roles at Carson Street, Miss Marshall, the police are happy to release you without further questioning.'

'I don't understand. Where is Louisa?'

'Mrs Hill is no longer your concern,' Sergeant Richardson said. 'And if you take my advice, she never will be again. I suggest from now on you put as much distance between yourself and Carson Street as humanly possible.'

'Do you mean we are to be freed, but you have every intention of ensuring Louisa and Jacob face a judge?'

'We do indeed.' The sergeant's dark eyes glinted with satisfaction. 'Sometimes the police are better off cutting their losses and keeping the gold of the mine rather than the coal surrounding it... if you understand me, Miss Marshall.'

Octavia snapped her gaze to Mr Holloway. If he had been sent by Nancy, surely she would have made it clear to him that Louisa's liberty was her priority? Excluding her husband Francis and the newly adopted Alice, there was no one Nancy loved more.

How will I live with the guilt if I am set free and Louisa remains imprisoned?

'But this isn't right.' Culpability coiled inside Octavia as the last words she and Louisa had spoken to one another resounded in her head. She gripped Adelaide's and Eliza's hands. 'We are a family at Carson Street. We need one another. No one works there under dure—'

'I advise you not to bite the hand that feeds you, Miss Marshall.' The solicitor widened his eyes again in warning. 'If you each sign a statement that you were unwilling participants in the activities at the house, you will be set free under caution today without prosecution. Unless, you understand, the police have further cause to arrest you.'

Sergeant Richardson crossed his arms, his gaze steely. 'An officer will escort you back to Carson Street where you will pack up your belongings and never set foot in the house again. Do I make myself clear?'

'But what of Louisa and Jacob? What of the house?'

'It will be closed with immediate effect. As for Mrs Hill and Mr Jackson, it's best you remember them as a sad event in your history and move on.'

'No.' She shook her head. 'This isn't right. Louisa and Jacob are decent, hardworking people who care for us deeply. You cannot possibly—'

'The choice is yours, Miss Marshall. Are you going to continue to defend your association with Mrs Hill and land yourself in further difficulty? Or do you wish to leave now while you can?'

Octavia stared at him before closing her eyes, all too aware of how Adelaide and Eliza trembled. What was she supposed to do now? Heavy responsibility pressed down on her. Disparaging the house was clearly the lawyer's strategy for ensuring freedom for her, Adelaide and Eliza, but how were they to walk out of the police station without a backward glance when labels of enforcing prostitution would hang over Louisa and Jacob?

Or could it be that the police lied in order to hoodwink her? It was entirely possible. Well, they clearly did not know her at all.

Octavia opened her eyes and lifted her chin. If she was free, she would be able to do more to help Louisa and Jacob than she could here, behind bars. 'We will leave now.'

'Good, then Mr Holloway will escort you, along with an officer I will assign to take you back to Carson Street.'

As soon as they were outside in the blessed fresh air, Mr Holloway bid her goodbye, telling Octavia to relay to Nancy and Francis that he would be in touch with them regarding Louisa and Jacob as soon as possible. The matter was being dealt with as a priority by his offices.

Octavia thanked him and watched him walk away, her mind racing. So much so that when a gentleman gently touched her elbow, she jumped. 'Oh, sir. You startled me.'

'I do apologise, miss.' The gentleman smiled, his brown eyes kindly, his moustache rising above his upper lip. 'I am a lawyer sent here by an associate of yours.'

'A lawyer? But we already have representation.' Octavia glanced along the street. 'What do you mean *sent by an associate of mine*? Who?'

'William Rose.'

'William?' Pitiful happiness jolted through her, but Octavia could not contain her smile. 'He sent you here to help me? To help us?'

'Indeed, he did.' The lawyer nodded, his gaze amused.

'I managed to briefly speak to the lawyer representing you before he entered the station and I am pleased to say he is going along the exact same route that I would have adopted myself had I been in his position. Therefore, I am happy to report this outcome to William if you do not see him before me.' Another smile. 'But that too seems very unlikely. Miss Marshall, do not lose hope for your friends. There is every possibility Mrs Hill and Mr Jackson will win over a judge. Of course, they will suffer a fine and the closing of the business, but both are preferable to a prison sentence. With men like William Rose vouching for Carson Street, any decent judge will dismiss the charges.'

Octavia glanced at Adelaide and Eliza where they stood in each other's arms, smiling through their tears. 'Do you know where William is now?'

'I don't, but please try not to worry. Your lawyer will do his best for Mrs Hill and Mr Jackson as he has you.'

She forced a smile. 'Thank you so much for being willing to help. It is deeply appreciated.'

'Not at all.'

He touched his hat in farewell and walked away. Adelaide and Eliza immediately stepped closer.

'What are we to do now?'

'Will Louisa be in prison for the rest of her life?'

'Listen to me,' Octavia said firmly as she glanced at the officer waiting for them nearby. 'We must not give up hope. I want you both to go back to Carson Street as the sergeant said and collect any belongings you have there. Think yourself lucky the house was not yet your home.'

'But what are you going to do?' Adelaide asked, her eyes wide. 'Where will you stay tonight?'

Eliza clutched Octavia's arm, her blue eyes blazing with

undisguised fear. 'You must tell us where you are going. We can't be without you now!'

'Of course you can,' Octavia snapped. 'I am going to see Nancy. She and Francis have already helped us so much. I will see you later.'

The officer stepped closer. 'You are going nowhere other than Carson Street, miss.'

Octavia looked back and forth along the street, feigning distress. She met his eyes and gripped his arm. 'Please, officer, I must check on my sisters before I return to Carson Street. They live just a short distance away and will be out of their minds with worry. I promise to come to the house in half an hour. Please, may I go to them? I am a free woman now, after all.'

The officer's indecision was clear before he glanced at the station doors. 'I could get in serious trouble for this.'

'Please, I'm begging you.'

'Fine, but I expect you at Carson Street within the next half an hour. Do I make myself clear? If you fail to arrive—'

'I'll be there. You have my word.'

Before he could change his mind, Octavia hurried away.

27

William stood stiff-shouldered and tense at his hotel bedroom window, glaring at a sky peppered with dark clouds that promised rain. It was barely two-thirty and it was driving him almost insane wondering how Octavia was faring, or whether Thomas had managed to ensure her freedom.

His friend had said he would send a message to the hotel but when William had gone to reception half an hour before no such message had so far been left.

He could not stand around here much longer. He had to do something!

How he wished he and Octavia had packed their bags and left for Manchester days ago. But there was every possibility his need to have her in his home had been fuelled by lust, his own conceit. And neither of these things would help her or protect her from the scandal and rejection she could receive if people uncovered her prostitution.

She would be molested, ostracised and discussed. All in a place to which he had brought her with the promise of a new beginning. William swiped his hand over his face, a painful helplessness lingering in his chest even if he felt Octavia would be better off away from Bath and with him where he could protect her and support her in every single one of her ambitions.

Initially, her interest in his business acumen had caught him like an eager child distracted by a sparkling, winking marvel. One who often looked at him with her wide blue eyes filled with admiration and an almost palpable need to learn as much as she possibly could from him.

What man would not be flattered by such adulation from a woman as spectacularly beautiful and desirable as Octavia?

Yet he was beginning to fear their entire adventure was grounded in his own vanity as opposed to the concern he should be feeling for Octavia's mental welfare.

He still held the hope that she might one day be his wife, but what of her life in between, even if she eventually agreed to wed him? Once in Manchester, she would be alone for the most part among a sea of strangers. With the time he had spent in Bath would come a mountain of issues to sort out at home and at the mills upon his return. What was Octavia to do when he was dealing with those problems and queries? Shadow him from meeting to meeting? Sit in his office and wait for him to return? Worse, sit all alone in his home amid Foley, Mrs Gaskell and his other staff while they stared at her with curious eyes?

There was no doubt in his heart or mind that he was falling in love, and even if she continued to reject him romantically, he swore to his very soul that he would not abandon her or her dreams. Not ever.

Was he insulting her by assuming her ignorant of the problems and challenges that lay ahead of them? Was he smearing her strength and courage before she had even been given the chance to prove herself capable of so much more than he could possibly know?

'God damn it, why am I standing here doing nothing?' he said aloud. 'I am not waiting for Thomas any longer. I will go to Carson Street and find out for myself what is going on.'

* * *

When William arrived at the Carson Street house, the front door stood wide open with nobody standing outside, so he walked straight into the hallway, 'Octavia! Are you here?'

High-pitched voices filtered down the staircase followed by the lower and somewhat impatient murmurings of a man. William took the stairs two at a time and marched towards one of the back bedrooms where the voices gathered in volume.

'We will take what we want, officer. Take your hands off me.'

'Don't you touch that! That is Octavia's.'

William stepped into the room to find clothes and trinkets, hats and boots thrown on the bed and scattered across the floor. 'Adelaide? Eliza?'

The two women and the uniformed constable all started and turned, staring at him with mixed expressions of surprise and suspicion.

'Who are you?' demanded the officer. 'You have no right to enter this property. Out you go, go on now.' He walked closer. 'This house is no longer open to the public, so if you're a regular visitor here, I suggest you scarper.'

Ignoring him, William looked to the two women. 'Where is Octavia?'

'She's gone to Nancy's. Are you... William? The man taking her to Manchester?'

Misplaced pride swelled inside him. 'I certainly hope so. Where does Nancy live?'

'Queen Square. Big fancy house on the north side. You can't miss it.'

'Thank you.' He faced the glowering officer. 'These ladies have the right to pack their belongings properly, officer. It would not do for them to be rushed from here without consideration or respect.'

The man guffawed. 'Respect?'

William stepped closer, his hand curled into a fist at his side. 'Yes.'

The young officer met William's glare before his cheeks mottled and he took a single step back. 'These ladies have exactly the time I allow them and not a minute more.'

'Of course, you are an officer of the law, after all,' William said slowly, his irritation rising. 'But if they tell me later that they were unduly treated in any way, I will be coming to the station to lodge my complaint first thing in the morning.'

With a final nod to a smiling Adelaide and Eliza, William inhaled a long breath and hurried down the stairs.

When he arrived at Queen Square, he made for the largest house on the north side, hoping against hope that it belonged to Nancy and Francis Carlyle and knocked on the door.

A few seconds passed before a young girl answered, her green eyes soft. 'Good afternoon, sir. Can I help you?'

His patience to see Octavia so thin, William glanced over her head into the hallway. 'I am looking for a Miss Octavia Marshall. Is she here?'

'She is, sir, but is busy with Mr and Mrs Carlyle. Maybe I could tell her you called and—'

'Nancy Carlyle, will you calm down and listen to me!'

The young girl spun around, and William watched as an auburn-haired woman burst into the hallway from the dining room, quickly followed by Francis, who made a grab for the woman's arm. 'Do you want me to tie you down?'

'You wouldn't bloody dare!'

Octavia came sharply behind them, her cheeks flushed as she scowled. 'Nancy, behave yourself. This is not going to help Louisa, is it?'

Suddenly all three of them looked towards the door.

William raised his hand. 'Hello, there. Apologies for the interruption.'

28

'William!' Octavia's stomach fluttered. She was so entirely elated to see him. 'You're here.'

'I am.' Shadows of relief and concern showed in his eyes as his gaze lingered on hers before he faced Francis and Nancy. 'Mr and Mrs Carlyle. I apologise for the intrusion.'

Francis stepped forward, his hand outstretched. 'Not at all. Come in, please.'

As the men shook hands, Alice closed the door before flashing a quick smile at Nancy and disappearing towards the kitchen. Nancy stared at Octavia, her eyes wide and eyebrows raised with clear expectation of an explanation as to why William was standing in their hallway.

Octavia had none to give her. How did he even know she was here?

Believing it safer if she opened the questions rather than Nancy, Octavia quickly approached him. 'Why don't we go into the parlour?' She took William's elbow. 'I suspect you have been to Carson Street. Did the lawyer you arranged to act on our behalf tell you we'd been released? Did you see Adelaide and Eliza?'

'They are being moved out of Carson Street by a police officer as we speak.' His concerned gaze swept over her face as they walked upstairs. 'Are you all right?'

'I'm fine...' She glanced over her shoulder at Nancy and Francis as they followed behind them. 'Especially for seeing you. It means so much to me that you would go to the trouble of finding a lawyer. Of trying to help us.'

'Not that we didn't have everything already in hand,' Nancy said purposefully and loudly, shamelessly revealing her eavesdropping. 'Francis and I thought of a solicitor immediately and dispatched ours to the station.'

Octavia rolled her eyes as they entered the parlour. 'I know you did, and Louisa and I expected nothing less from you. As grateful as I am to you, it does no harm to extend my appreciation to William too.'

Francis sat and patted his wife's knee once Nancy was sat alongside him, causing her to shoot him a glare as he smiled genially at William. 'Your willingness to help is duly noted, sir.'

Once Octavia and William had taken a seat opposite Francis and Nancy, Octavia tried her best not to slip her hand into William's, her heart so unexpectedly filled with joy at seeing him, and considering the way he looked at her with such care, she imagined he was feeling the same way. If the nights she had spent locked up behind bars had made her realise her feelings for William, then they had also made her realise how little time they might have left together. After all, she would never leave Bath without Louisa and Jacob having gained their liberty too.

'So...' Nancy blew out a shaky breath. 'Now we must think what to do to help Louisa and Jacob. Every minute they spend in that station is another minute closer to them being brought in front of a judge and then Lord only knows the outcome. We must take steps now in the hope it assists their case.'

Octavia considered the lawyer's words when he'd spoke to her at the station. 'Louisa's arrest is a little more complicated than everyone else's.'

Nancy frowned. 'What do you mean?'

'As the house's madam, the law holds her more culpable for the business. The lawyer suggested that myself, Adelaide and Eliza were working at the house under duress so that we might be freed.'

'What?' Nancy's eyes bulged. 'Well, I hope you put them right!'

'I did, but...'

'But what?'

Octavia swallowed, knowing she needed to tell Nancy what had happened between her and Louisa. She braced herself against Nancy's inevitable onslaught. 'But I fear my protestations did little to help. I'm just as concerned about Louisa as you are. Especially considering we had... cross words the last time we spoke.'

'What do you mean, cross words? What did you say to her?'

Guilt mixed with defensiveness and Octavia lifted her chin, determined to stand her ground even if fear shrouded her heart that she risked losing the love of the best friends she'd ever had. 'I told her that our arrest had not changed my decision to go to Manchester. If anything, it has strengthened it.'

'How? Can't you see the three of us need to stick together now more than ever? That if one of us is in trouble, we all are?'

'Of course I do, but—'

'You're leaving anyway?' Nancy's grey eyes darkened. 'How could you say that to her? After all Louisa has done for you, I cannot believe—'

'If you'll let me finish,' Octavia said, holding her glare and all too aware that Francis and William were exchanging glances. She had no doubt Francis was warning William to refrain from intervening. 'These arrests have made me realise the life I have been living for the past few years is over, Nance. I don't want it anymore. I want to learn, grow and change. Just like you and Louisa. I want to stretch my wings, learn new skills...' She swallowed, praying that her next words did not weaken William's respect for her but also wanting to hint that her feelings for him were deepening. 'Maybe even meet a man I might fall in love with like my best friends have. Is that so bad?'

For a long moment, Nancy said nothing, her grey eyes shining with what looked to be – but couldn't possibly be – unshed tears. Eventually, she shook her head, her cheeks red. 'You would consider leaving even with Louisa and Jacob banged up?'

'Of course not.' She glanced at William. 'I have no intention of leaving until they are free.'

He nodded, his tender gaze on hers.

'And if they aren't freed?' Nancy asked. 'Then what?'

Octavia sighed, suddenly feeling completely helpless. 'Then... I don't know.'

'I understand what you are saying and I want you to be happy, truly I do,' Nancy said. 'But when there is a chance Louisa might not see the light of day for many days or weeks yet, you should not have told her you are still leaving.'

'Maybe not, but I would never lie to her either, Nance. She is upset, scared and probably feeling as though I intend abandoning her, which is not the case at all.' She looked at Francis and William. 'We must do everything we can to ensure Louisa and Jacob are released too. I'm sorry, William, but our plans will have to wait. I won't abandon my friends. I understand if you have to leave but—'

'I gave you my promise, Octavia. I'm going nowhere without you.'

Relief flooded through Octavia that he would wait for her... however long that might take. She looked into his eyes and hope swelled her heart that maybe her mention of finding love had not terrified him as much as it had her. Or maybe he did not associate love with her at all.

She forced a smile. 'Thank you.'

He winked. 'You're welcome.'

Nancy huffed. 'If you two could stop making damn googly eyes at one another and concentrate on the task in hand, it would be appreciated.'

Octavia faced her, inwardly cursing the heat that rose in her cheeks and Nancy's knowing stare. 'Well, as your lawyer clearly knows what he is up against, we will urge him to speak to as many of our clients as possible. Surely having some influential character witnesses or at least statements will go some way towards softening a judge.'

'I agree,' said Francis as he rose from the settee and looked pointedly at Nancy. 'But, as my wonderful wife has a babe in her belly, I would prefer the two of you remain here for the time being.' He turned at William. 'Mr Rose, would you care to accompany me to my lawyer's office? Two voices have to be stronger than one in matters such as these.'

'I'd be delighted, sir.' William stood and looked at Octavia. 'I want to do all I can to help... for however long that might be.'

Unable to resist touching him, Octavia reached for his hand. 'Thank you.'

He squeezed her fingers, his brow furrowing. 'Where will

you stay? When I was at Carson Street, it was clear the police intend closing your home with immediate effect.'

Loving the way he had referred to the Carson Street house as her home, as though it was a perfect house in a quiet suburban street rather than a brothel, Octavia smiled. 'Go with Francis. I'll be fine. The police have ordered that I go back to Carson Street, so, I'll decide what to do after I've finished there. I will come and find you later.'

'Octavia will be sleeping here for the foreseeable, Mr Rose,' Nancy said. 'There is no need for you to worry. Rest assured, we ladies know how to look after one another.'

'What?' Octavia froze. With tensions as high as they were between them, she very much doubted their arguments were over, and with Nancy being pregnant Octavia refused to be the one to put her baby at risk. 'No, Nancy. My staying here is not a good idea.'

'Very well,' William said firmly. 'How about I book you a room at my hotel?'

She turned. 'What?'

'Why not? I will request adjacent rooms. As neither of us will be leaving Bath anytime soon, it makes sense.' He leaned over her and brushed his lips over her cheek. 'Once you've collected what you need from Carson Street, go back to the hotel, and I will meet you there.'

William nodded to Francis and they left the room. Soon after, the front door slammed.

'Well.' Nancy slapped at her skirts, her colour high. 'He's a quite the bossy so-and-so, isn't he?'

Octavia struggled to stem her smile. 'And you're not?'

Nancy glared. 'This is not funny.'

'Am I laughing?' Octavia stood and made for the drinks cabinet. 'I need a quick gulp of something.'

'Help yourself... then I think you should concentrate on running a bath.'

Octavia poured a generous glass of claret. 'I can't. I need to go back to the house. Adelaide and Eliza are there with a constable. I've already been here far too long.'

Nancy stood. 'Then I'm coming with you.'

'Oh no, you're not.' Octavia took a generous mouthful of wine. 'Francis would never forgive me if you came all the way across town and then started lugging belongings from the house. You stay here; I'll be fine.'

'But—'

'I mean it. The baby comes first.'

Nancy opened her mouth to protest and then slumped before returning to the sofa and sitting down. 'Fine.' A few seconds passed before she spoke again. 'So...' She sighed, dropping her head back. 'Are you falling in love with him?'

Octavia tightened her fingers on the stem of her glass, took another fortifying sip. 'I don't know.'

'You don't know? Well, you'd better hurry up and work it out because the man seems to think you're his to do with as he will.'

'Don't be so obtuse. William cares about me. Respects me. More than that, I admire his brain and his ambition. He makes me believe I can be more. Have more.' She pulled back her shoulders. 'And, when we are in Manchester, I know he will look after me.'

'*If* you get to Manchester, of course.' Nancy raised her eyebrows. 'But, yes, I believe if your move north happens, Mr Rose might just look after you.'

Octavia smiled. 'Everything is going to be all right, Nance. We will get Louisa and Jacob free and our lives will go on as we want them to – I'm sure of it.'

'Maybe. It's just...'

'What?'

'You hardly know William despite your claims otherwise. I love you. If Louisa and Jacob are released and you swan off to the north, how will we know you are all right?'

'Surely the fact William secured us representation and sent a lawyer to the police station proves his willingness to do all he can for Louisa and Jacob. Doesn't that show something of his character? Won't you please give the man the credit he deserves?'

'Fine. You know best, I'm sure.'

But, despite her assertions in William's defence, fear stirred inside Octavia. She had no idea if William would always be the kind, considerate man he was now. He could change. Turn into a monster when she was miles away from the only people she could really trust. How could she be certain she wasn't misjudging him as she had so spectacularly her father?

'The way you are looking at me speaks volumes,' Nancy said quietly. 'Just be careful. That's all I ask.'

Octavia looked deep into her heart and only a resounding certainty whispered through her that going to Manchester with William was the right thing to do. 'All I know is that William is the catalyst for the change I want in my life. I have to follow that.'

But her friend had closed her eyes and was already softly snoring, her pregnancy clearly taking its toll. Octavia inhaled a long breath as she thought of William and how he was willing to stay in Bath and wait for her, willing to help Louisa and Jacob in any way he could.

It felt wonderful to have him in her corner. To have someone she could rely as well as Louisa and Nancy.

And when she returned to the hotel, she intended showing

him just how much she appreciated him being in her life; the uncertainties of their future be damned.

29

Leaving the coffee shop located at the bottom of the steep slope of Gay Street, William was happy that he had accepted Francis's suggestion that they share a cup of coffee after they had seen his lawyer. William still found Francis Carlyle as amiable and forthright as he had the first time they met and hoped that he might get to know the theatre manager even better in the future.

He shook Francis's offered hand, the rain dripping from the brims of their hats. 'Well, we have done all we can for now. I'm confident your man will have Mrs Hill and Mr Jackson released in no time.'

'I fear we have a long way to go before they're out of the woods.' Francis frowned as he pulled up the collar of his coat. 'All we can do is hope for a good outcome. I'll return to the house and see what Nancy and Octavia are up to. Would you like to come back with me?'

'No, I'll head back to the hotel. I'm sure Octavia will be on her way there soon.'

'I'd like you to know, despite my wife's impulsive outbursts, we both suspect you will do right by Octavia.' His gaze slightly hardened. 'I hope you do not prove our instincts wrong.'

William held the other man's gaze. 'I want only the best for her.'

'I'm glad to hear it.' Francis nodded. 'Well, goodbye for now.'

Francis walked away and was soon swept up in the crowds bustling back and forth along the busy street, umbrellas glistening under the increasingly heavy rainfall. Manchester would be even more dreary this time of year and William couldn't help worrying Octavia would be disappointed by what could be seen as a dismally grey city even in the sunniest of weather. Yet Manchester was a city he loved to his very soul and he hoped Octavia would come to feel the same.

She was so dynamic, so willing to open her eyes and see things differently. He believed her to be a woman who would undoubtedly thrive wherever she might be, and her time in Manchester would prove no different. With Octavia beside him, who knew what might be written in their futures?

William smiled as he headed for the hotel, excited for what lay ahead for them. He could already picture her face upon seeing his mills, the questions she would ask, her curiosity about everything and everyone. He was certain her enthusiasm would only serve to remove his occasional weariness and reignite his excitement for a business that didn't quite consume him the way it once had.

Everything would look brand new through her eyes – even the problem of announcing their engagement could not quite take the shine from his expectation. But first they must ensure the release of Louisa Hill and Jacob Jackson or else he had no doubt Octavia would remain in Bath.

* * *

Once he arrived at his hotel, William strode directly to the reception desk and reserved a room for Octavia.

'We have Room 34 available, sir. It is located just along the corridor from yours.'

'Wonderful. Thank you.'

The young man behind the hotel desk reached for the keys hung on a board beside him. 'Will your associate be arriving shortly?'

'She will, yes.'

'Very good, sir. Once your associate arrives, let us know, and we will see her belongings are taken to her room immediately.'

'Thank you.'

William turned just as Octavia entered the lobby. His breath caught to see her looking so beautiful after she had washed the station cell from her clothes, hair and face. It only made him admire her more that she seemed to have no idea of her beauty. The door attendant immediately leapt to attention, relieving her of her dripping umbrella and coat.

She looked up and her gaze met William's. She smiled, her whole face seeming to light up at the sight of him.

Walking forward, he resisted the overwhelming urge to take her into his arms and kiss her. Instead, he took her elbow and led her towards a small table in front of one of the windows facing the street. 'Tea?'

She nodded, her gaze dropping to his mouth. 'Please.'

Something had changed in her. Her gaze was almost hungry on his, her lips slightly ajar as though expectant for his kiss. Desire stirred inside him and William looked around for a waiter, lest he act on his sudden yearnings.

Once the tea was ordered, he settled back in his seat, watching her and trying to fathom her feelings. 'Has something happened?'

She stared at him before lowering her gaze to her lap. 'Why do you ask?'

'You seem different to when I left you at the Carlyles'.'

'I suppose I am.' She lifted her head, her bright blue eyes happy. 'Despite Louisa and Jacob still being imprisoned, I know we will get them freed and I know I will still come to Manchester with you. I feel... empowered. Content. Maybe even a little proud.'

He could not drag his eyes from hers as she continued to talk, the blue of her gaze brightening under the lobby lights as her fervour for her friends' release and her future beside him escalated. God, he was well and truly caught... and that meant he was in a whole lot of trouble too.

Never in a million years did he think heartbreak would be on his agenda – not William Rose who thought only of business, his wealth and his family's future. Now, he thought of more than his parents' and sisters' happiness; he thought of his... and Octavia's.

'...I've realised that asking for what I want, doing what I want, does not make me selfish.'

Octavia's voice broke through his reverie and William blinked. 'Of course not. I'm surprised to hear you say such a thing. You deserve the life you want as much as the next person,' he said, his defence of her immediate. 'Who has suggested otherwise?'

'No one, but it is how I have spoken to myself for far too long. Just because I am going to Manchester, that does not mean I am turning my back on my friends or thinking only of myself. This move will make me happy, just as the theatre does Nancy and independence does Louisa.'

'I feel you are trying to convince yourself rather than me.'

'Maybe I am. A little.' She exhaled, her shoulders slightly lowering. 'But no matter what our lives might entail going forward, you should know that I will always be there for Louisa and Nancy should they ever need me.'

'I would expect nothing less. Your loyalty is to be admired, not condemned.'

'Thank you.' She smiled as she sat up straighter. 'I intend holding on to this change in myself for as long as possible.'

'Good.' He looked deep into her eyes, trying to gauge her sincerity. He loved witnessing her possible happiness because it made him think of his own life, his own dreams as much as hers. 'You know, all I ever wanted was to ensure my family never reverted to the poverty we once knew, but…' He ran his gaze over her beautiful face. 'I have also come to learn, from seeing you with your friends and they with you, that no amount of money can make up for love.'

She smiled, but he did not miss the flicker of uncertainty in her eyes.

Before he could question her further, the waiter came to the table. 'Your tea, sir, madam.'

As the tea paraphernalia was laid out and their cups filled, William carefully watched Octavia as she smiled at the waiter, seeming to avoid looking at him. At last, they were left alone again.

'Octavia?' he asked, quietly. 'Did I say something wrong before?'

'Not at all.' She waved her hand. 'Ignore me. Please, tell me about the meeting.'

Concern whispered inside him. Maybe she wasn't quite as confident about moving to Manchester as she wanted him to believe. Or maybe the fate of Mrs Hill and Mr Jackson continued to plague her and possibly could for a long time yet. He cleared his throat, determined to do his best to keep her spirits lifted.

He told her that Louisa and Jacob were likely to be

summoned in front of a judge in the next few days, but the Carlyles' lawyer was confident that her friends would face a hefty fine and the closure of the house, rather than imprisonment.

'So, it's highly likely the house will have to cease business?' Octavia grimaced. 'Louisa has such plans. This will not be welcome news.'

'Surely she would welcome that rather than a prison cell?'

'Of course. In time. But Louisa is fiercely independent, and the house is her domain. She's already fighting Jacob about starting a family after they are married in a few weeks.' She sighed, her eyes glazing with worry. 'If they marry at all. With everything that has happened, I wouldn't be surprised if Louisa wants to delay the wedding until the New Year.'

'Will Jacob agree?'

'I very much doubt it. He loves every inch of her. Heart, body and soul. All he wants is to make Louisa his and spend the rest of his life making her happy.' She dropped her gaze to her cup, added a lump of sugar. 'William?'

'Yes?'

'We should go upstairs once we've finished our tea.'

She met his eyes, hers dark with a sudden and unmistakable hunger.

His groin stirred awake. 'Yes, I think maybe we should.'

30

Octavia stretched before wriggling deeper into the soft comfort of the bed in her hotel room. Her lovemaking with William had been infinitely sweeter, more intimate, than when they had lain together before, his caresses and care profoundly shifting something inside of her. It was as though she could physically feel her heart thawing. And, as scary as that was, for the first time since she had begun her pitiful journey into prostitution, Octavia felt alive and filled with purpose and – dare she think it – the possibility of love.

But she had to keep strong. Had to bear in mind how her need to lie with William again would inevitably alter things between them. Bring them closer, and with that intimacy, the risk of complication and emotion. Something she could not afford to give in to easily when her side of their pact – being his fake fiancée – had been carried out, whereas his part of the deal was yet to begin.

'What are you thinking about?' William's gaze was teasing as he stood at the foot of the bed, securing his tie. 'Just a few moments ago you looked entirely sated. Now you look distracted, even a little worried. You do know it cheers a man to know he can satisfy a woman?'

She lifted her eyebrows and tried to hide the longings and fears that stirred inside her heart. 'But am I *any* woman, Mr Rose?'

'No, you are most definitely not...' He came to the side of the bed and sat, trailing his finger across her collarbone and lower to the curve of her naked breast. 'You are most definitely one of a kind.'

Octavia shivered, arousal pulling low in her stomach. 'And pray you never forget it.'

He leaned forwards and kissed her, his tongue teasing hers. Octavia lifted her hands to his strong, broad shoulders, easing him closer as she deepened the kiss, wanting to pull every part of him inside her.

This new, intense want of him had taken her by surprise. Yet she knew it was connected to her certainty that despite Louisa and Jacob's incarceration they would be freed and she would find her destiny in the north. She held a new, liberating strength that compelled her to think and desire more than mere survival.

She wanted to thrive. To celebrate. To conquer.

And she had no doubt William was at the core of everything she was feeling and enjoying.

Slowly, he pulled back and gave a low whistle. 'You need to get dressed before I forget about eating... again. I've booked us a table for dinner, remember?'

'Where are we going?'

'A small but fantastic restaurant on Pulteney Bridge,' he said, pushing to his feet and walking to the mirror. 'They serve the best goulash I've ever tasted.'

'Well, then...' Octavia smiled, amused by his excited gaze in the mirror's reflection. 'I am not one to keep a man from his goulash.'

'Are you making fun of me, Miss Marshall?'

'Of course.'

Turning abruptly, he strode across the room towards her, his hands raised in claws as he growled. Octavia squealed as he leapt atop her and tickled her until she had to beg for mercy...

* * *

An unforgivably long time later, Octavia slipped her hand into the crook of William's elbow as they descended the hotel's steps. The day's heavy rain had eased, leaving the early evening dry, clear and cold with a welcoming, undeniably Christmassy feel. No matter how hard she tried, she could not stop smiling as she revelled in her new-found optimism.

Even though the Carson Street house was facing closure, she had no doubt Louisa and Jacob would rise to the challenges they were certain to face. As individuals they were made of the strongest mettle. Together, they presented an impenetrable barrier that nothing or no one would destroy.

Octavia inhaled a long breath as though absorbing her friends' strength to see through all that was calling her forward with William. She glanced at him as he stared ahead, his brow furrowed. Concerned, she followed the direction of his gaze.

A band of women stood in front of an ornate marble fountain in the centre of the street, some waving newspapers and placards, others holding lit lanterns that cast an eeriness onto their faces, contorted with venom and spite. Although all were elegantly dressed, their coats and hats seeming of fine quality, their posture upright and dignified, their unified rancour was palpable in an unusual show of female public outrage.

'Down with the Carson Street harlots!'

'Remove the depravity of these homewreckers from our streets!'

'Such strumpets have no place in our city!'

William's hand tightened on hers where it now trembled on his arm. He urged her away from the melee. 'Keep walking. Ignore them.'

'How can I?' Octavia demanded, rage simmering inside of her. 'Look at them. Listen to what they are saying about me and my friends, about the house.'

'Believe me, I would like nothing more than to march over there and give them a piece of my mind, but there is little chance of any of them listening to reason.' William glanced again at the women, his jaw tight. 'Which is exactly why we should leave. Let's go.'

'I will do no such thing.' Octavia's heart beat fast as she pulled her arm from him. 'These women are not your usual troublemakers. They are ladies of class and wealth by the look of them. Why would they take it upon themselves to make such a public demonstration?'

'I have no idea, but—'

Octavia stormed forwards, her body tense with anger. She merged with the crowd watching the women, their arms raised as they yelled and cat-called their support.

She glanced at a woman beside her, hoping she did not recognise Octavia as one of the prostitutes these women slandered before she could find out what was happening. 'What is this all about?' she shouted above the racket. 'Why are they protesting?'

'Because of this, I expect,' the woman yelled, pushing a newspaper towards Octavia. 'Down with the slut and her keeper, I say.'

Octavia scanned the headline.

One of Bath's most prominent madams is taken into custody!

She read further, sickness coating her throat.

Mrs Hill, along with the doorman – who clearly does so much more than stand at her door – were arrested…

William joined her and slid the paper from her hands. 'What's this?'

Instead of answering him, Octavia surged between the sea of bodies to the front and stood before the woman shouting the loudest among the vigilante group. 'Whatever happened to the notion of women sticking together?' Octavia yelled. 'Can you not see that women like Louisa Hill are doing what they must in order to survive? That prostitution is not a choice but the result of desperation?'

'If you do not support us, then be on your way,' the woman retorted, her eyes bulging with anger. 'Clearly, you are neither married nor have children. Otherwise you would be standing alongside us and working to put a stop to these disgusting houses.'

'There would be neither the houses nor the prostitutes if it weren't for the men who visit them!' Octavia fumed. 'Do not turn against your own sex for utilising all that they have. Look to the men. *Your* man if it is Carson Street causing him to stray from your fireside.'

The woman's glare lit with such savageness there could be no doubt that Octavia had perfectly summed up this woman's home life and rage. 'I said, be on your way!'

Shaking with a dangerous mix of pride and anger, Octavia

shook her head. 'You should be ashamed of yourself. At least the women in this house are not turning on one another. At least Louisa Hill and Jacob Jackson are doing all they can to offer these girls protection and prevent them from having to hawk on the streets. Shame on you!'

Furious, Octavia spun around and knocked straight up against William's chest.

He took her elbows in his hands, steadying her, his gaze boring into hers. 'This is not the time. They won't listen to you.'

'But I have to do something.'

He tightened his grip, glared over her head towards the protestors. 'Listen to me. You cannot reason with people like that. We are helping Louisa and Jacob by securing them representation and ensuring they have a firm and solid voice to speak for them in court.' He met her eyes. 'They will be all right, I promise.'

'You cannot promise that. No one can.' She threw out her hand towards the crowd. 'And this sort of public display will only further fuel people's misplaced disgust, their ignorance.'

'That may be so,' he said, his gaze determined, his grip unyielding. 'But I will not risk you being attacked or worse by aggravating these people more than they already are. You really do not want to see how angry I will be or what I will do if anyone should lay a hand on you.'

She opened her mouth to protest but the fiery passion, the anger in his eyes, dissolved the words on her tongue. He wanted to protect her. When was the last time any man had stepped forward to do such a thing?

'Fine.' She swallowed, drew her arms from his hands and crossed them in front of her – almost as though the action might protect her fragile heart. 'I'll not do anything else.'

'Good.' Admiration softened his gaze. 'You dealt with that

woman wonderfully, and seeing you confront her, challenge her, only deepened my certainty about you.'

She scowled towards the women. 'I barely started with what I wish to do to that woman.'

'Come with me.'

Before she could object, he moved her through the crowd. Without care, he roughly pushed people to the side until, as last, they were free of the throng.

He pulled her into an alleyway.

He took her chin between his thumb and forefinger, turning her face to his. 'You fascinate and amaze me, Octavia. You make me want to learn more about you, spend time with you, and having you arrested will not help our plans going forward, will it?'

'I fascinate you?'

He smiled. 'And amaze me.'

Moved by his words and the ferocity with which he spoke them, Octavia looked away.

'Can I kiss you?' he asked, quietly.

Her heart picked up speed under the force of her growing love for this man. It was as she had feared. Their lovemaking at the hotel had been more than sex for them both. They were no longer whore and cull, but man and woman.

She took a long breath, lifted her head and threw caution to the wind. 'Yes. Yes, you can.'

His kiss was gentle, yet firm, unspoken promises and hopes passing between them. Slowly, he eased back and brushed a curl from her cheek. 'You do not need to fight with women like that. They should not matter to you. Louisa and the others are stronger than them, as are you. You want to come to Manchester. To learn business. Yes?'

'Yes, but—'

'Then that is what you shall do. As God is my witness, Octavia Marshall, the stars will align so that you come to Manchester and I will teach you all I know. Whether it's next week, next month or next year, I will wait for you and together we will make it happen. I promise.'

Her heart beat fast as she looked into his eyes and saw his sincerity. He would wait for her... 'William, I never thought...'

'Never thought what?'

She shook her head, tears burning the backs of her eyes. 'I never thought I would ever escape this world, have the chance to *be* more, achieve more or find another way to become the woman I should have been before my mother died.'

'But now you feel differently?'

'Yes. Yes, I do.'

He kissed her again, his lips almost bruising hers, their previous tenderness turning to passion.

31

The day of Louisa and Jacob's court hearing broke with bright, hazy sunshine glinting over the early morning frost atop Bath's sandstone buildings. The ironic beauty of the sunlit stone was not lost on William as he was sure it wasn't on Octavia, Nancy or Francis, who sat alongside him in the courthouse's public gallery.

Now, only doom and darkness shrouded them as Louisa and Jacob stood a foot apart in the dock, the stalwart connection between them palpable, despite the gravity of their situation. William stared at their hands – so close, yet so far apart – and could only imagine how deep Jacob's yearning was to take his fiancée's hand.

Glancing at Octavia beside him, William took her fisted hand from her lap and held it in his own, hoping she took solace in his being there. 'Are you all right?'

Her eyes glistened with tears as she faced him. 'Look how they are standing so strong and upright beside each other,' she said, nodding at Louisa and Jacob. 'They are unbreakable. No matter what the judge might say.'

William stared at her friends, inexplicably proud of them despite barely knowing either. Their composure and dignity were beyond impressive. Shoulders back, heads held high. 'I am sure he will see they do not belong in a prison cell.'

'I pray you are right, but I fear Louisa and Jacob will be nothing more than a whore and her boxing keeper in the judge's eyes.' Octavia exhaled a shaky breath, her fingers gripping his. 'They do not deserve this. They deserve to be happy and married. Living and working side by side.'

Cursing an alien feeling of helplessness, William squeezed her hand and focused on what was playing out below them. The inside of the court was dismal and filled with a tangible doom. The wood panelling and ornate high ceiling imposing and emanating an atmosphere of reprisal rather than mercy. The walnut desks and chairs were occupied by clerks, laymen and Francis's solicitor, Emmett Holloway.

'Your honour—'

'I have heard enough, Mr Holloway.' The judge's voice boomed around the room, his white whiskers and moustache matching the tufts of hair above his overly large ears. 'I will address the accused and then give my decided punishment.'

Octavia's sharp intake of breath sounded loud in the now silent, cavernous room and William's heart picked up speed. God, how he wished he could remedy this for her.

'It appears to me, Mr Jackson and Mrs Hill,' the judge continued, 'that you are not only living in sin, openly and wantonly, but you have also drawn innocents into your house of depravity.' He peered over his half-rim spectacles as booing and heckling bellowed from the public gallery. 'However, you have had several well-respected members of society come forward in your defence.' The judge raised his voice. 'They suggest that, although your house is most certainly one of ill repute, it is also run fairly and without unnecessary or indeed, as far as has been attested, a single act of violence or mistreatment of the other poor souls from whose sacrifice you have drawn profit.'

Octavia gripped William's hand to such an extent that his blood pulsed beneath her fingers.

'Your supporters' claims have gone some way to softening my view of your somewhat unseemly enterprise. However...' The judge peered over his spectacles, his mouth twisted with distaste. '...I far from approve and, therefore, uphold that your residence on Carson Street is to remain closed without condition or excuse from this day forward. As for you, Mr Jackson, and you, Mrs Hill, I am ordering a public offence fine of £30 to be paid forthwith by each of you. Your names will also be added to a list whereupon if either of you should be found in any way committing the slightest misdemeanour, a custodial sentence will be passed without hesitation.'

He banged the gavel down causing Octavia to jump beside William before she flung her arms around him and began to weep. 'They're free. They're free!'

William pressed a firm kiss to her cheek and they stood with a clapping Nancy and Francis and stared down at the dock where Louisa and Jacob looked up at them. Louisa smiled, her violet eyes shining. Jacob merely winked, his back still ramrod straight as though half expecting the judge to change his mind – or maybe the giant of a man was already plotting his revenge on the people who had put him here today.

William turned to Octavia. 'Do Louisa and Jacob have the means to pay such a substantial fine?'

'Whether they do or not, all of us will band together and make sure it is paid.' Octavia swiped her cheeks, her eyes alight with happiness. 'They are free. That is all that matters.'

William hoped she was right, and Louisa and Jacob truly felt free when their entire world had been turned on its axis.

'Come on then,' Nancy said, tugging on Octavia's arm. 'Are we getting out of here or not?'

The two women embraced, looking into each other's eyes, tears shimmering on their cheeks before they walked along the gallery hand in hand. William gave a final glance around the courtroom, sending up silent thanks to God, before nodding at Francis and letting him lead the way out of a place William suspected neither of them wished to enter again.

The sun still shone brightly as they emerged onto the courthouse steps where, after a short wait, Louisa and Jacob joined them. Encircled by Octavia and the others, they hugged and kissed, shouted and laughed as William looked on from where he stood a little way away from them.

As he watched Octavia with the people she loved, their love and support of her palpable, William vowed to remain strong and be all that she needed him to be, in the hope that one day Octavia Marshall would become his wife.

Forcefully burying the apprehension that once his work life consumed his every waking moment again, Octavia would no longer look at him as she did now, that she would find him lacking, William stared ahead.

As much as he tried to rid himself of his need to provide endlessly for his family, he could not, and guilt twisted in his gut that once he was in the midst of the dust, sweat and toil of his mills he would spend every available minute at his endeavours. He still had so much he wanted – needed – to do and he could not provide any guarantee that his life in the north would make Octavia happy as it did him.

But, as God was his witness, he would do all he could to try and find a way.

She turned, and when her gaze fell on him, her smile slowly dissolved, her happy eyes clouding with concern.

Leaving her friends, she came closer. 'William? What is it?'

He forced a smile and slid his arm around her waist. 'Are you happy?'

'More than I can say.' She sighed and dropped her head against his shoulder. 'Will you just look at them? The relief they must feel to be able to return to Carson Street. As the house is fully paid for and owned by Louisa, I can't see how the authorities can remove them even if they have to close for business. They will be fine.'

He turned his gaze towards Louisa and Jacob where they stood on the courthouse steps, their arms tight around each other as they kissed deeply, not caring about the people around them or the judgement that might be directed their way.

'All right, that's enough.' Nancy laughed, tugging at Jacob's coat. 'Put each other down. We've got some celebrating to do.' She looked across at William and Octavia. 'Come on, you two. We're going to the White Hart.'

Octavia tugged William forward and they joined the group, linking arms with Nancy.

'I'm going nowhere until I've washed and changed,' Louisa said, pinning Nancy with a stern glare. 'The White Hart might not be the Pump Room, but it isn't Bath's police station either. I'm filthy, and I am not setting foot inside any establishment looking like this.'

Nancy rolled her eyes. 'Yeah, of course, that's why you want to go back to the house with Jacob... to get changed.'

William smiled as Louisa swatted Nancy's arm. 'Behave yourself.'

'Just go, the pair of you.' Nancy laughed again and took

Octavia's hand. 'Meet us at the pub when you've finished... washing.'

As they walked, Nancy called out to someone along the street, releasing Octavia's hand. Octavia pulled William closer to her.

She looked into his eyes and grinned. 'How soon can we leave for Manchester? Louisa and Jacob will be all right now. They have each other, after all. We will write back and forth, and I will return for their wedding but, for now, I am free to go whenever you like.'

'Don't you want to stay to make sure your friends aren't further harassed?' he asked, not wanting her to leave before she was entirely ready. 'Those women on the street—'

'Will regret coming within ten feet of Carson Street if Nancy has anything to do with it.' She shook her head, her gaze glazing with thought as she stared at Francis and Nancy. 'Louisa and Nancy are the dynamic duo, William. I am a mere extra, I promise you.' She faced him. 'They think they need me, but they don't. Not really.'

He brushed a curl from her cheek. 'And that doesn't bother you?'

'It has in the past, but not now.' Her bosom lifted as she inhaled. 'Now nothing matters to me in Bath the way it once did. Come, let's catch up with Nancy before she accosts the entire city to join our celebrations.'

He gripped her hand, halting her. 'Octavia, I need to be sure you want to do this. I do not really have any idea of my family's reaction to you despite them knowing about our betrothal. I like to think they will adore you.' He smiled, hoping his words did not scare her. 'But the simple fact is, it will be impossible to prevent them from meeting you for long. My parents might be put off for a while, but as for my eldest sister Elsa, she is a different kettle of fish altogether.'

He didn't miss the flicker of apprehension that flashed in her eyes even as Octavia smiled, her fingers squeezing his. 'Of course, I must meet your family. How will we explain my involvement in learning your business if they do not believe us to be a couple, interested in one another's lives? No matter what challenges we face, I will not allow you to renege on your side of the bargain, so all will be well.' She raised her eyebrows. 'That is what this is all about after all. What we promised each other.'

'Absolutely.'

'Good. Now, let's join the others.'

She tugged on his hand and William followed. For him, at least, their leaving, their relationship – everything – had become about so much more than business.

It seemed that was not the case for Octavia, and it pained him just to think how deeply and how quickly he had fallen for her.

32

Octavia stood back from the open bags and boxes on her bed, the deluge of belongings a stark testament that she would soon be gone from Bath. She pressed her hand to the nerves leaping in her stomach. Today was the day she left Carson Street, left Louisa and Jacob, Nancy and Francis, and boarded a train to Manchester.

Although she had no doubts she was doing the right thing – that she must embrace this new adventure heart, body and soul – she could not stop worrying about not being here if anything else should befall the friends who had come to mean so much to her.

She walked to the window and stared towards Parade Gardens, now woefully empty of the people who chose to promenade amongst the park's trees and flower beds in spring, summer and autumn. Winter was a desolate time in any city, yet she feared Manchester would be even more so than Bath.

Her conversations with William had led her to build up a picture of an industrial, entrepreneurial metropolis, buzzing with innovation and invention. Its smoky, factory-filled skies belying the glittering nature of its wealth and growing monetary success. That vision turned her mind to Jacob and Louisa's visit to the Great Exhibition in London last year and their stories of the wonders they had seen, touched and experienced. Considering Jacob's enthusiasm for industry and invention, Octavia could not help but puzzle over his seemingly purposeful distance from William.

Could he be envious of William's extensive success? The way he had forged a prosperous legacy in industry? Octavia frowned. She could not imagine Jacob wasting time envying anyone. She had never met a man so self-assured and comfortable in his path. Not to mention that he now deemed his number-one priority in life was to protect her, Nancy and Louisa. Anything or anyone who threatened their safety was, more often than not, quashed with a single look rather than violence.

She would miss Jacob as much as she would Louisa and Nancy.

Turning away from the window, Octavia battled her melancholy. Manchester would be wonderful, a place of miraculous adventure filled with life-enhancing lessons and delight. She would forge new relationships with wonderful people, find joy in her new work and grow into the woman she always believed herself destined to be.

There was no need for fear or self-doubt. The entire world would soon be hers.

Smiling, Octavia picked up a book from her bedside table and put it into a bag containing the things she wanted with her on the train. Putting her hands on her hips she surveyed her packing. She was just about done, just one or two more things...

There was a knock on the door.

'Come in.'

Louisa walked into the room and glanced at the bed. 'How are you getting on? It looks as though you are almost finished.'

'I am.' An unexpected lump formed in Octavia's throat as she looked at her friend and she quickly plucked a chemise from one of the open cases and refolded it with her back turned. 'I'll start bringing everything downstairs shortly.'

'Nancy has just arrived to say goodbye but got waylaid, unable to resist finding an excuse to vex Jacob. She'll be up when she's finished, no doubt.' She shook her head. 'I hope she isn't in the mood for tormenting everyone. She told me she specifically wants to speak to William before you both leave. I assume he will be here before long?'

Dread dropped into Octavia's stomach. She wanted to leave her friends with only love between them. She prayed Nancy would be amiable. 'Do you think she plans to harass him?'

'Most likely.' Louisa arched an eyebrow. 'And you'd be best advised to let her get on with it. You know she won't let you go until she's said her piece. I'm sure William can hold his own with her.'

'So am I, but I have no doubt he'll be dragging me onto the train once Nancy has finished with him.' Octavia laughed.

Louisa smiled, her eyes glinting with what looked to be tears. Her friend's sadness was more than she could bear and Octavia strode forward. They embraced, their arms tight around one another as quiet sobs escaped them, tears trickling over Octavia's cheeks.

She could not be this weak, this afraid, when she craved a new life with her entire being. Her friends would be fine with or without her.

Octavia pulled back, swiping her fingers under her eyes. 'You'd think I was never coming back.'

'If you and I can't keep hold of our emotions, I dread to think of the fuss Nancy is going to make.' Louisa laughed through her tears. 'She'll be clutching on to your skirt hem as you're heading out the door.'

'I wouldn't put anything past her.'

Louisa ran her hand over the surface of the dressing table, empty but for a lace doily and a box of handkerchiefs. 'We are going to miss your austerity, you know. Who is going to keep us in line when you're gone?'

'I can't imagine Jacob allowing either of you to run amok.'

'He's worse than ever with you leaving. Plus, he seems entirely intent on finding out who instigated the prying into our affairs.'

'I assumed the alderman, Alexander Middleton, was the instigator.' Octavia frowned. 'It was him who came here shouting and ordering us around the night we were arrested, after all.'

'Yes, but Jacob has since found out he is merely a figurehead, the man who likes to take the glory. There is a whole band of people working together to get the brothels closed and...' she rolled her eyes '...the city free of depravity and debauchery. I am concerned that Jacob will not let our arrest go unpunished. He's even mentioned taking another boxing match just to vent some of his fury.'

'Surely not? I assumed his fighting days were behind him.'

Sharp, confident footsteps sounded on the landing and then Nancy burst into the room, her arms wide. 'I'm here, girls, never fear!'

'Never fear?' Louisa put her hands on her hips, her gaze teasing. 'We were enjoying the brief peace and quiet.'

'Peace and quiet be damned.' Nancy strode past Louisa, straight for Octavia, her expression stern. 'So, you are actually going through with this madness then?'

Octavia braced for Nancy's challenge. 'I am. Anything you want to say to me, you'd better say it now. And, be warned, I will not be standing silently by if you intend reprimanding William when he gets here. The decision to go to Manchester with him is mine and mine alone.'

Nancy's grey eyes wandered over Octavia's face as though she searched for something. Octavia stayed perfectly still. What was she looking for? Fear? Doubt? Happiness? With Nancy there was no telling what she was thinking.

'Well?' Octavia lifted her eyebrows. 'Have you anything more to say?'

'Two things actually. One...' Nancy peered over Octavia's shoulder towards the bed. 'Have you packed enough of those books you like so much? Lord only knows what the bookstalls are like in Manchester.'

Octavia bit back her smile. 'I have.'

'Good.' Nancy sniffed. 'And two, how much longer are you expecting me to stand here without a cuddle?'

Her smile breaking, Octavia pulled Nancy into a firm hug and held her. 'I love you so much, you pain in the backside woman. Don't ever change, do you hear me?' She eased back and held Nancy at arm's length, tears building in her eyes once again. 'Even when you're a mother, I expect you to be just as stubborn, just as foul-mouthed, and just as likely to stand on a table in the White Hart and sing your heart out.'

Nancy grinned, her eyes glinting with mischief. She smoothed her rounded belly. 'Whether boy or girl, this one will love the stage, considering who its mother and father are.'

'You're going to be wonderful as the star in Francis's play, you know.'

'Indeed, and I will expect to see you in the front row on opening night along with Louisa and Jacob.'

'I'll be there, I promise.'

A tear rolled over Nancy's cheek and she quickly wiped it away.

Louisa stepped closer and took each of their hands. 'No matter how our lives have changed and continue to change, the three of us and Jacob are a unit. A family. Nothing and no one will take that away from us.' She exhaled a shaky breath. 'The house might be closed—'

'For now,' Nancy interrupted, her grey eyes turning steely. 'If you want to open again, Lou, we'll find a way.'

'Maybe.' She smiled. 'But all I care about right now is that the three of us never drift apart and always remain the very best of friends.'

Nancy tutted, but Octavia saw the worry in her eyes. 'Of course we will.'

Octavia swallowed. She owed it to them to admit her vulnerability despite the stalwart front she had fostered for so long. 'I am scared, you know. Not of losing your friendship, but afraid that moving to Manchester might come to be the biggest mistake I could've made, but...' She squeezed their hands, desperate that they hear and understand. 'I have to go. Have to see a different way of life. Find out for myself whether I can succeed in business. I need to do something...' she took a deep breath '...to ensure my future security through my own hard work.'

Louisa frowned. 'You have always worked hard.'

'I know, but this will be different.'

'And your ambition is admirable,' Nancy said as she slipped her hand from Octavia's and walked to the bed. She sat down and fingered the clothes spilling from one of the cases before lifting her gaze. 'But what of William? I see the way he looks at you. This is no longer just about business for him. You do know that?'

Octavia's heart swelled with pleasure but also a hefty dose of fear. If William's feelings for her matched hers for him, then how would they ever maintain a business relationship? How would they keep up the pretence of their feigned engagement? She couldn't think further ahead when she still did not know him enough to be sure he would deliver on what he had promised.

If they married, he would be entitled to every penny she had.

She pulled back her shoulders, her determination rising as she walked forward and sat on the bed beside Nancy. 'I can't say for sure it is still only about business for me either, but I do know I will never surrender what I have earned and learned over the years just for the chance of a little romance. You know me better than that. I would never be so foolish after all that each of us has been through.'

Louisa came closer and gestured with her hands for Octavia and Nancy to stand. She took their hands. 'We are all grown women and entitled to act on what we believe to be best for us.' She looked at Nancy. 'Octavia included. Let her go, Nance, with our blessing.'

The three of them put their arms around one another and Octavia inhaled the familiar scent and warmth of the two women who had rescued her, had faith in her and loved her, making her the woman she was today.

She cuddled Louisa and Nancy close. 'Long live the ladies of Carson Street.'

33

William stared through the carriage window as he and Octavia trundled through Manchester's streets on an absurdly grey December afternoon. It was close to two o'clock so he had no doubt that once he and Octavia arrived at his home, the staff would all be there. With their morning duties completed, they would now be rushing around, busy with last-minute preparations for their master and his fiancée's arrival. He blindly reached for Octavia's hand where she had sat bolt upright beside him since they had alighted from the train and hailed a carriage.

No matter her protestations, he sensed her nervousness.

'Is something wrong?'

Octavia's question broke through his contemplation and William forced a smile. 'Not at all. The house isn't too far away now. We will arrive in the next ten minutes or so. What do you think of the city so far?'

'I...' Rare hesitation showed in her gaze before she slumped her shoulders. 'It does not quite reflect the picture I had built in my imagination, but it is nice enough.'

'Nice enough?' Although disappointed that she was not

immediately impressed by Manchester, the city surely warranted a little more animation than that? 'Are you not impressed by the new buildings? The innovative architecture?'

'Well, yes... the buildings are grand indeed. And enormous.' She laughed. 'I'm sure Manchester will grow on me in time, William. There's no need to jump to its defence quite so soon.' Her beautiful blue eyes glittered with teasing. 'And neither am I fooled that whatever is worrying you is bound in whether or not I like Manchester. What is it? You can tell me anything, I hope.'

William battled to find the words of warning he felt duty-bound to share with her. Words that had encircled his mind for the majority of their journey. No matter how he'd prefer to think Octavia entirely happy and excited about her decision to come to Manchester, he could not help feeling protective towards her considering the possible hurtful speculation her arrival might cause.

'William?'

He cleared his throat and shifted in his seat so that he faced her directly. 'Octavia...'

'Yes?'

Come on, man. Just bloody well say what you need to say... 'Whether you realise it or not, my feelings for you have grown throughout the time I have spent with you in Bath and now, more than ever before, I have the need to look after you. To protect you.' He exhaled a shaky breath, tightened his fingers on hers. 'What I'm trying to say is, I'm falling in love with you, and I am not going to take kindly to any judgement sent your way from my parents or anyone else.'

'You're falling...' Her eyes were wide, her mouth slightly open. 'I don't know what to say.'

That you are falling for me, too? 'Then say nothing. I just want you to know I will do everything in my power to protect you and if I fail...' He drew in a long breath. 'That failure will damn near break me, I swear to you.'

She smiled softly. 'You do know how tough I am, don't you? That I am more than capable of looking after myself?'

'Yes, but when a man desires a woman as I desire you—'

'Desires me?' She arched an eyebrow. 'Ah, are we talking of your love or lust for me?'

It was clear she was trying to ease his seriousness and William relented, not wanting to increase her tension more than necessary.

He winked. 'I must admit, keeping to the laws of propriety is going to be difficult. Keeping my hands off you even more so. But I will endeavour to behave and allow my family to believe us in love if not completely intimate.'

A slight blush darkened her cheeks. 'Hmm, despite the desire not being entirely one-sided, I'm sure we'll manage well enough.'

The desire not being entirely one-sided... but clearly the falling in love is.

He cleared his throat. 'I have only told my staff the bare minimum about you, but I worry that would have done little to prevent any chatter and assumption taking hold in my home the moment my letter to my butler was opened, read and shared.' He inhaled a long breath. 'Which means there is every possibility my staff will either welcome you with long-awaited glee as my future bride, or worse, as an unmarried, unchaperoned woman who has no business staying with me until you have a band of gold on your finger.'

Concern shadowed her gaze before she pulled back her shoulders and smiled. 'I will be perfectly all right. I have dealt with far worse than disgruntled men and women in my time.'

'I'm sure you have, but—'

'Everything will work out as it's supposed to,' she said, casting a glance over his shoulder towards the window behind him. 'I can be as good an actress as Nancy if the situation warrants it.' Her eyes met his. 'As long as we keep my previous occupation from them, what other problems could there be? I mean, of course it's not entirely conventional that an unmarried couple stay under the same roof without other family members staying, but your staff are hardly going to protest when you pay their wages.'

'I am thinking more of my family. My mother and Mrs Gaskell, my housekeeper, like to talk... a lot.'

'I see.' Her brow creased. 'Then I will just have to charm your family when I meet them, won't I?'

'Then you will need all your charm tomorrow evening.' He grimaced. 'A letter arrived for me at the hotel before I left this morning. My mother is beyond excited to meet you and informed me that she has made all the arrangements with Mrs Gaskell for a meal at my home tomorrow.'

Her colour ever so slightly paled, her smile strained. 'It seems our biggest challenge is coming sooner rather than later in that case. Things will be smoother after I've met your parents, I'm sure.'

'And my sisters too, I'm afraid.'

'Your sisters too?'

'Yes. Could we not consider that it might be better if you meet them all at the same time?'

'A single deluge, you mean?' She inhaled, her bosom rising. 'Fine. Yes. I can do that.'

He lifted her hand to his lips, pressed a kiss to her knuckles. 'I know you can. I never doubted it for a minute, and I will be right beside you and I will not let them bully you, I promise.' He lowered her hand. 'Not that they ever would. My family are hardworking, down to earth and welcoming. You'll see that for yourself soon enough.'

'Then I look forward to meeting them,' she said, before slipping her hand from his and looking out of the window, the discussion seemingly closed for now.

William stared at her profile and pulled his lips together, trapping any further words. The tight line of her jaw and the stiff set of her shoulders showed her anxiety, despite her valiant act of nonchalance. She was clearly no less worried about what kind of reception lay ahead than he.

The increased bump and jolt of the carriage signalled that they had now turned from the main thoroughfare and joined the tree-lined street where William's grand townhouse stood just a short distance away.

As the carriage rolled closer, William's apprehension gave way to prideful determination that no one at the house, or indeed within his family, would undermine his care and love for Octavia. They – even more than he – had believed he might never fall in love or even marry without love, but he had fallen and deeply... who knew if the marrying part might come later?

Deep in his gut – in his heart – William knew Octavia belonged beside him and, in time, everyone he cared about and loved would feel the same.

Purposefully burying the prospect of anyone finding out about Octavia's past and the unthinkable repercussions, William raised his chin and breathed deep. All would be well.

They passed through the gates and ascended the sloped path that would deliver them adjacent to the house's portico. He squeezed Octavia's fingers. 'Welcome to my humble abode.'

He opened the carriage door and stepped outside, glancing towards the house's front door as it opened. Foley emerged first, followed by Mrs Gaskell, young Ada his housemaid and, finally, his conscientious footman, Arthur Nightingale. They formed a welcoming line that William suddenly wished was not in any way the norm.

Would Octavia be impressed by the formality or profoundly discomfited?

Taking his hand, she stepped out of the carriage and stood beside him, her tension palpable through the stiff grip of her fingers.

He looked into her eyes, willing her to feel his love for her. 'Everything will be all right,' he said, quietly.

She nodded, before lifting her chin and smiling. 'Of course it will.'

He faced his staff as he drew Octavia closer. 'Well, this is quite the welcome. Everyone, let me introduce my fiancée, Octavia Marshall. Darling? These are my staff...'

Her fingers tightened on his, quite possibly because of his endearment, but William led Octavia along the line as though he had not noticed. The difference in Foley's and Mrs Gaskell's notably cooler welcome compared to the kinder greetings of the younger staff irked, but William was neither surprised nor – so far – perturbed, having expected as much. He was glad he had warned Octavia of potential teething problems, even if she had denied there was any cause to worry.

'Right then, let us go inside. It's far too cold to be standing around out here for very long.' William waved his hand towards the entrance and his staff hurried inside ahead of him, leaving him and Octavia to follow. He gently took her elbow. 'So far, so good. Pay no mind to Foley and Mrs Gaskell. They will come around.'

She nodded, but her eyes were wide as she stared at the sandstone columns beside her and then at the portico roof. 'William,' she whispered. 'This house is beautiful... and big.'

Pleased that she was already impressed, he smiled, hope stirring deep inside of him that she might come to love his home as he did. 'It is my pride and joy. Well, along with my mills, of course.'

'It's wonderful.'

'It means everything to me that you are comfortable here. I want you to treat my home as though it were yours.'

She stared at him, indecision warring in her beautiful, slightly apprehensive gaze. 'I will. Thank you.'

He led her inside and they discarded their coats and hats as Foley and Mrs Gaskell stood awaiting William's instructions. 'Have you put Miss Marshall in the bedroom I requested?' he asked.

'I have indeed, sir.' Mrs Gaskell shot a pointed glance at Octavia, her brown eyes clouded with suspicion. 'Although close to your own, it is a decent distance along the landing should anyone ask.'

Maybe he should have reprimanded Mrs Gaskell for her words and tone but instead, William found himself entirely amused. 'And who would have the right to ask anything about what goes on in my private home, Mrs Gaskell?'

'Well, sir...' She bristled. 'Mrs Rose, for one, I should think.'

'Mrs...' Octavia's voice was somewhat higher than usual. 'Mrs Rose?'

Mrs Gaskell's eyes gleamed with satisfaction. 'Indeed, miss.'

Any semblance of a smile William might have had vanished as he locked his glare on his housekeeper. 'And why would my *mother* have issue with anyone I invite to stay here? Have you ever known an occasion when she has questioned my decisions or choices?'

'Well, no, but she might well question Miss Marshall, considering—'

'I think it best we leave any further storytelling or speculation unsaid, don't you?' William snapped, pleased that Mrs Gaskell at least had the decency to blush and dip her eyes to the polished floorboards. 'Now, Foley, please sort things out with the carriage driver and then take Miss Marshall's belongings upstairs. Mrs Gaskell, could you arrange for tea to be served in the drawing room in half an hour or so?'

'Yes, sir.'

'In the meantime, I will give Miss Marshall a quick tour of the house and garden.'

Octavia stood ramrod straight beside him, her gaze following Mrs Gaskell as she bumbled towards the kitchen stairs, muttering loud enough for both William and Octavia to hear.

William shook his head. 'Ignore her. She likes to think she has a level of authority in the house, which sometimes leads her to mistakenly believe she can take liberties with her conversation. I will be sure to remind her that is not the case.'

'She certainly doesn't approve of my being here. For a moment there' – Octavia laughed shakily – 'I thought you might have a wife in the attic, and I'd walked straight into a scene from *Jane Eyre*.'

He smiled, his lips itching to kiss away the line between her brows and bring some colour back to her abnormally pale cheeks. 'No, no wife... yet. Come, we'll start the tour with the lounge. It has a balcony and you look as though you need some air.'

She released a shaky breath. 'That would be most welcome.'

34

Octavia pushed a final pin into her hair and rose from the dressing table in William's guest room. Light and tastefully decorated in shades of pale green and cream with a huge double bed, complete with exquisitely embroidered coverings, the ambience of such a beautiful space had left Octavia refreshed after a surprisingly peaceful night's sleep. When she had exclaimed over the room yesterday, William had laughed and told her it was the most feminine of all the rooms in the house and where his married friends slept when they came to visit.

She had found it hugely pleasing that he entertained – even if she had the distinct impression every soirée would be connected in some way to business.

Octavia wandered to the window and surveyed the long, narrow garden.

The corner of a small seating area was just visible beneath the window and a paved pathway ran from the flagstones to what would almost certainly be a vegetable patch come spring-time. She smiled to see a small walled area at the very bottom of the lawn housing a steel-wired aviary, the birds' bright feathers catching the morning sunlight.

The entire garden had surprised and delighted her, providing a deeper insight into who William was, how much he enjoyed his home, despite the hours he worked. But her good thoughts faltered as Octavia stared beyond the garden to the smoking chimneys of the many factories and buildings in the distance, the winding edges of the canal just visible.

She constantly sensed the bustle and industry of Manchester, the never-ending toil of its thousands of working men, women and children. She smelled the smoke and oil, heard the clanging and banging of machinery and saw all that had passed by the carriage windows on their journey from the train station to the house.

But she had also moderated her initial disappointment of the city when speaking with him, all too aware of just how much he loved Manchester and clearly wanted her to feel the same.

Yet, she had been shocked and dismayed to see so many thin, emaciated people on the streets, their sunken eyes and outstretched hands beseeching all who passed them. Evidence of poverty and hunger, filth and squalor seemed so much more prevalent here than in Bath.

She had been shocked again when they had hardly travelled any distance at all before entering a clearly wealthier area of the city where everything was brighter and gayer. The houses and frontages of shops painted and decorated with a falsity of privilege that had made Octavia feel sick and guilty. How could two such extremes exist barely streets apart?

There was no denying the vast monetary divide in Bath, but it felt far worse here. Maybe that was due to Manchester's obsessive sense of industry, but she could not help being annoyed that William had not mentioned the vastly different margins in all the time they had known one another. Or could it be he thought her impervious considering some of the terrible sights and experiences that could be found in Bath? Or maybe he had purposely kept the truth of many people's existence from her, for fear she would change her mind about coming to Manchester? No, she was being unfair.

Her upset could just as easily be blamed on her own lack of investigation. She just hoped William knew the depth of her mettle by now and was confident that the state of the city, although upsetting, would not deter her dreams of making a success of herself.

Turning from the window, she gave a final glance around the room as excitement knotted her stomach for their planned visit to one of his mills after breakfast. Last night, they had taken a small nightcap together, and he had talked enthusiastically about all she could expect to see the next day. His love for his mills had been tangible and soon Octavia found herself excited to see all that he had described.

As she came down the stairs, murmured conversation drifted from the dining room and Octavia braced for another run-in with Mrs Gaskell. The housekeeper's attitude towards her had not softened at all the previous evening, her expression and clipped responses were more than enough to tell Octavia that in Mrs Gaskell she had found her biggest adversary so far.

The maid, Ada, was as sweet as they come, the footman shy and unassuming. As for Mr Foley, she had no idea of his opinion of her, considering she had yet to even manage to obtain eye contact. The butler seemed to believe formality was the only way to give service to William and would stick by it at all costs.

Pulling back her shoulders, Octavia planted on a smile and strode confidently into the room. 'Good morning.'

'Octavia.' William turned from where he sat at the dining table. 'I hope you slept well?'

Mrs Gaskell stood beside him holding a dish in one hand and a fork in the other, her brown eyes immediately darkening.

'I did, thank you.'

'Good, what would you like for breakfast?' William asked, his eyes happy, making him appear oblivious to the string of tension stretching across the room between Octavia and his house-keeper. 'Mrs Gaskell has prepared bacon, eggs, bread. How about some grilled tomatoes? They are fresh from the market.'

Octavia took a seat opposite him. 'Anything is fine, thank you.'

'Very good.' He looked at Mrs Gaskell as she finished serving him several rashers of bacon. 'Mrs Gaskell, a plate for Miss Marshall, please.'

'As you wish, sir.'

The housekeeper cast a glance at Octavia as she left the room and Foley entered with a rather exaggerated clearing of his throat. 'Ah, good morning, Miss Marshall.'

She dipped her head. 'Mr Foley.'

The butler's tone clearly insinuated he thought her tardy, but Octavia restrained her smile. There was something she liked about Foley. She liked that his loyalty and duty to William was obvious in all he did and whenever he was present. Considering how William had mentioned his butler several times, Octavia could only assume the fondness and respect was mutual – the butler holding himself with authority and constant deference, his attention barely leaving his master for a moment.

Which only led Octavia to believe that William's content-ment, ease of mind and general happiness was Foley's ultimate, maybe even only, priority.

Foley walked to the buffet table and retrieved the coffee pot.

As he filled William's cup and then Octavia's, Mrs Gaskell returned, panting for breath as though she had run to the kitchen and back, clearly fearful of missing anything. She laid a plate in front of Octavia containing every single one of the foods William had mentioned.

Octavia laughed. 'Thank you, Mrs Gaskell, but I really don't think I'll be able to eat all this.'

'Of course, you will.' William smiled, his gaze amused. 'Moreover, you'll need the sustenance in preparation for your trip to the mill today.'

She picked up her knife and fork and nodded at Mrs Gaskell. 'Well, thank you, Mrs Gaskell. This looks delicious.'

'You are welcome, miss.'

The housekeeper lingered a moment longer beside Octavia before muttering something inaudible and returning to the buffet table, where she and Foley then stood to attention should either of them be beckoned by William.

'So...' Octavia tried to think of something to say as she dragged her study to her plate. There were no staff at the Carson Street house, Louisa having decided the fewer people who knew the goings-on inside the house, the better. So this depth of servility was somewhat unnerving. She cut into a rasher of bacon. 'What can I expect to see at the mills? Will you be showing me everything? I do so wish to see it all.'

'I will certainly endeavour to show you as much as I can. I also want you to ask as many questions as you wish. Your interest in my business is wonderful and I intend to embrace it fully. I'm sure my parents will be equally impressed by your enthusiasm when they meet you later.' He glanced towards his staff as though checking Foley and Mrs Gaskell were listening. 'They will also be pleased that your family are of a grand standing in Oxfordshire. With your father owning such a wonderful estate, I'm sure they will want to hear all about what you got up to when you were growing up.'

Octavia stared at him, words flailing on her tongue, her mouth dry. Why hadn't William warned her that he would talk about her childhood? Her home? Was this supposed to test her nerve? A challenge to prove herself in some way?

'Octavia?'

She swallowed. 'I... yes... I loved my home. My parents raised me to know a lot about running an estate. My mother especially felt it important that I know how everything worked and that the privilege I enjoyed was made possible because every person, every tenant and member of our staff, had a hand in our family's prosperity.'

William's eyes lit with satisfaction. 'Just so. And I suppose you were expected to make a grand match? I hope I do not disappoint.'

Nerves knotted Octavia's stomach. He was turning the subject to marriage? Now? 'Stop teasing me, William. You know you are more than a match for me.' She shot him a glare, glad that Foley and Mrs Gaskell stood behind her. 'We will make the perfect pair, will we not?'

He laughed and turned his attention to his food.

Octavia stared at his bowed head as realisation dawned. This was a purposely staged show for the benefit of Mrs Gaskell. This was about snobbery. Clearly, William's housekeeper thought herself qualified to deem another's place in the world, probably assuming Octavia entirely brazen by staying here unchaperoned. William was merely using Octavia's background, her breeding, to override Mrs Gaskell's preconceived conclusions and no doubt extricate some of the poison the housekeeper had every intention of dripping into his mother's ear.

Picking up her tea, Octavia hovered the cup at her lips. 'And I truly believe our match will have even deeper meaning through our joined industry. Although I was entered into society and enjoyed all the privileges that brings, it is important to me that I use my education and experience to serve others.' She sipped her tea, carefully returned the cup to its saucer. 'It is my utmost wish to have my life mean something. To do something businesslike of my own. Something that will help others and help me, too.'

William raised his head and glanced with what looked to be unease towards his staff. 'I know how keen you are to work and help me, my love, but all that can come in due course. For now, I will show what I can and introduce you to my family.' He flashed her a smile, his eyes wide as though relaying a silent warning.

His gaze grew more and more intense on hers as the silence stretched. He did not look at her with amusement now, but with genuine challenge. Maybe even a little irritation. Was he doubting his decision to involve her in his work now? Was he warning her to bite her tongue? Remain quiet? Toe the line? Instead of being angered by the possibility, Octavia found herself almost pleased, hoping he was a little fretful about her forthrightness in front of Foley and Mrs Gaskell.

After all, she hadn't agreed to come to Manchester for love. She had made that very clear from the beginning. She came here to learn, to work, not to be William's puppet and not to carry out their fake engagement forever.

She might have begun to fall for the man, but her principles and ambitions had not changed. Neither had her suspicions nor her fear of trusting someone. If she was to obey the rules, so would he.

She speared a piece of tomato. 'Didn't you tell me you do not necessarily believe that women should be at home for every hour of every day?'

A muscle flickered in his jaw, his eyes never leaving hers. 'I did say that, yes.'

She smiled sweetly. 'Which is just one of the many reasons I fell in love with you. You are a man different to any other I have ever met. Forward-thinking, progressive. A man I wish to learn from so that I might stand side by side with him and make a happy home and life for us both.'

His gaze lingered on hers before briefly dropping to her mouth. 'Then I can't wait for this breakfast to be eaten so you can see first-hand a workplace where all are welcome. Men, women and children.'

They resumed eating for a few minutes before Octavia glanced at William from beneath lowered lashes.

His shoulders were stiff, his jaw tight.

She inhaled a deep breath. Today would be interesting, to say the least.

35

Standing outside William's mill, Octavia watched him walk towards the building, having agreed to come back in an hour or two once he'd had time to be updated with regard to the mill's goings-on since he had been in Bath.

Pride filled her as she waved to him where he stood at the grand entrance, the indomitable master of his domain. The red-brick building loomed large behind him, its countless windows shining grey and black, its chimneys puffing huge clouds of smoke.

Her gaze drifted to the great golden arch with *Rose Textiles* moulded in fancy italic letters sitting in pride of place over tall green gates. She couldn't wait to see inside. William had achieved so much, on such an impressive scale, but as he watched her now, his unwavering stare and set expression left her in no doubt that their conversation at breakfast had made him question the plausibility of their plans as much as it had her.

They were very different people with – quite possibly – very different agendas. Now they had added love, sex and emotion into the melting pot, their arrangement was beginning to falter, becoming a lot more fragile than Octavia had allowed herself to acknowledge.

She headed for the parade of shops that separated the wealthy district from the poor. Familiarising herself with the neighbourhood local to William's house might go some way to making her feel she belonged here.

His change in attitude and demeanour since they had arrived in Manchester should not have come as a surprise. Had he not warned her that he worked long hours? That the mill and the building of a fortune were his absolute priority after he and his family had pulled themselves out of poverty? But that did not mean she would sit back and accept the dire scenes she had witnessed on their way into Manchester. She had every right to ask questions and challenge him. He knew she was here, first and foremost, to ensure her future security.

She would utilise calmness and patience as she had so many times before. After all, both had been perfected by the necessity to calm angry culls – not to mention Nancy. Admittedly, her mediation had done little to appease her father, but her experience with him had strengthened her humanity. It would be to William's detriment if he ignored her wish to discuss the disappointments and reservations she now harboured. As much as she had been shocked by some of the things she had seen so far, it only made Octavia all the more determined to find an industry with which she could help others.

She entered the main shopping street and slowed her pace, taking the time to observe everything around her. Despite the heavy grey cloud and drizzle, the thoroughfare bustled with grandly dressed ladies and top-hatted gentlemen amid an array of umbrellas. Dotted between the gentry, the dirty faces of the street sellers emerged and shrank, flower sellers and lacemakers holding out their hands in supplication and hope.

The contrast to the extravagant displays behind the lattice windows of the dress boutiques, cake and bookshops was stark, but Octavia refused to surrender to the sympathy that rose inside of her. She must bury her emotion and think only of what good she could do going forward. What actions would make her new life here worth something. How she could learn from, as well as support William, at the same time as fulfilling her own purpose.

She came upon a shop with tables of books outside and stopped, her eyes immediately drawn to a copy of *Shirley*, the second novel by Currer Bell, which Octavia had yet to read. Excitement mixed with guilt. Reading was her pleasure, not part of her plan to orchestrate a new, pioneering life change.

Yet the temptation was too strong, and she picked up the book. Smiling, she clasped it to her bosom and entered the shop. Plans or no plans, she also deserved to enjoy times of happy solitude.

A bell tinkled her arrival and Octavia inhaled the familiar, beloved smell of dusty books and paper. The sensory comfort warmed her and instead of heading straight to the counter to pay, she opted to take a quick peek at what other volumes the shop had to offer.

'Rose is his name. He owns a mill not too far from here and at least two others on the outskirts of the city, I believe.'

'And his first name?'

'William.'

Octavia quickly stepped out of view of the two gentlemen. Hidden behind a floor-to-ceiling bookshelf, she peered around its edge. The men were well dressed, around fifty years of age, their almost identical ivory-topped canes and elaborate moustaches exhibited like badges of honour.

'Then the man must be one of the wealthiest in Manchester.' One of the gentlemen sniffed, his beady eyes surveying the immediate space around him. 'In which case he could easily afford to buy himself a position on the local council. If he is a true businessman, he should be open to more opportunity than cotton.'

'They say his interests are family and cotton only. He rarely socialises outside of his intimate circle.'

'Clearly the man considers himself an enigma!'

The men laughed heartily, making Octavia wince and she pulled back, leaning her head against the books behind her, her mind racing. Did William know he was a topic of conversation around town? That his business and his personal life were discussed as people wandered around?

'Well, whatever the man is, he is running those mills at a pound a pace, I can tell you,' one of the men declared. 'It's rumoured his mills are run as fairly as possible with regards to his workers, but the man does not surrender profit for pampering. I heard a woman suffered a crushed arm at one of his mills. Had to be amputated. And then, just this week, a child was rushed to the infirmary having lost two fingers collecting cotton wisps from beneath the looms.'

Octavia closed her eyes, shock reverberating through her. Crushed limbs? Amputation? Lost fingers? William was aware of all these things yet continued to profit from such suffering? What else had he failed to tell her? Humiliation burned hot at her cheeks that she might have been so naïve as to accept whatever William chose to show and share with her. Surely he would never be so callous, so conniving, to keep her from seeing the full picture of his life?

What if he pretended to care nothing of her occupation as a whore in his affection for her, but in truth had chosen to bring her here under the wrongful assumption that she would turn a blind eye to humanity in favour of wealth and a grand home?

The men congratulated each other on their canny surmising of William and his mills with a clap to one another's shoulders before walking past the shelves where Octavia stood. She narrowed her eyes and stared at their retreating backs until they opened the shop door and ambled, still laughing, along the street.

Her heart hammering, Octavia's mind reeled. Had she given William her trust too quickly, too blindly? Tears pricked her eyes and she squeezed them shut, willing all her self-belief to the surface. She was neither stupid nor averse to learning. She was in Manchester because she wanted to be and would make her leap of faith work out, come what may.

And if that meant confronting William about what she had learned this morning... so be it.

After hurriedly paying for her book, Octavia strode from the shop. The moment she stepped outside, she released her held breath and marched along the busy street, praying she was headed in the right direction for William's mill. With all she had learned that morning, she suddenly felt incredibly alone, missing the support of Louisa and Nancy, their advice and love.

Her need to do more and be more meant she had immersed every ounce of her faith and trust in William, and now Louisa and Nancy's questions and need for reassurance she was doing the right thing echoed in Octavia's ears like the tolling of a hundred bells. Would her quest for stability and respect mean forsaking her authenticity and integrity? Did William claim to be falling in love with her but really just wanted a wife who turned a blind eye to the darker side of his industry? That would be more sacrifice than she could bear.

Swiping angrily at the tears that dared to fall from her eyes, Octavia stormed forward, passion burning hot inside of her. She would not surrender who she was, the woman for whom she held so much pride. The last few years had been hard, tougher than she ever could have imagined, but her experiences had changed her from a child who wanted for nothing to a woman who cared about, sympathised and empathised with others who had nothing.

The selfishness her father had accused her of, the narcissism she had believed she possessed, was no more. Of that much, she was finally certain.

36

William led Octavia up the iron steps to his office and onto the small, riveted platform outside. Walking to the railings, they stood side by side and stared down at the workers below. The power looms whirled and cranked, puffs of white cotton swirled through the air, but not hovering like persistent snowfall as the fragments had a few months before. The wheel he had installed blew air through the vast room, alleviating the danger to his workers' lungs from the threads, but little could be done to banish it completely.

'What are your first impressions?' Purposefully burying his concern that Octavia might hate all that he loved, he looked at her. Her expression was stony, her beautiful blue eyes scanning the rows and rows of machinery and people. 'Octavia?'

Her gaze drifted to his and William tried not to stiffen at the lack of enthrallment in her eyes that he had hoped for.

'It's... interesting.' She faced the work floor again. 'Even though my research provided me with good insight into what I could expect when I came here, I don't think I fully fathomed the number of people you have working here, or how exhausting it must be labouring as they do each day.'

'My workers are treated fairly, Octavia. I stand by a minimum age of employment, provide meals and help with rent and sickness. I offer a humane and sought-after package, believe me.'

'According to whom?'

Defensiveness simmered low in his stomach and William stepped away from the railing, held his hand out towards his office. 'Let's go in here and talk.'

She intently stared at him before moving to scan the entire workroom once more. Dropping her hands from the railing, her chest rose as she inhaled a deep breath before she turned and entered the office ahead of him.

Tension inched across William's shoulders as he closed the door and walked behind his desk. Octavia stood at the window and stared outside, her brow furrowed.

Lacing his fingers, he placed his hands on the desktop, trying to calm his growing irritation. 'What do you want to say to me, Octavia?'

'Through my reading I discovered mill owners often work their people harder than even those unfortunate enough to find themselves in the workhouse. That workhouse children can leave by the age of fifteen, yet many are contracted to eighteen, or even twenty-one, at the mills.' She looked at him, her gaze unreadable yet her jaw so very tight. 'Is that true of your business? Do you contract children to stay here until they are adults?'

'I do, but that is industry practice. I am not doing anything out of the ordinary. However, I am doing better than most as the majority of my workers have chosen to stay at Rose Textiles far beyond their contract completion.'

'I see.'

'It's business, Octavia.' He held her gaze, determined that she neither smother him with guilt nor undermine his long-earned experience and authority. 'We have barely scratched the surface of what my business comprises, yet I feel you already stand in judgement of my mill *and* me.'

Her skirts brushed the dusty floor as she came forward and slowly lowered onto the chair on the other side of the desk. She placed her purse on her lap, her eyes on his. 'I am not judging you. I am merely saying I was naïve despite my reading.'

Her gaze was colder than he had ever seen before, her cheeks pink.

Swallowing in a bid not to blurt anything defensive, William leaned forward. 'Mill work is hard. Brutal. But it is also the future. An enterprise that will take the innovation and invention of so many and make this country one of the most powerful in the world. If you want to be a part of industry, of doing something towards making life bigger and better for all, you need to accept there is often a darker side to becoming wealthy.'

'Maybe so, but it's difficult to accept that when the people who work for you are no different, no less desperate to survive, than I was when I was on the streets. They are doing what they must, with little hope of ever earning enough money that their situation might change.' She glared at him, her cheeks red. 'That is not something I find easy to stomach. Not when I have been in that place myself.'

'As have I,' William said, hating her distress but also a little disappointed by her naivety. 'But I clawed my way to where I am now, as have you. You have money because of the wealthy, Octavia. They were your clients and they paid you. I have money—'

'Off the backs of the poor. Do you not see how stricken and overwhelmed the people working here seem? Their eyes slitted against the fibres and dust, blood on fingers and knuckles. I only had to walk through the workshops to notice those things.'

He clenched his jaw. 'I am doing my best for them, I assure you. It's a hard life in the mills, but there are also people begging on the street, living a dozen and more to one room.' He stood and stalked to the office window, his heart beating fast as he stared towards the workroom before abruptly turning. 'I am not a slave driver, Octavia. Nor am I a mill owner who expects his workers to toil when they are sick or exhausted. I do all I can to ensure that no one here gets to either of those points without my overseers or myself noticing it.' He fisted his hands in his trouser pockets. 'I thought you had a good idea of the intensity of mill work. Of what it takes to produce the cotton that is becoming the backbone of this country's success.'

She stared at him before the fire in her eyes slowly lessened. 'Maybe in the back of my mind, in the depths of my foolishness, I had imagined something... less harsh. Less merciless.'

'And you have placed the blame of your preconceptions at my door?'

'Not at all,' she said, her gaze once again hardening. 'I don't blame anyone for my failings but myself. But despite my reading and the meetings I attended with you, the accounts I listened to were most certainly made by the men profiting from this business, not the workers. Just as the accounts given to people about the enjoyment of brothels is shared by the men who use them, not by the whores who work there.'

The strike was quick and deep. 'You think I am like that? A man who only relays the aspects of his business that he gets to enjoy?'

She looked away from him towards the window. 'No. No, I don't.'

'Then why say—'

'Because I'm afraid, William.' She snapped her gaze to his. 'Afraid of my decision to come here. Of what it is I wanted to make happen. How I wanted my life to change and grow and improve.' She stood and walked towards him. 'Come with me.'

She opened the office door and led him onto the platform. 'When I look at these people – these young men, women and children – I realise that, once again, I had built up a selfish ideal in my mind. Something that served *me*. That gave me the courage and reason to leave Bath and start anew somewhere else.' She shook her head, her shoulders dropping. 'And because of that, I realise it is wrong of me to confront you when I really know nothing. A few books, reading and research are not enough to justify my outburst.' She faced him, her gaze regretful. 'I'm sorry.'

He briefly dropped his chin, despising her obvious despair. 'Apology accepted. It's going to take a long time before you fully understand all that happens here. You do know that?'

'Yes.' She looked away from him. 'At least, I do now.'

Fear pulsed inside of him. Yes, he was disappointed she was not as excited about his enterprise as he'd hoped. Yes, he was fearful she was not quite the woman he thought her to be but... he still wanted her. If she had doubts about what she had seen thus far, she could easily leave, return to Bath and he truly did not want that.

He followed her gaze across the workroom as he gripped the railing. 'There are sides to my enterprise that are ugly. I cannot deny that.'

'And you clearly know the same is true of prostitution.'

He drew in a shaky breath, slowly released it. 'I shouldn't have referred to that before. I'm sorry.'

Over and over again, she had told him how she wished to leave her life as a whore behind. That having faced some of the worst men in society, she was ready to move on. Such a life had made her strong and fearless, but he had also assumed it would have made her a realist too.

Uneasy, William faced her. 'Do you wish to leave? I won't stop you if that is what you want.'

Her brows rose, her beautiful eyes widening with disbelief. 'You really think me so weak that a shock or two will lead me to flee? Turn away from what I have seen, what has moved and angered me and return to a place of safety?' She huffed a laugh and faced the workshop floor once more. 'Oh, how much more we must learn before we really know one another, William.'

Unable to bear looking into her eyes lest he saw disappointment or even disgust, he forced himself to look at the room's activity as though for the very first time.

The sight was far from pretty.

Could he really continue in his wish that he and Octavia marry one day? God only knew what his parents and sisters would make of her forthrightness, her stamina and steel. Traits that he loved about her could easily be misjudged and condemned. But surely not by his family? Not by the people who had raised him to face adversity head-on?

He had so fervently insisted to his family that his work would lead to their higher standing in the community, riches and prosperity for all. Before Octavia, a faraway plan had lingered in his consciousness that he would one day marry a well-connected woman, raising his status in society, maybe even presenting their daughter at court and a having a son who would become his protégé.

Now he saw and loved a woman who was once a prostitute. A woman he refused to forsake or lose, no matter what.

'William?' Her fingers curled around his forearm but still he could not look at her. She sighed. 'I suspect I have seen far from the worst of what goes on in your mills, yet that merely makes me all the more determined to see more. I have no wish to leave. Will you please look at me?'

He briefly closed his eyes. He had purposely chosen to first show her the mill that had experienced the fewest problems, accidents and sickness of late. Hoping that, once she was settled in his home and life, she would be impressed and interested enough that he might go on to show her his two other mills, where discord arose more often.

William looked at her and time stood still. The cacophony of noise, yelling, shouting and machinery drifted into silence until it was just him and her standing there, looking into each other's eyes.

Could it be that Octavia was no more certain of what lay in their future than he? Could this wonderful woman who seemed so sure of everything she did and said was not the person he had put on a pedestal but, instead, a person who had all the flaws and apprehensions of any human?

He swallowed against the dryness in his throat. 'Octavia—'

'This isn't the worst of it, is it? What I have seen here today, what I saw when we travelled to your home? There is more, isn't there?'

He opened his mouth, words of protest battling on his tongue. He would not lie to her. 'Yes.'

She stared into his eyes before slipping her hand from his arm and giving a curt nod. 'Then I shall see it all.'

He stood straighter, determined that his love for her would not override the common sense that had held him strong through every decision he had made for his family, his business, his entire life. His family's wellbeing would remain a top priority forever and he had to be certain that Octavia was the woman he wanted – needed – or else regret it for the rest of his life.

'And if you continue to hate what you see?'

'Then I either come to terms with it or do all I can to improve it.' She smiled softly, her eyes on his. 'As I suspect you do every day.'

His gaze dropped to her mouth, to the lips he would never tire of tasting before he looked at the chocolate-brown hair he would never tire of touching. Hope once again burned inside of him. 'Good.'

'But tomorrow, I think my efforts should be concentrated at home.'

'Home?' *Does she mean Bath?*

'Yes, if I am to remain here...' Her eyes glittered with the mischief he loved so very much. 'I think it imperative I make some headway into the affections of your staff, don't you?'

37

Making headway with William's staff had fallen to the wayside when Octavia had returned home to find Mrs Gaskell, Mr Foley and the other staff running around making mad-dash preparations for that evening's meal.

Three hours later, Octavia stood in her bedroom, her stomach jumping with nerves as she critically assessed the dress she had selected to wear tonight – according to young Ada, Octavia looked like a duchess. Admittedly, the emerald-green velvet dress edged with black at the skirt's hem and cuffs was one of her most elegant. And she hoped the set of matching jet necklace and earrings added enough illusion of wealth that William's family would have no possible reason to suspect her a prostitute – or former prostitute.

There was a discreet knock at the door and Octavia drew in a deep breath, planted on a smile and turned, instinctively knowing William stood on the other side. 'Come in.'

He strode into the room, looking good enough to eat in a black dinner suit with white shirt and tie, his eyes bright and his smile wide. Desire pulled treacherously at her core even though she was still a little mad with him after their discussions at the mill.

'You look incredible,' he said, stopping in front of her and kissing her cheek.

'Thank you. You look very nice, too.'

He winked, sending a flutter through her stomach. 'They are here. Their carriage just pulled up outside.'

'What?' Octavia's admiration of his handsome looks was obliterated by a surge of panic. 'Your parents and your sisters? All of them? But they are early.'

'No doubt because they are desperately keen to meet you.' He stepped back, his admiring gaze grazing over her from head to toe. 'You are going to knock them dead. Trust me. Come.' He offered her his arm. 'We will go down together.'

As they moved towards the door, Octavia tightened her grip on his arm. 'William?'

He stopped, his hazel eyes concerned. 'Yes?'

'I'm... Are you sure about this?'

'About you meeting my family? Of course.'

'I mean about how we are deceiving them.'

'We have no other choice if you are to remain here with me, in my house. I want to keep up my side of our bargain and this is the best way forward if we are to safeguard our reputations.'

A whisper of inexplicable hurt passed through her that he could still be so entirely logical when everything was no longer so easy for her. The day had thrown more and more light on how much she would have to stomach in business and in life if she was to succeed and make the money she desired.

She forced her shoulders back and held his gaze. 'Yes, you're right. We must do what we have to.'

'They will be so pleased I am engaged that any other reason why you might be here will be ignored, believe me. You don't have to do anything more than be your usual wonderful self.' He smiled, his gaze warm. 'I promise that will be enough.'

Octavia forced as much authority into her voice as she could muster. 'Maybe so, but our talk today opened new realisations for us both. Me of my naivety that business is terribly tough sometimes. And you—'

He blew out a heavy, almost frustrated breath. 'We cannot return to this now. My parents are here. Please, Octavia. Enough.'

Octavia's heart quickened with annoyance as she rolled her lips tightly together, her eyes narrowed. How dare he speak to her as though she was little more than an ornament with which to dazzle his family!

'Let us get through this evening,' he said, quietly. 'And then, later, we will talk. You're right, we need to rethink what we want to do going forwards, but please, tonight be my loving fiancée, Octavia. That's all I ask.'

What was he saying? That if she just went through with this final charade, then they would devise an explanation of a necessary and unexpected separation so that she could leave Manchester if that was what she wanted?

Anger and hurt simmered deep in her stomach as tears burned the backs of her eyes, but she held firm. 'Fine, I will act as you wish tonight,' she said, firmly. 'Then we talk.'

With her arm linked in his, they walked downstairs.

Octavia held her head high and the smile she had perfected at Carson Street was welded in place, despite her heart feeling as heavy as clay and her confidence wavering horribly.

But as they descended the stairs and she met the stares of William's mother, then his father and finally his sisters, she forced her best play-acting skills to the fore for their sake more than her own. They looked at her with such hope, such friendliness, such kindness... How was she to disappoint them? She could not and would not think how they would feel upon learning of her and William's break-up whether that be tomorrow or weeks from now.

Before she could even think of something to say in greeting, Mrs Rose rushed forward, her kindly eyes – so much like her son's – glinting with tears of happiness. 'Oh, my dear, you are extraordinarily beautiful.' She laughed, taking Octavia's hand and easing her from William's grasp. 'William said you were pretty, but the boy clearly has no idea of prettiness versus exquisite beauty.'

'Thank you, Mrs Rose.' Octavia smiled. 'You are too kind.'

'Not at all. Come, let us get seated, shall we?'

'Mother—'

'Come along, William, your fiancée and I know the way, do we not, dear?'

Octavia couldn't help but smile at the distress on William's face and the satisfied, amused look of his sisters behind him. Clearly, Mrs Rose was a force to be reckoned with when it came to her children's happiness and, for now, her focus was entirely on her son's... seemingly to his sisters' delight.

The meal passed with much laughter and amusement on Octavia's part as William's family regaled her with stories of him as a child and adolescent, his success barely mentioned even though his parents' pride in him lit their eyes.

It was almost as though his business acumen and prowess were applauded but it was not that which made his family so very proud of the young, impoverished boy who grew up to be a wealthy, caring and dynamic businessman.

That came from his care for his family, his quiet modesty and, Octavia learned, his goal of building an enterprise that did everything it could to drive forward better opportunities and care for its employees. Shame writhed inside her that she had so vehemently scolded and judged him without allowing the time to find out what lingered beneath the surface of what she had seen at his mill.

'So, Miss Marshall...' William's father's voice boomed across the table as he leaned back in his chair, his ample stomach stretching the buttons of his waistcoat. 'You have been brave enough to take on my only son. I don't know whether to congratulate you or warn you, but either way, William will ensure you are cared for and loved for the rest of your days – I can promise you that.'

Octavia dipped her eyes to the table as heat rose in her cheeks. Oh, how she deceived him! If only his father's sentiment were true... She lifted her gaze. 'As I will love and care for him, Mr Rose.' She glanced across the table at William.

The way he looked at her seared across the table and deep into her heart.

His eyes were filled with genuine love; there could be no mistaking it and Octavia drew in a steadying breath. She could not afford to believe his feelings were still steadfast when she had voiced so much criticism, was still so filled with horror about certain aspects of his life. Moreover, his request that they talk had not been voiced in tenderness. Of that much, she was certain.

Mrs Gaskell and Foley approached the table to clear the dessert dishes and plates and William stood. 'Let's go into the drawing room. We can have an after-dinner drink.'

The party rose from the table and walked upstairs to the drawing room. As Octavia entered the room behind William's parents, he slid her a wink of encouragement. Smiling, she silently congratulated herself on getting through the meal relatively unscathed when Elsa, the elder of William's two sisters, gently touched her elbow.

'Miss Marshall?'

Octavia turned, trying to decipher the inclination behind the cool yet pleasant look in Elsa's eyes. She smiled.

'Would you walk with me? I thought we could take a stroll around the room while William prepares the drinks.'

'Of course.' Octavia's smile strained as Elsa slid her hand into the crook of her elbow.

They walked in silence for a few steps, the gazes of William and his family almost palpable as they burned into them. Doing her best to appear relaxed, Octavia smiled softly, her gaze drifting about the room with feigned interest.

'So,' Elsa said, so quietly Octavia wasn't sure at first if she had spoken. 'I'm not sure that my parents do, but I see all too clearly what is going on between you and my brother, Miss Marshall, and I'm not sure how long you think you will be able to keep up the charade.'

Octavia swallowed, her heart picking up speed. 'What do you mean?'

'I have always had an interest in people's thoughts and feelings. Their reactions to situations and to others who might be in their company. In fact, I have become increasingly skilled at reading people. William, in particular.'

Octavia glanced uneasily towards William where he stood at the drinks cabinet with his father, both laughing and smiling as the older man clapped his hand onto William's shoulder. 'And?'

'And I have surmised that things are not as you and he claim them to be. For one, this is the first time we have met you, yet you are engaged to my brother. A man who values his family above everything else. So his complete failure to even so much as mention you to us during your courtship speaks volumes.'

Octavia stared at her before looking away, heat rising over her neck. If Elsa suspected there was an element of convenience to the engagement, which for Octavia there no longer was, she could cause untold trouble and upset...

'I... wanted William to tell you and your parents about our courtship weeks ago, but instead he wrote to tell you about me just before we came here, insisting it would be a nice surprise to have me arrive in Manchester with him.'

'I see. And what of the speculation your sudden appearance is bound to evoke from his few friends and the neighbours?' Elsa protruded her bottom lip but her eyes sparkled with amusement as she looked at Octavia. 'I can't say he's ever done anything so entirely reckless before.'

Octavia raised her eyebrows. 'Getting engaged is reckless? I'm not sure William sees it that way.'

'It is most certainly reckless if the engagement ruffles feathers or in any way suggests you accepted his proposal for something other than love.' Elsa studied Octavia before she looked towards William. 'Not that it is unusual for women to accept marriage for money, of course.'

The heat from Octavia's neck leapt into her cheeks. Indignant, she struggled to keep her face relaxed as they continued to walk. 'I do not need William's money. In fact, I was hesitant in accepting his proposal because I am more than aware it is me who will lose *my* money once we are wed.'

A hint of satisfaction lit Elsa's eyes. 'Well, that is most gratifying to hear, Miss Marshall. Most gratifying, indeed. But you do not strike me as a woman who would be content as little more than an added necessity to William's life.'

'Never,' Octavia said, firmly. 'In fact, I am not inclined to allow anyone to use me as a convenience or decoration, including your brother.'

Elsa grinned as she drew Octavia to stop at the window, purposefully facing out into the darkened driveway. 'Your offence pleases me,' she said softly. 'I would hate to think my probing has been in vain. At least now I know I am entirely right about the authenticity of William's feelings for you and yours for him. Otherwise, I might have had to box his ears a little first and then yours.'

'What do—'

'For all William's secrecy about bringing you here, for all the rapidity of your engagement, my brother is completely and profoundly in love with you, Miss Marshall.' Elsa grinned. 'And that pleases me more than anything. I just had to tease a little truth from you about your feelings too. I am beyond happy that you will clearly meet William as an equal... in every way. At first, I feared my brother had fallen hopelessly in love but you were not as invested as he. I see now, that is not the case at all.'

Octavia opened her mouth to say something – anything – but nothing came into her mind, only her heart. She looked across the room and William met her gaze, his brow furrowed and his eyes dark with concern.

She smiled and his eyes immediately brightened, his face relaxing and, in that moment, Octavia knew their love was no longer a charade to anyone. Including her...

38

'And then of course, with Nancy being Nancy, she ended up walloping the poor lad just as he leaned in to kiss her cheek!'

William smiled, thoroughly enjoying Octavia's story and the look of delight and love in her eyes as she spoke about her friend. His parents and sisters had left about an hour before and now he and Octavia were enjoying a glass of wine – or two. Seeing her so happy, so ridiculously and heart-rendingly beautiful, he was loath to raise the topic of how, when the time came, they would announce their broken engagement – especially now that his family had embraced her so emphatically.

He loved her but would also accept losing her if the dark side of his world was too much for her to shoulder. He had spent too many years, too much blood, sweat and tears to forgo his ambitions now – even for love.

He put down his glass, his smile dissolving. 'Octavia, we should talk.'

The happiness seeped from her gaze. 'Yes, I have things I need to say to you, too.' She dabbed her napkin to the corners of her mouth. 'Why don't you go first?'

A horrible, unwelcome tension shrouded the room, exacerbated by the way it had rung with her laughter just a few moments before.

Leaning back in his chair, William forced his gaze to remain on Octavia's. 'I know you have found a lot of what you have seen in the area and at my mill shocking, disconcerting, maybe even horrifying, but this is life in a growing city and it is life in a factory. I hate that you have been so upset and disappointed by what you've seen but, as much as I'd like to change things, I cannot do so overnight. So...' He exhaled a shaky breath, a horrible slash searing his heart. 'If you wish to go, then we—'

'I was in a bookshop today and there were some gentlemen there talking about you. Talking about a little girl whose fingers had been crushed, a woman who had lost her arm.'

Even though it was inevitable that people – strangers – spoke about and judged him, shame ignited his anger. 'I see.'

'As do I.' She lifted her chin, her gaze steady. 'Maybe I should not have judged you so quickly, but I do think it's barbaric that these things are going on... and in your mills no less.'

Defensiveness rose inside him and he clenched his jaw. 'You do not understand what I am saying at all.'

'I understand perfectly. Whatever your practices, they require improvement.'

His immediate reaction was to retort in anger, but he refrained, his heart hammering. He sensed more to her words than care or disgust. 'What do you want me to say, Octavia? The industry is tough. It is hard work and labour of such severity that most would not withstand it for any amount of time, but my workers are strong, willing, and understand that—'

'If they do not work, their families will die. I'm sorry, William, but as hard and real as that truth might be, I cannot just stand aside and condone it.'

He squeezed his eyes shut, controlling the urge to grab her shoulders, make her understand and not look at him as though the blame for the country's poverty and struggles lay with him.

'The wealth of Great Britain will inevitably mean growing opportunities for all.' He opened his eyes, pinned her with a stare. 'Yes, industry can be brutal, but you benefit from cheap cotton as much as anyone else, do you not? Your linens and handkerchiefs, cloths and garments, they are all made by those labouring for me and others like me.' He stood and pushed his hand into his hair. He stared at her before snatching his gaze away, choosing to pace back and forth rather than look at her. 'You did not grow up as I did, Octavia. You were born into a life where your family depended on servitude, whereas I came from poverty and know what it is to live and work like the young who work for me.' He stopped and faced her. 'I will never ignore how they live and struggle. I am doing my utmost to ensure they are always in work. I will not accept judgement from you or anyone else.'

He had never known her be so quiet for so long. He held her gaze and she stared back at him, her cheeks flushed and her blue eyes burning with... anger? Shock? Fear?

It was impossible to tell, so William stood entirely still, feet firmly planted, his gaze unwavering on hers.

She drew her gaze from his to her wine glass and stared into its ruby depths before lifting it to her lips. She drank deep, her eyes meeting his over the rim before she lowered the glass to the table. 'I came here wanting to immerse myself in your business without fully thinking through what that might mean to my own integrity. But, as I have told you before, I don't want to go home. I want to stay here and prove to myself, prove to you – maybe even prove to my father – that I am made of stronger stuff than I realised.'

Relief whispered through him, diluting his anger. He released his held breath.

'But,' she continued, 'I meant it when I said you must show me everything. Not just what you determine to be as much as I can manage, but all of it.'

She stood and walked towards him, her eyes burning with passion and vitality as she grasped his hand. The contact sent a jolt of lust, desire and love through his chest. God, how he wanted her. Her courage, her passion, even her damned defiance suddenly ignited his arousal, making him long to kiss her, touch her, make love to her.

'If, after everything I have said and done since I have been here, you can't, or won't, involve me in absolutely everything, then...'

He dropped his gaze to her lips. 'You will have no choice but to return to Bath.'

'If it becomes clear that our reasons for uniting, for making the audacious decision for me to come here, were wrong and selfish, then yes.'

'That won't happen.'

Tears glistened in her eyes, her passion palpable. 'I cannot waste any more of my life worrying if I am doing the right thing. If I am being selfish. Being ashamed when I make a wilful turn or that I have sold myself out of necessity.'

The sudden pain and fear in her eyes were heart-rending. 'Octavia.' He gripped her fingers. 'You have no reason—'

'I have every reason. Life is short, William, and the things I have done, the things that have been done to me, cannot be changed, but *I've* changed.' She looked deep into his eyes. 'It is not enough for me to be here and in love with you. I have to know that my life will one day count for something. That I did good in this world.'

He stared at her, probably loving her more than ever in that moment, but also feeling like the devil. The time had come for brutal honesty before one, or both, of them became so entangled in what they dreamed – rather than what was real – that each would be left unhappy, unfulfilled, and possibly married to someone they had grown to wholly resent. As she had to accept the darkness, he had to accept she was a human being with flaws and imperfections just the same as he.

'You're right. I will show you everything. I will answer your questions, let you talk to whomever you please, see my books... whatever you wish. I truly want to give and teach you all that you imagined when you came here.' He raised her fingers and pressed a kiss to her knuckles. 'But if you are to remain here, you will have to accept the darker side of the cotton industry. If you think you can do that, then I will strive to give you all that you want. Do everything in my power so that you are happy in Manchester... happy to be with me.'

The silence pressed down on him until all William heard was his own heartbeat.

He had allowed himself to fall so deeply in love that he believed theirs to be a true meeting of hearts. A coming together of two people who loved, cared and wanted to do so much for one another. He had to believe that was true because he had never loved a woman as he did her, a woman so strong, who proved her bravery and defiance in every word and challenge to him. That was the partner he had longed for and looked for his entire life and he had finally found her. If he lost Octavia now, it was entirely possible he would never find anyone like her ever again.

'I want to marry you, Octavia,' he said quietly. 'I want you to bear my children and be happy here. I want you to love and understand my business and be there for me to consult, discuss and decide with.' His heart lifted as her gaze softened. 'I want *you* more than anything in the world.'

Leaning forward, she dropped her gaze to his mouth before ever so gently brushing her lips to his. 'And I want you, too.'

He smiled, relief washing through him.

39

Octavia stared at William as he slept beside her, his head sharing her pillow, his legs entwined with hers. Having to do their utmost to avoid his staff hearing or suspecting their love-making, they had made love like illicit lovers... or maybe a whore and a cull, she couldn't be sure. Hidden. Secret. Shameful.

And now the flames of their passion had died down, Octavia was left wanting.

Wanting reassurance, a promise that she would not regret giving up her life in Bath and coming to Manchester – that, somehow, she would manage to accept William's life and business, despite the sickness and doubt that continued to coil in her stomach.

She had shown such cowardice yesterday evening by asking him to take her to bed. Resorted to what she knew best as a way of averting his attention from her vulnerability and insecurity. She had used seduction as a decoy – a distraction – so that she might gain the upper hand and exert her power. More than that, to have him believe her strong and resolute in her decision to stay in Manchester and make a life here. That she trusted him completely.

She gazed towards the window.

The winter's morning light was still at least an hour away, but she could hear the soft twittering of birds in the eaves, indicating dawn would arrive before long. Most maids who worked in grand houses were expected to have the home's fires lit by five or six in the morning. All too soon young Ada would start her morning chores.

The end to her and William's time alone together ebbed ever closer.

Yet Octavia did not want William to wake until she had found her inner strength again and was able to face him with a confident smile, have him believe all was well. He had agreed that she could see all aspects of his business, no matter how upsetting they might be. She, in turn, had agreed that she would endeavour to withhold any emotional reaction and accept that some of business's worst moral problems were not always immediately solvable.

But it wasn't just her possible inability to embrace William's work and home worrying her. It was that, even now, as she lay in his arms, she worried she would not come to feel either the respectability or the security she craved.

She had only been here a matter of days, but already she feared that Manchester would not deliver the freedom and growth she had so desperately anticipated. Worse, she had no doubt of what potentially blinded her, of what she had allowed to envelop her in false hope.

Her need to be successful, to harness her inner dream of being seen as confident and driven by those around her, had come to consume her. Her move to Manchester had acted as a catalyst that would somehow, someday, mean she could stand tall and proud in the face of critics should it ever be revealed what she had done in order to survive.

She did not want to live in shame and secrecy for the rest of her life, hiding her whoring and begging. Why should she when her deeds had led to her being alive today to tell the tale? Yet now, more than ever, she was terrified of failing in her endeavours both financially and emotionally. For if she failed now when opportunity lay all around her, surely she was destined to always fail?

Octavia closed her eyes.

Suddenly it felt that the only way to truly rid her conscience of all she had done would be for her and William to marry. Surely then, once she was the respectable Mrs William Rose, the melancholy and fear striking deep in her heart would vanish. As would the mocking face of her father, his expression twisted with scorn at the depth of her dishonourable way of life.

Warm tears slipped from beneath her closed lids just as William stirred beside her.

She snapped her eyes open to find him watching her, his brilliant blue gaze concerned. 'Why do you cry, my love?'

'I'm just so happy,' she lied, hastily wiping her cheeks and forcing a smile. 'That is all.'

His frown deepened. 'The truth, Octavia. Please.'

Her disgrace intensified as she stared into his eyes. How was it he could see her so clearly when so many others had looked at her and saw only what she allowed them to see? 'I want us to marry as soon as possible.'

His gaze travelled over her face, her lips, before he slipped his arm from beneath her neck and pushed back the covers. Octavia's heart beat faster as he swung his feet to the floor and leaned his forearms onto his thighs, his head bowed.

'Why the sudden urgency?' he asked quietly.

'My feelings have deepened for you, become stronger since I came here.' Her words and emotions clogged painfully in her throat. 'My wish to embrace your work and home more profound. That is all the proof I need to know I belong here... with you. Why delay in making our union permanent?'

'And your fears about your money becoming mine? They have vanished?'

Octavia swallowed. That fear remained rife in her consciousness.

He glanced at her. 'As I thought. Plus, I am yet to show you all of my factories. What if you see things there that you want no part of? I thought that next step had been agreed between us.' He turned his head and spoke over his shoulder. 'When I said I wish us to be married, I meant in time. Not immediately.'

Sickness unfurled in her stomach. He spoke so quietly, his tone guarded. Had he had doubts through the night? Changed his mind about wanting her for his wife just when she had so vehemently come to want him for her husband? Her fingers itched to reach for him, to touch his smooth skin, feel his hard muscles beneath her fingers.

He shifted on the bed and faced her, his jaw tight. 'Tell me the truth of all you are feeling right now. In this new light of day.'

So, he has had doubts, too. 'I love you, William.'

'As I do you, but what is it that sticks so sorely in your throat that you cannot share it with me?'

Words flailed on her tongue until she dropped her chin to her chest, a treacherous tear falling from her lashes. 'I just wanted us to marry.'

'Why?'

'Because...' She inhaled a shaky breath, slowly released it as his gaze bored into hers. 'I still feel my father's judgement despite not having seen him for years. I know he would look at my being here, in your bed, as little more than further evidence that I am no better than the whore I have been these past years. No different than if he had found me at Carson Street. Our lying together so secretly last night...' She shook her head. 'It made me feel as though I am your mistress despite our engagement. If I am to be your true partner, I need us to marry.'

He slipped beneath the covers and drew her into his arms. She laid her head on his chest, his embrace so comforting, her relief escaped her lips on a sigh, her shoulders lowering.

'There is more to your angst than the need to be married, Octavia.'

'There isn't.' She shook her head. 'That is what I need. To know we are husband and wife.'

'And you think a wedding will destroy the demons in your heart and mind? The demon who takes the form of your father's image whenever you sleep?'

She closed her eyes. 'It is not every time I sleep.'

'I have slept with you a number of times now and every time you have shaken in your slumber, whimpered and muttered incoherently.' He touched his finger to her chin, lifting her eyes to his. 'And then you cry.'

Octavia's heart hammered to see such deep fury in his eyes. No sympathy or care. Just an innate fury that was undoubtedly directed at her father. A man he had never met.

She dropped her gaze. 'Maybe marrying you wouldn't completely destroy the pain and doubt my father has provoked in me, but it would certainly help.'

'This urgency to marry has nothing to do with your father. This is about something else. Something about yourself that you are afraid to face and make peace with.'

Her desperation became humiliation, and she lifted her chin

from his fingers, inched away from him. 'If you believe that and think we should wait, then there is nothing more to say. I will deal with my fears as I always have.'

'How?'

'By swallowing my pride and biding my time. By believing I need rely on nobody but myself.'

A muscle flexed in his jaw, his gaze hard.

Octavia's heart pounded, self-loathing rippling through her. Why did she always resort to such superior behaviour when things were not going along as she wanted?

He slowly rose from the bed. 'I should return to my own room before Ada awakes. We will talk more later.'

'What?'

'I'm leaving. I think it for the best.'

'But we cannot just leave this conversation undone.' Octavia grasped his arm as he neared, her bravado crumbling. 'Please, William, I love you. Let us be married and start living the life we both want.'

He pushed his legs into his trousers, reached for his shirt. 'I will marry you, Octavia. But not until you love yourself as much as you claim to love me.' He finished buttoning his shirt and then came towards her, cupping her jaw in his hands. 'Your past would not still affect you like this if you loved yourself as I love you. I can't marry you until that is no longer true.'

'But how am I to do that when—'

'Do you really believe that once we are married you will be truly happy?'

'Yes.'

He shook his head, a vehemence in his eyes Octavia could not understand, before he picked up his boots from beside the bed. 'Then I will not marry you, Octavia. Not while you believe that I can heal all that aches and hurts inside of you by putting a band of gold upon your finger.'

Pain slashed her heart as his every word stabbed inside of her. Everything he said was true, but what was she to do to cure her pain, her anguish and self-loathing other than by embracing all she had done? Of telling people openly and honestly?

'That's not fair,' she said. 'You once believed a fake marriage to me would solve your problems, did you not?'

'And that's what you want?' he demanded. 'A fake marriage where you are not wed to a man who is your equal but a man who is little more than your route to respectability?'

'No, of course not.' She shook her head, frustrated that her words were making things worse rather than better. 'I'm just saying—'

'That your want of me might be for reasons you have yet to accept.'

Tears pricked the backs of her eyes and she blinked them away. Why could he not hear her? 'William, please.'

'No.' He marched towards the door. 'We will speak later.'

The door closed behind him, and Octavia sank onto the bed, crossing her arms tightly around her. She loved William so much, yet it seemed her love was not enough for either of them. Maybe they would always need more...

But would she ever have any more to give?

40

William stood in the hallway and shrugged into his overcoat. The hour was barely seven o'clock, but he needed to leave the house, get far away from Octavia. Frustration continued to roll through him, no matter how hard he tried to calm himself.

How could she lay such unadulterated expectation on his shoulders? The pain in her eyes had been so profound, so heart-breakingly raw, if he had not known any better, he would have assumed she had lain not with him but with a cull last night. How in God's name was he supposed to heal a pain so deep? She had to at least meet him halfway in her recovery from all that she had been forced to endure over the years since she had fled from her father.

'Mr Rose, sir. Wherever are you going?' Mrs Gaskell emerged at the top of the steps leading from the kitchen. 'You have not eaten.' She widened her eyes. 'Nor shaven from the looks of it.'

'Something of urgency has arisen at one of the mills, I must go.' He reached for his hat. 'Tell Foley I am happy to walk this morning.'

'But there has been no post, sir. How did you hear of any urgency?'

He scowled at his housekeeper, who was equally wily and familiar with William's ways as his mother. 'Just believe things to be as I say they are, Mrs Gaskell. Please.'

Her cheeks flushed and she dipped her head. 'So I am to serve just Miss Marshall for breakfast? I see. Leave that with me, sir.'

He glanced at the oak staircase. 'Better still, ask her if she would like to take breakfast in her room this morning.'

Interest lit Mrs Gaskell's eyes as she followed his gaze towards the stairs. 'Has she taken ill in the night?' She faced him. 'Might you have already seen her this morning, sir?'

William swallowed, his annoyance rising. 'No, but as she is a guest in my home, and I wish to afford her every hospitality, I imagine breakfast in bed would be welcome.' He arched an eyebrow. 'Am I clear?'

She took another glance towards the stairs before meeting his gaze, with undisguised disapproval. 'Yes, sir.'

After grabbing his hat from the stand, William marched to the door.

Once outside, he breathed in the cold air with relish, welcoming its pinch against his cheeks. He strode along the gravelled pathway and out into the street, walking in the direction of town where his nearest mill stood within grassland not more than a mile away.

William stared resolutely ahead, almost oblivious to the street traders and mill workers who passed him, hurrying to their places of business with so much more vigour than William could muster that morning. Thoughts of Octavia, his family and marriage swam in his mind, his mill work not taking up any of the space it usually occupied.

Over and over again, his parents had warned him that if all he allowed to consume his time and mind was work and wealth, it would be to his detriment in the end. *Look for love, William. Find a woman to cherish and give you a family to have and hold. Show your heart to others, not your wealth...*

Well, that was what he had done with Octavia and now he understood that their marrying would not make her any happier than she'd been before she knew him. He could not do it. He would not marry her knowing she believed him the answer to the deep, unremitting pain inside of her. She had to forgive herself. Stand proud in her decisions.

His parents were wrong. Love was not the answer to happiness.

Falling in love, marrying someone you believed your equal, your soul mate, someone who understood you completely, would not guarantee a life of contentment. Security, ambition and innovation had always given him huge pleasure and satisfaction and would again if he could not find a way to have Octavia whole and healed.

Liar.

* * *

Half an hour later, William reached the huge entranceway to the mill and stormed forward, his boots crunching on the gravel. The familiar smoke and industry of the mill enveloped him, and he breathed a little easier. The clanging and banging, screeching and screaming of the machines echoed his footsteps as he made for his office.

Wisps of cotton filled the air like drifting snow, the workshop hot and stuffy. Men, women and children swiped their brows and pushed their hands into the base of their backs as they watched him walk by from beneath lowered lids.

William lifted his chin and marched forward, annoyed that none of the usual pride that filled him when he walked through his domain surfaced. Octavia's shock and revulsion at the things she had witnessed had shown in her eyes and expression more than once and it was that image that appeared in his mind's eye now.

He stalked up the iron steps to his office and slammed the door.

Before he even had time to remove his coat, there was a firm knock on the door and one of his foremen entered. 'Good morning, sir.'

Hissing a curse, William took off his hat and began to unbutton his coat. 'Hastings, good morning.'

'I wanted to book some time in to sit down with you and go over this month's figures, sir.' He lifted the two ledgers in his hand. 'We are a couple of days past our usual catch-up.'

'Is there anything to worry about?' William sat at his desk and picked up a note atop a pile of paperwork left for him by his assistant. He scanned the request for his signature on several of the papers and looked at his foreman. 'Hastings?'

'Not so much of a problem, sir, but...' The foreman pulled out the seat on the other side of the desk and held the ledgers in his lap. 'Orders are coming in at such a rate the weavers are struggling to keep up. I think now is the time to increase working hours. Maybe decrease lunch breaks. It's well known that you like your workers to have ample—'

'No, absolutely not,' William said firmly. 'My regulations are in place for the workers' sake and the sake of my business. If needs be, we will take on more people. I refuse to allow my employees, no matter how much they might say they want the extra work, to labour themselves into the ground. I've seen it elsewhere, Hastings. People cannot work productively when they are exhausted.'

'But surely if we just offer a couple of extra hours a day to a select few?'

Octavia's anguished face came into William's mind again. 'No. Have a quiet word with a few of our best workers, with an offer of work to their family members, friends or whomever else they think up to the job. Then we'll see where we stand in a week or two.'

Hastings frowned, clearly disagreeing with William's thinking. 'If you're sure.'

'I am. This is my business, and I will run it how I see fit.' William stood and walked to the window, staring out over the workshop floor. 'Things need to be made more humane in our factories, not less, if this country is to truly flourish as the government claims it will.' He turned, pinned the foreman with a stare. 'Taking advantage of those less fortunate, those in dire straits, does not sit well in my conscience and it shouldn't in yours either.'

The other man stood. 'Well, whatever you are doing, you are doing something right. This month's profit is well up on where we were this time last year. Make no mistake, you are on the path to becoming a very wealthy man, Mr Rose. Even wealthier than you are already.'

William briefly closed his eyes, not wanting his foreman to see how his words pained him rather than pleased him. 'I will see you at three o'clock this afternoon to go over the books.'

'Right you are, sir.'

Hastings left the office, closing the door behind him, and

William watched him descend the steps, his gut churning with
unease and his thoughts about Octavia and what she was doing
right now.

41

Octavia heaved her bags from the bed to the floor and stood with her hands on her hips for a final look around William's guest room. Nausea coated her throat and her stomach twisted with doubt that leaving was the right thing to do – but what choice did she have? She had nothing more to give William than her honesty. Every hope she had for their future had crumbled when she realised that until she stood entirely on her own, she would never know if she was strong enough for anyone else.

And William deserved a wife who knew herself and loved who she was completely.

For now, she could not imagine herself ever being that blessed and her fear had been revealed to William in all its awful shame. She was a coward. She was selfish. All she cared about was her own self-preservation.

She could curse her father as much as the life she had adopted after she fled him. Every moment of his assault, every image of his face contorted in rage and grief, still haunted her. She had endured more abuse at her father's hands than anyone else's – even the culls she had lain with. How would William ever understand how much that humiliation had shaped who she was today? Her father's treatment of her was tattooed on her heart, a permanent reminder that the man who was meant to love her unconditionally, in truth hated her.

Swiping her cheeks, she took a final look about her, satisfied all her belongings were packed and ready to be taken downstairs once she had commandeered some help.

Opening the bedroom door, Octavia peered onto the landing.

Downstairs, footsteps and general hubbub sounded, revealing William's staff were diligently going about their duties. She regretted that she was about to disturb Mrs Gaskell when it was only really Arthur she had any need to bother – unless he had driven William to work. Why had she not considered how else she was to get to the station without Arthur taking her? Or maybe he was seeing to the horses somewhere and would be free to take her after all?

She took a deep breath in a bid to settle her nerves and walked downstairs, knowing she had no choice but to face William's staff and she would do so with confidence. They had no say in what she did or didn't do – and neither did William.

Once she reached the hallway, she walked as soundlessly as possible to the coat cupboard and extracted her outercoat and hat. She put them on and then stood still, listening. Fighting her treacherous smile at Mrs Gaskell's extraordinarily off-key singing, Octavia approached the dining room door.

She entered and cleared her throat. 'Good morning, Mrs Gaskell.'

'Oh, Miss Marshall.' The housekeeper spun around from where she stood dusting the windowsill. 'I didn't even hear the stairs creak. You're as quiet as a mouse.'

Octavia's stomach knotted with trepidation. 'I came to say

goodbye and ask if Arthur is available to take me to the train station. I'd walk, only I have a lot of luggage and I'm not entirely sure I wouldn't become lost.'

'I'm sorry, I'm not sure I understand.' Mrs Gaskell slowly put her rag in the basket next to her, fit to bursting with cleaning paraphernalia. 'You are leaving?'

Heat crept up Octavia's neck, but she lifted her chin. Nothing or no one would stop her from going now she was decided. 'I am.'

The housekeeper's brow furrowed, her brown eyes somewhat sceptical. 'And without Mr Rose's knowledge? Do you really think that is fair to the master when you and he are engaged to be married and he has shown you such kindness? Opened his home to you, had his staff tend to your needs, and given you every minute of spare attention he possibly can in his hugely busy life?'

Irritation mixed with pride and Octavia firmly held her gaze. 'I am still my own woman, Mrs Gaskell, and free to come and go as I please. Mr Rose is hardly keeping me here against my wishes and it is my wish to return to Bath. Now, if you would be so kind as to tell me where I can find Arth—'

There was a knock at the front door and Octavia froze.

Mrs Gaskell's eyes lit with triumph. 'If I could ask that you wait here just a minute, miss. I'd better answer the door.'

Octavia crossed her arms and stared at the ceiling, counting the seconds until she heard Mrs Gaskell exclaim happily at the sight of whomever was at the door. 'Oh, madam, come in, come in,' she cried. 'I'm sure Miss Marshall will appreciate a surprise visit from you this morning. Here, let me take your coat.'

Dread fell like lead into Octavia's stomach. Surprise visit? When she heard Elsa's soft murmurings, Octavia dropped her arms and shot her gaze around the room, looking for somewhere to hide. God above, what was she to do? Hide behind the sofa?

'Here she is,' Mrs Gaskell announced as she entered the room, Elsa behind her. 'You might want to relieve yourself of your hat and coat, Miss Marshall. The master's sister has come visiting.'

Octavia pulled back her shoulders and purposefully met Mrs Gaskell's gleeful gaze. 'I am quite all right, thank you. If you leave me and Elsa, I will explain that I was just about to make my departure.'

'Your departure?' Elsa frowned. 'Where are you going?'

Instead of answering her, Octavia stared at Mrs Gaskell until the housekeeper shot her a glare and reluctantly left the room, closing the door none too gently behind her.

'Has something happened, Miss Marshall? Where is William?'

Briefly closing her eyes, Octavia faced William's quite lovely sister. 'I'm afraid I am leaving. Things... William and I... We...'

Sympathy bloomed in Elsa's hazel eyes, so like her brother's. 'I see.' She walked across the room and took a seat in one of the two chairs in front of the fireplace. 'Please, won't you join me? Just for a moment?'

Octavia looked towards the door. She had two options. She either gathered her courage and faced Elsa's questions with honesty or she barrelled to the door and fled to the station without luggage or direction.

Deciding the first option might leave her with a modicum more dignity, Octavia sat alongside Elsa.

'You know, Miss Marshall, it was clear to me just how deeply you and my brother feel for one another at dinner last night but, as you are fleeing before you've even been here long enough to see your bed sheets changed, I assume your engagement is no more. Well, I think that is a shame, indeed.'

Octavia's mouth dried, but she refused to allow Elsa to see the success of her clipped admonishment. 'William and I had a long conversation,' Octavia said, looking the other woman directly in the eye. 'And we both know, deep in our hearts, that now is not the time for us to marry. Or even remain engaged. Whether that changes in the future, I do not know.'

'I see.'

Elsa's gaze lingered on Octavia's before she opened her bag and fingered through its contents before pulling out a leather wallet. Opening it, she withdrew what looked to be a well-thumbed ink sketch. Her mouth curved into a wistful smile as she studied it.

Curious, Octavia leaned forward in her chair. 'What's that?'

Elsa held it out. 'It's a sketch of me and my family when we were younger. Much younger.'

Octavia took the picture and an unexpected lump formed in her throat to see a beautifully drawn mother, father and two little girls, no older than six or seven dressed in little more than rags, their ill-fitting clothes torn and patched. The long street where they stood stretched into the distance. The dilapidated terrace houses on either side seemed to lean in, close enough to crush the young family in the foreground.

Yet each of William's kin smiled as though happy and content amid the squalor all around them.

Octavia swallowed. 'Where is William?'

'Working at a nearby mill. He wouldn't have been any older than eight or nine, but he persuaded someone to take him on regardless.' Pride rang in Elsa's voice, her eyes filled with adulation for her brother. 'This picture was drawn by a local artist. A man working for the paper was doing a piece on the city's poorest areas or something similar and asked Pa if he could sketch our picture for a penny or two.' She met Octavia's gaze, smiled wryly. 'He was hardly likely to say no, was he? Anyway, even at such a young age, William was determined to achieve all he set out to do. Make sure his family got out of the slums even if he had to break his back doing it.' She waved her hand, encompassing the dining room. 'And, as you can see, he did exactly that. Ma, Pa, me and my sister live in even better luxury these days than William and he wouldn't have it any other way.'

Words stuck in Octavia's throat. She did not need to be told how wonderful a man William was, how generous and kind. She knew that all too well.

'He worked his way up, and nearly to the bone,' Elsa continued. 'Until he was near-running someone else's mill. Bought that owner out, then another...' She shook her head, love burning in her eyes. 'The rest is history.'

Staring at the picture again, tears pricked Octavia's eyes. 'Why are you showing me this?'

'What do you feel when you look at it, Miss Marshall? What do you feel that you somehow shouldn't?'

Octavia looked closer at each of the smiling faces, the way the husband had one arm slung around the shoulders of his wife, his other hand clutching the hand of the eldest daughter. The mother holding the youngest girl tight to her side.

Octavia swallowed. 'Happiness... I see happiness.'

'Exactly. And it does not seem right, does it? All that filth and poverty surrounding us and you can still feel our happiness. Now, why would that be?'

'I don't know.'

'Because we were genuinely happy. We had each other to love and trust, no matter our difficulties, no matter our empty bellies or any illnesses we might suffer.'

Octavia slowly laid down the sketch, her heart aching with love and admiration for William's goodness. Why had she ever thought herself the right woman for him? She could never be this selfless, this concerned for others. 'It's a wonderful picture, but it is not enough to make me stay.'

'And who says I want you to? William deserves all of you or nothing at all.' Elsa laughed, her brown eyes amused. 'Your life is your own, Miss Marshall. It doesn't mean anything to me. The trouble is, if your life affects my brother's happiness...' Her smile dissolved. 'That is a different matter entirely.'

'You don't understand—'

'I understand more than you give me credit for and I'm not so blind that I cannot see you are here for something more than romance. Or that you and William becoming engaged in Bath, far away from here, happened because the pair of you initially had reasons to do so that had absolutely nothing to do with love.' She leaned back in her chair, her canny gaze pinning Octavia to her seat. 'But as soon as William wrote home about you, as soon as we read and reread the way he spoke about you, we knew he had fallen in love. Hook, line and sinker, whatever might have passed between you before then. So, the question is, Miss Marshall, do you really love *him* or was everything I surmised before entirely wrong?'

A rush of panic swept over Octavia and she abruptly stood, feeling like a rabbit caught in a trap.

Wringing her hands, she opened her mouth and closed it again before a frustrated growl rose in her throat. Mortified that she had made such an unseemly noise, she paced back and forth, her cheeks hot.

Elsa laughed. 'Is that your answer?'

Octavia shot her a glare. 'I shouldn't even have to answer such a question.'

'Why not? I think I've every right to ask. I love my brother, Miss Marshall, and there is little possibility that I will sit here and let you run away without first giving me a worthy explanation.'

'Fine. I love him.' Octavia planted her hands on her hips. 'But I do not feel about my family the way he feels about his. Last night I realised the relationship I have with my father still affects who I am today, and I have no idea when that is likely to change. William told me he cannot heal what happened to me and that I must look inside myself and...' Octavia pursed her lips together. 'It does not matter what else he said. I just need to go.'

'I see. So because William most likely knows you better than anyone else, you are running away without as much as a goodbye to the man you claim to love?'

'I've left him a note. It's on his bed.'

'A note...' Elsa protruded her bottom lip, her eyes flashing with annoyance as she gave a dismissive wave. 'Well, that's all right then.'

'I've had enough of this.' Octavia glared. 'I have no argument with you. Please, just let me leave and go on with your life as though I were never here.'

'You know, William hasn't a spiteful bone in his body and I suspect, deep down, you know he would never ask you to do anything he didn't believe in his heart was good for you. Am I right?'

Octavia's heart ached with a sudden want for William to walk through the door. He was such a good, good man. 'Yes. I know how good he is and that's why I can't—'

'Then all you need to do is trust him. William looks after everyone, and if you are at the top of his list, he will never, ever let you down or allow you to be hurt in any way.' Her gaze softened. 'Please, Miss Marshall, don't run away from him. Not like this.'

Indecision warred inside Octavia, her love for William telling her to stay; her common sense telling her to flee. Yet hadn't she found it in herself to trust Louisa and Nancy when she had been nothing but a street walker, taking culls in alleyways and doorways? Learned how to trust and love again, lean on others as she once had her parents? How could she not give the same devotion to William when she had money, means and the freedom to leave whenever she might choose? She was not reliant on him as she had been her father and Louisa. She needed nothing from William other than his heart.

'If you walk away now,' Elsa said quietly, 'you will regret it for the rest of your life. I can promise you that. You are enough for him, Miss Marshall. If he chose you, you must believe you are all that he wants.'

Octavia drew in a long breath, then shakily released it. *I am enough.*

The mantel clock ticked off the seconds as Octavia stood completely still, her heart steadily beating as possibility and hope swirled inside of her. Imaginings of her life with William and all they might do ran through her heart and mind, making her suddenly want to grab on to every beautiful moment.

An unexpected and wholly wonderful confidence swept through her and Octavia smiled, standing tall. 'I need to go to William at the mill.'

Elsa grinned. 'Indeed you do, Miss Marshall. Indeed, you do.'

42

William shoved the papers on his desk aside and dropped his head into his hands, scoring his fingers into his hair. It was barely noon. Yet, for the first time for as long as he could remember – possibly forever – he wanted to leave the mill and go home.

Every figure, every notation on the documents he was due to review and discuss with his overseer later that afternoon annoyed and frustrated him. The only person he wanted to talk over his problems and their possible solutions with was Octavia. Not because he believed her yet prepared to help with his current dilemmas when she still had so much to learn, but because she understood *him*. Understood how passionately he wanted to make his mills a place where families wished to work from generation to generation. Where the reputation of Rose Textiles was second to none for product, production and progression.

No matter how much he stressed his wish for change and improvement to his senior staff, blank incomprehension remained on their faces. He needed to take some momentous action. Maybe bring his weavers, workers and collectors into a meeting, promote them into the hierarchy where they could have a voice and ensure William understood every one of their issues and complaints.

He stood and walked to his office door, stepped onto the iron landing. Gripping the railing, he narrowed his eyes and scanned the workshop.

God, he wanted Octavia here. Standing beside him and seeing what he saw as he knew she eventually would. Never had he felt so understood by anyone outside of his family and there was no way on God's earth he would contemplate losing her. If the trauma of her father's violence still haunted her as much as it clearly did, then he would dig deep and find the patience and temerity to wait until she found the courage to heal those wounds.

He'd been wrong, arrogant, to insinuate she was alone in her struggle, that he would not help her. How could he know how it felt to lose a beloved mother and have a father you loved, and thought you knew, turn into someone unrecognisable? Someone capable of hurting you, heart, body and soul?

His parents could almost be deemed too loving, too caring. God above, they had enveloped Octavia in that love and care the moment they set eyes on her. In fact, their love and welcome could have risked being entirely overwhelming if anyone had been foolish enough to mention grandchildren to his mother...

Warmth rose in William's chest, and he returned to his office. He had to go home. Had to speak to Octavia. Tell her all would be well. He just needed her beside him – always.

He grabbed his coat and hat and put them on before sweeping up the papers from his desk. He hurried down the steps onto the workshop floor, scanning the busy, clamouring space for Hastings so he could tell him he would review the books at home and return later that day for a meeting about his decided way forward.

And that was when William saw her.

He stopped.

Despite the smoke and dust filling the air, Octavia's dark curls gleamed beneath her bright red hat, her smile wide as she said something that had the three grown men surrounding her looking at the floor or, if they were self-assured enough, directly at her, their lips curved in amusement, their gazes pitifully adoring – not that William could blame them.

What in God's name was she doing here? How did she even get here? Knowing Octavia, she would have had absolutely no qualms about boldly walking through Manchester's dark, grey streets with the same savvy she had walking the glorious, architectural streets of Bath. His stomach lurched. Just thinking about what might have happened to her raised the hairs at his nape.

The workers parted as he shouldered past them towards her. Octavia's smile dissolved as she intently listened to what one of his workers explained to her, his arm outstretched towards the mechanical loom beside him, the colour rising in his cheeks as he gesticulated. She nodded, her brow furrowing, her back straight.

William slowed his pace, mesmerised by her attention and keen interest until he stood less than three feet away from her turned back.

'And this is your wife?' she asked the man, turning with a smile to the woman standing a little away from her. 'How do you do, madam?'

Octavia held out her hand but the woman neither took it nor stepped forward, only nodded before dropping her gaze to the floor and then turning back to spooling the cotton she was working on. The amiable conversation suddenly drew quiet as one by one the workers looked past Octavia to William. His heart sank to see how quickly the delight and relaxation in their faces was replaced with sombreness and concentration as they all returned to their tasks, leaving Octavia standing adrift in a snowstorm of floating cotton.

She turned. 'William.'

He walked forward and took her hand, not caring that his workers saw their touch or the love that was undoubtedly etched on his face. 'What are you doing here?'

'I came to find you, of course.' Her gaze drifted over his face. 'I have much to learn, do I not?'

He smiled, every part of him wanting to take her in his arms and kiss her. 'You do.'

'And not just about mill work, I fear.' She stepped closer and stole her hand into the crook of his elbow, urging him in the direction of his office. 'I have been forced to see the error of my ways by your somewhat loyal sister.'

The soft amusement and, dare he think it, fondness in her tone cheered William more than he could say.

'Might I ask which one?'

'Elsa.'

'Ah.'

He smiled. If she liked Elsa, the rest of his family would be no problem whatsoever. Elsa was a force of her own making.

They walked to his office and William shut and locked the door, not wanting anything or anyone to disturb them. There was so much he had to say to her and there was no possible way he could contain his words until they returned home.

'I am so glad you are here,' he said, as she stared at him with her wide, glorious blue eyes – happy eyes. 'After this morning, I thought you might take it upon yourself to leave. Go back to Bath. I'm so glad you—'

'I did take it upon myself to do just that. My bags were packed and waiting in my room.' She put her purse on his desk. 'And I am none too pleased how well you know me, William Rose. I have no idea how you are so intuitive about me, your staff, your workers...' Her gaze softened. 'Everyone.'

A weight lay heavy in the pit of his stomach. To think of her coming so very close to leaving... 'And Elsa changed your mind?'

'No, not just Elsa.' She took his hand and led him into a darkened corner of his office as far away from the window as possible. She raised her hand to his cheek. 'Your entire family changed my mind.'

'My entire family?' He shot his gaze towards the door as though his parents and sisters might suddenly appear. 'What do you mean? Did they all come to the house?'

'No.' She laughed. 'Elsa showed me an old sketch of them. They were happy, William. A true family in every sense, and it's clear you are still a happy family all these years later.' She softly brushed her lips to his. 'That is what I have been looking for. I want to feel as your family do. I want a husband I can stand beside in good times and bad and know everything will be all right, that he will never betray or turn me away.'

'Octavia, you have to believe that I would never—'

She put her finger gently to his lips, her eyes shining with happiness. 'I know you'll never hurt me. I believe that deep in my heart. I want to work and live beside you to make your business just how you envision. I want to learn the tasks and jobs of your mill workers and your staff at home. I want to be such a part of your life that it will lead me to forget all the hurt that has scarred me until I am free and clean again.'

'And I want that, too. More than anything. I wish I could heal you, I really do.' He brushed a stray curl from her temple, praying she heard him. 'But all I can do is help in any way I can so that you are able to heal yourself and be free of past hurts. It's the only way.'

'I know that now. Not from what you or even Elsa said.' She smiled, wiped the tears from her eyes with trembling fingers. 'I realised the two people who have been side by side with me for months taught me that a long time ago, if I'd had the heart and mind to listen.'

He dropped his shoulders. Of course... 'Louisa and Nancy.'

She nodded. 'We have come so far together, have had so much happen to us that I neglected to see, to truly understand, all that they are to me. All they have done to shape me into the woman standing before you today.'

'And I have every confidence you are no less of a strength and influence to them.'

'I hope so, but the point is, I love you as Louisa loves Jacob and Nancy loves Francis. That is something to be celebrated, not be afraid of, not to withhold or fight against.' She wrapped her arms around him, her gaze boring into his. 'I love you, William. I want to start our life together, right here, right now.'

All the love and passion he felt for her swept through him and William covered Octavia's mouth with his, seeking her strength and solace to soothe the tentative fear of losing her that had haunted him all day. Their tongues teased and their lips bruised until he pulled back and drowned in her delighted eyes.

Smoothing his hands down her body to her waist, William pulled her close. 'I will spend the rest of my life making you happy. Mills or no mills, grand house or hovel.'

'You'd better.' She smiled. 'But can I take the mills and grand house over the no mills and hovel?'

He laughed and kissed her again.

EPILOGUE
CHRISTMAS EVE, BATH

Octavia took William's hand as she stepped from the carriage onto the pavement outside the Carson Street house, Nancy's laughter ringing loudly as she clamoured out behind Octavia and straight into Francis's arms. He planted her on the ground with a firm kiss.

'You are a scoundrel, Francis Carlyle!' She laughed, swatting him on the arm. 'Don't you know I'm a respectably married woman with a baby on the way?'

Francis grabbed her hand and unceremoniously pulled her as close as Nancy's belly would allow and growled into her neck, sending Nancy into more screaming laughter.

Octavia grinned and slid her hand onto William's arm as she stared at the facade of the house where her life had truly begun. 'This house means everything to me and always will.'

'I know, and if Louisa and Jacob have anything to do with it, it will always be theirs, which means you can visit whenever you want.'

She nodded, trying her best to blink back the tears pricking her eyes. 'We've all changed so much, I'm not sure if it would be easier for all of us if Louisa sold it and started afresh somewhere new.'

The rumble of carriage wheels behind them made them turn before Louisa and Jacob's grand wedding coach came to a stop at the kerbside. The white exterior glinted beneath the lamplight as dusk fell, the satin ribbons festooning the horses' bridles, door handles and lamps waving in the late December breeze encompassing both wedding and Christmas.

'And here they are!' Nancy shouted, holding out her arms. 'The blushing virgin bride and her gentleman husband. Ladies and gentlemen, Mr and Mrs Jacob Jackson.'

Octavia laughed as Louisa and Jacob alighted from the carriage, their smiles wide and their eyes shining with happiness. Octavia immediately rushed forward to embrace them, she and Nancy elbowing each other in jest as they fought for supremacy in offering their congratulations.

'Will the pair of you stop jesting and jousting like children?' Louisa laughed, pulling them both into her arms and kissing them firmly on their cheeks. 'We are above such nonsense now. No longer whores, but married women.' She raised her eyebrows at Octavia. 'Or soon-to-be married women.'

Octavia pulled back and put out her hand so her friends could inspect her diamond and sapphire engagement ring *again*. 'I am, indeed. A date will be set as soon as the new year comes around. Your invites will be the first I write, I promise.'

'They'd better be,' Nancy said, frowning and patting her belly. 'But please make the big day in the summer so I can fit into a nice dress rather than a matron's frock.'

'As if you could look less than perfect in anything,' Octavia said, love for her friend swelling inside of her. 'You are one of the most beautiful people I know.'

'*One* of the people?' Nancy planted her hands on her hips

and frowned. 'As soon as this baby is born, I clearly need to up my game.'

The friends laughed as Louisa linked her arms with theirs and they stood side by side staring up at the Carson Street house. A sea of emotions washed over Octavia, the sudden stillness and silence between them so much more powerful than any words or actions.

Jacob slowly approached, leaving Francis and William talking by the road.

Octavia struggled harder than ever to hold back her tears as the big, broad, gentle giant Jacob Jackson stood in front of the women and eyed them each in turn. His midnight-blue gaze was as sombre as always, yet love burned in their depths along with a hefty dose of his habitual protectiveness.

'What have you got to say then, Jacob?' Nancy asked, standing taller. 'Never known you to be so quiet.'

He rocked back on his heels, a slow smile curving his lips. 'I'm just thinking how you and Octavia have finally grown up enough to match Louisa in your sensibilities. It warms my heart that I played a part in your maturity.'

'Played a part—' Nancy spluttered. 'I beg to differ. You are little more than a thorn in mine and Octavia's side. Isn't that right, Octavia?'

'Absolutely.' A tear rolled over Octavia's cheek despite her smile. 'But I love him, all the same.'

Jacob winked at her, and she pulled away from Nancy and Louisa to embrace him. She squeezed their stalwart guardian tight before Nancy pulled her away to have her hug, too.

Louisa stepped forward and slipped her hand around Jacob's waist. 'If you've quite finished, I'd like my husband back. It is our wedding day, you know.'

Arms linked, the four of them exchanged a smile and started

up the steps into the house, William and Francis following behind.

Octavia breathed deep. Whatever trials, tribulations and triumphs were waiting for them in the future, the six of them were friends for life. Of that, she had absolutely no doubt whatsoever.

* * *

MORE FROM RACHEL BRIMBLE

The next instalment in The Home Front Nurses Series, is available to buy now by clicking on the link below:
https://mybook.to/4HomeFrontBackAd

ACKNOWLEDGEMENTS

I'd like to thank Boldwood for giving this book a second outing! I am so proud of The Ladies of Carson Street trilogy and having the third and final instalment taken care of by such a fabulous publisher is wonderful.

Also, huge thanks to the librarians at my local library who are always so supportive tracking down the random research books I request and offering their help with records and archives.

Finally, I want to thank my lovely, faithful readers for reading everything I write and taking the time to contact me via email and social media. I love hearing from you!

Rachel x

ABOUT THE AUTHOR

Rachel Brimble is the bestselling author of over thirty works of historical romance and saga fiction. The first book in her series, *The Home Front Nurses*, is set in Bath.

Download your exclusive bonus content from Rachel Brimble here:

Visit Rachel's website: www.rachelbrimble.com

Follow Rachel on social media here:

- facebook.com/rachelbrimbleauthor
- x.com/RachelBrimble
- instagram.com/rachelbrimbleauthor
- BB bookbub.com/profile/rachel-brimble
- tiktok.com/@rachelbrimble

ALSO BY RACHEL BRIMBLE

The Home Front Nurses Series

The Home Front Nurses

Dangerous Days for the Home Front Nurses

Winter Wishes for the Home Front Nurses

The Pennington's Shop Girls Series

A New Start for the Shop Girls

The Shop Girls Get the Vote

A New Start for the Shop Girls

Christmas for the Shop Girls

The Shop Girls' Farewell

The Ladies of Carson Street Series

The Widow's Vow

The Foundling's Fortune

The Wife's Reputation

Sixpence Stories

Introducing Sixpence Stories!

Discover page-turning
historical novels from your
favourite authors, meet new
friends and be transported
back in time.

Join our book club
Facebook group

https://bit.ly/SixpenceGroup

Sign up to our
newsletter

https://bit.ly/SixpenceNews

Boldw**oo**d

Boldwood Books is an award-winning fiction publishing company seeking out the best stories from around the world.

Find out more at www.boldwoodbooks.com

Join our reader community for brilliant books, competitions and offers!

Follow us
@BoldwoodBooks
@TheBoldBookClub

Sign up to our weekly deals newsletter

https://bit.ly/BoldwoodBNewsletter